'RASSELAS' AND ESSAYS

ROUTLEDGE ENGLISH TEXTS

GENERAL EDITOR: T. S. Dorsch, M.A. (Oxon)
Westfield College, University of London

Volumes in the series include:

ELIZABETHAN LYRICAL POETS, edited by Patricia Thomson

ELIZABETHAN VERSE ROMANCES, edited by M. M. Reese

POETS OF THE EARLY SEVENTEENTH CENTURY, edited by Bernard and Elizabeth Davis

DRYDEN: 'ABSALOM AND ACHITOPHEL' AND OTHER SATIRES, edited by B. D. Greenslade

POPE: SATIRICAL POEMS, edited by J. Chalker

JOHNSON: 'RASSELAS' AND ESSAYS, edited by Charles Peake

WORDSWORTH: 'THE PRELUDE', BOOKS I–IV, edited by P. M. Yarker

BYRON: 'DON JUAN', BOOKS I–IV. edited by T. S. Dorsch

'RASSELAS' AND ESSAYS

SAMUEL JOHNSON

EDITED BY CHARLES PEAKE

LONDON

ROUTLEDGE & KEGAN PAUL

Published 1967
by Routledge & Kegan Paul Ltd
Broadway House, 68–74 Carter Lane
London, E.C.4

Printed in Great Britain
by Richard Clay (The Chaucer Press) Ltd
Bungay, Suffolk

SERIES EDITOR'S PREFACE

THE ROUTLEDGE ENGLISH TEXTS are designed primarily for the use of sixth-form pupils and undergraduates. Each volume is edited by a scholar who is an authority on the period which it represents and who has also had experience of teaching and examining at the school-leaving or the undergraduate level. The aim is to provide, in the introductions and notes, both sufficient explanatory material to enable the texts to be read with full understanding, and critical commentary of a kind that will stimulate thought and discussion.

The series will include both single works of some length and collections of shorter works. Where a work is too long to fit within the limits of size necessarily laid down for a text-book series—such a work, for example as *The Prelude*, or *Don Juan* —it will normally be represented by a single extended extract of several consecutive books or cantos rather than by an abridgement of the whole, since an abridgement runs the risk of losing the cumulative effects that are important in a work of some scope. In the anthologies a few authors of a particular period will be well represented, in the belief that a reasonably thorough study of a limited field is more profitable than a superficial study of a wide field, and that a more than passing acquaintance with an author is of value in itself.

T. S. DORSCH

CONTENTS

INTRODUCTION

EARLY CAREER

According to Johnson, when he and David Garrick arrived in London in March 1737 there was twopence-halfpenny in his pocket and three-halfpence in his companion's. Garrick protested that the story was exaggerated, but, whether or not the details were correct, there can be no doubt that Johnson, at least, was badly in need of a source of income. He was then twenty-seven years old; he had had to leave Oxford without a degree through financial difficulties; his father, an unsuccessful Lichfield bookseller, had died in 1731, and the business, such as it was, was being carried on by Johnson's mother. Johnson himself had tried school-teaching, without much pleasure or profit, and, after his marriage in 1735 to a widow twenty years older than himself, had set up his own school, but with little success. David Garrick was one of his pupils, but there were very few of them.

Johnson had tried, again not very profitably, to supplement his income by literary work. He had published in 1735 a translation of Father Lobo's *Voyage to Abyssinia*; had written to Edward Cave, publisher and editor of the newly founded *Gentleman's Magazine*, offering to supply poems, dissertations, or criticisms, but without result; and he brought with him to London the manuscript of an unfinished tragedy in blank verse, *Irene*. Presumably he hoped to find in London greater opportunities of earning money as a writer, and possibly the chance of interesting someone in his tragedy.

Since early childhood his health had been poor (although in physique he was tall and strong) and his appearance was not improved by the scars, nervous starts, and gesticulations which his illness had left. His appearance at about this time was described by his step-daughter, Lucy Porter:

> ... his appearance was very forbidding: he was then lean and lank, so that his immense structure of bones was hideously striking to the eye, and the scars of the scrofula were deeply visible. He also wore his hair [i.e., did not wear a

wig], which was straight and stiff and separated behind: and he often had, seemingly, convulsive starts and odd gesticulations, which tended to excite at once surprise and ridicule.

Few people, however, would have dared to show the amusement they may have felt at the oddity of appearance and manner which remained with Johnson all his life, and those who made closer contact with him found other reasons for surprise. The painter Hogarth, seeing Johnson at a distance, 'concluded that he was an idiot', but, having heard him talk, 'actually imagined that this idiot had been at the moment inspired'.

Even before his arrival in London Johnson had earned a reputation in Lichfield as a talker and a man of learning. He had read very widely, had an extraordinarily retentive memory, and seemed able to apply all the resources of his intellect to any topic presented. The energy of his mind was matched by that remarkable readiness of speech to which Boswell and many others testify; Ozias Humphrey, the painter, after having heard Johnson, wrote that 'everything he says is as correct as a second edition'. Add to these qualities great force of character, and one can understand how Johnson, despite physical handicaps and an unpropitious beginning, never lost confidence in his own genius.

Little is known of his early months in London. He was certainly poor, but presumably found some prospects of employment, for, although he returned to Lichfield after a few months, towards the end of 1737 he came back to London, this time bringing his wife with him. In 1738 he began to write for, and later helped to edit, the *Gentleman's Magazine*; the work was probably not well paid, but it provided a living and became more and more regular. Gradually he took over the writing of the 'Debates in the Senate of Magna Lilliputia', in which, by using barely disguised names, the magazine evaded the prohibition against reporting parliamentary debates; working from rough notes of the speeches, Johnson invested the speakers with his own form of eloquence, but, as he said later, 'took care that the Whig dogs should not have the best of it'. His first real impact on the literary world was made in May 1738 with *London, A Poem, in Imitation of the Third Satire of Juvenal*, a work which was very well received and brought

Johnson the praise of Alexander Pope and ten guineas in cash. But at this period Johnson was essentially a hack-writer, writing to order (though not in conflict with his principles), and being paid in accordance with the quantity produced. To the great writers of Queen Anne's reign there were few creatures lower than a Grub-street hack, but Johnson was proud of having earned a living with his pen, and later, when he was the most distinguished literary man in Britain, said concerning his edition of Shakespeare:

> I look upon this as I did upon the Dictionary; it is all work, and my inducement to it is not love or desire of fame, but the want of money, which is the only motive of writing that I know of.

This and some similar remarks (for instance, 'No man but a blockhead ever wrote, except for money') are obviously exaggerated; Johnson had other motives and often described them. It may have been partly for money, but not merely for money, that he wrote his moving *Life of Richard Savage* (1744), the poor, unbalanced, Bohemian poet with whom he had been friendly in his early years in London; and his *Miscellaneous Observations on the Tragedy of Macbeth* (1745) was hardly likely to bring in as much money as a novel might have done. Johnson was, perhaps, merely commenting humorously on what he considered to be his natural indolence, and reflecting the attitude of a man who has had to write to earn his bread.

That his name was, as yet, not widely known among the reading-public is shown by the fact that it was not included on the title-page of any of these works, but he was beginning to acquire a reputation among the booksellers (who were also the publishers of the time). Consequently, when in 1745–6 a group of them combined to consider the joint publication of a dictionary of the English language, and were in need of a professional man of letters with the scope of mind to plan such a work, and the learning, application, and powers of exact expression necessary to its completion, Johnson was the obvious choice. The contract was signed in 1746, and in the following year Johnson produced *The Plan of an English Dictionary* which demonstrated how clearly he foresaw the nature and problems of the task he had undertaken, and which in itself was, by the brilliance and clarity of its argument and exposition, an assurance of the quality of the projected attempt 'to preserve the purity and ascertain the meaning of our English idiom'. The work which appeared in 1755 was not the first English dictionary, but by the accuracy and discrimination of its definitions and the range and interest of its illustrative quotations it set a new standard. The eccentricities of humour and prejudice which were allowed to colour a few famous entries have stayed in men's minds, but they are quite untypical of the dictionary as a whole. By it Johnson's reputation was made; he became known as 'Dictionary Johnson', and even the familiar title of 'Doctor' (he was awarded an honorary doctorate by Dublin in 1765 and by Oxford in 1775) was a delayed result of the great *Dictionary of the English Language*.

2

THE PERIODICAL ESSAYS

In 1750, after three or four years of harmless drudgery as a lexicographer, partly as a relief from his labours, Johnson began a new periodical, *The Rambler*, each number consisting of a single essay and costing twopence. The identity of the writer was no secret; Johnson was known as the author of the magnificently sombre poem, *The Vanity of Human Wishes* (1749), and, less happily, as the author of *Irene*, which had at last been produced, and had been received in a way sufficient to discourage any ambitions Johnson may have had as a dramatist. The periodical essay had declined from the hey-day of *The Tatler* and *The Spectator*: Addison and Steele had had many imitators but no equals, and most recent periodicals had been caught up in the political or literary wars of the time. *The Rambler No. 1*, which appeared on Tuesday, 20 March 1759, showed no sign of this last fault, but it conspicuously lacked the lightness of touch of Addison and Steele, despite the author's expressed intention to 'endeavour the entertainment of my countrymen', and to 'follow the national taste through all its variations, and catch the *aura popularis*, the gale of favour, from what point soever it shall blow.'

But Johnson had other intentions, concealed from his readers. Before beginning, he had written a 'Prayer on the Rambler':

Almighty God, the giver of all good things, without whose help all labour is ineffectual, and without whose grace all wisdom is folly, grant, I beseech Thee, that in this my undertaking thy Holy Spirit may not be withheld from me, but that I may promote thy glory, and the salvation both of myself and others: Grant this, O Lord, for the sake of Jesus Christ. Amen. Lord bless me. So be it.

Some readers may have felt that *The Rambler* was more concerned with their 'salvation' than their 'entertainment'. At any rate, although the essays continued to appear twice a week for two years (Johnson was responsible for all but four of the two hundred and eight published), it had little popular appeal or sale. Few would disagree that as a periodical to be read over breakfast or in the coffee-house *The Spectator* was incomparably superior to *The Rambler*. The latter has less variety, is

far less easy and conversational in manner, and often dis-
courses on subjects unlikely to provide a pleasant morning's
reading. *The Rambler No. 175* began:

> None of the axioms of wisdom which recommended the
> ancient sages to veneration seems to have required less
> extent of knowledge or perspicacity of penetration than the
> remark of Bias, that *the majority are wicked.*
>   The depravity of mankind is so easily discoverable, that
> nothing but the desert or the cell can exclude it from notice.

In its own way that is admirable—so striking as to arouse one's
curiosity as to how the author can proceed—but it is not what
we look for in a twopenny periodical, and it is not altogether
surprising that in his last number Johnson observed that he
had 'never been much a favourite of the public'.

In one month *The Rambler* discussed the following topics
(the titles were supplied in the collected edition):

144. The difficulty of raising reputation. The various species
      of detractors.

145. Petty writers not to be despised.

146. An account of an author travelling in quest of his
      own character. The uncertainty of fame.

147. The courtier's esteem of assurance.

148. The cruelty of parental tyranny.

149. Benefits not always entitled to gratitude.

150. Adversity useful to the acquisition of knowledge.

151. The climacterics of the mind.

152. Criticism on epistolary writings.

Admittedly this was a particularly serious month, and some of
the essays in it were not so lacking in humour as their titles
suggest, but Johnson differs from his predecessors as much in
the character as in the frequency of his seriousness.

The Spectator may complain of the wrongs done by society
and sympathise with its victims, but *The Rambler* develops a
fullness of pity and indignation with a stylistic energy and
rhythmical vigour which is quite new to the essay:

If those who pass their days in plenty and security, could visit for an hour the dismal receptacles to which the prostitute retires from her nocturnal excursions, and see the wretches that lie crowded together, mad with intemperance, ghastly with famine, nauseous with filth, and noisome with disease, it would not be easy for any degree of abhorrence to harden them against compassion, or to repress the desire which they must immediately feel to rescue such numbers of human beings from a state so dreadful. (*No. 171*)

The difference in manner reflects a difference in character and experience. Steele and Addison were men of rather conventional piety; Johnson was intensely religious: they knew little of the wretchedness and poverty out of sight of the fashionable world; Johnson had lived in contact with it. But, besides, there was a difference in quality of mind. Addison and Steele differed from each other in many respects, but both were men of high intelligence and wide reading; Johnson, however, had intellectual powers of far wider range and deeper penetration. Although his essays vary in kind and quality, there are very few where one is not conscious of a powerful mind at work, examining experience and trying to draw from it some useful general conclusions

This can be felt even in the organisation of the essays. Clearly there is no single pattern of argument, but very characteristic is a scheme where Johnson sets opposing ideas one against the other until he arrives at an embracing generalisation, a maxim of practical morality, or, often, an illuminating image or analogy. *No. 47*, on 'The proper means of regulating sorrow', is a good example. It begins by differentiating sorrow from other human passions as not leading to some satisfaction: it is 'unavailing misery'. Yet, on the other hand, it springs from love, and only the inhuman can escape it. Then, as it must be accepted as desirable or pardonable, it must be limited in degree and duration. The counter-statement follows: once admitted, sorrow often becomes so dominant as to become habitual. Johnson now states the Stoic remedy—that we should avoid attachments which cannot be ended without sorrow. But such an unattached life would be merely 'a state of neutrality and indifference', and would shut out happiness without successfully excluding misery. The solution, therefore, must lie, not in the avoidance, but in the mitigation of sorrow.

B

Johnson considers and rejects the suggestions that the sorrowful may be relieved by bringing them into 'scenes of merriment' or by confronting them with greater evils suffered by others; the first, he says, is often impracticable and the second may do more harm than good. He concludes that 'the safe and general antidote against sorrow is employment' and that time assists in the cure. The solution, then, is to have plenty to do and to make time pass quickly by moving rapidly from one occupation to another. The figurative conclusion is intended to fix this in the reader's mind:

> Sorrow is a kind of rust of the soul, which every new idea contributes in its passage to scour away. It is the putrefaction of stagnant life, and is remedied by exercise and motion.

However condensed the argument and generalised the terms, there is always the sense of Johnson weighing each abstraction, his own or others', against first-hand experience—the quality which, perhaps, above all others distinguishes him as a moralist.

The *Rambler* essays are the writings most quoted in support of the assertion that Johnson's style is verbose, polysyllabic, over-manipulated, and pompous. As for verbosity, it would be difficult to find writings of comparable length so full of matter. Similarly, too much is made of his uncommon words. Extracted and listed, such words may look odd and affected, but distributed through two hundred and eight *Ramblers* they occur infrequently and rarely obscure the sense. In *The Idler No. 70* Johnson defended the use of 'hard words' on the grounds that they avoid diffuseness and allow the writer to discuss matters for which everyday terms are insufficiently subtle or discriminating. But he also used them with a different intention, as he explained in the concluding *Rambler*:

> When common words were less pleasing to the ear, or less distinct in their signification, I have familiarised the terms of philosophy by applying them to known objects and popular ideas, but have rarely admitted any word not authorised by former writers.

By 'the terms of philosophy' Johnson meant what we would call 'technical terms' or 'scientific terms', and if some of the uses of such terms which he introduced have remained Johnsonian curiosities, it is equally true that many of them have become part of our language. But, by the nature of things, his successful innovations pass unrecognised, while the failures catch the eye.

Johnson's occasional use of unusual words should not be confused with his frequent use of abstract or generalising terms. Whatever reasons may be offered for this latter aspect of his style, one must be his conviction that it was an important part of the writer's job to find the general truth in the multitude of particulars. He believed that as the phenomena observed by the scientist remained unexplained until they can be embraced in a general hypothetical system, so from human experience the writer must draw general truths which will serve as a practical guide to living. Imlac's observations about 'the business of the poet' (in *Rasselas*, Ch. X) are typical. The modern taste is for implied moral discriminations and judgements rather than for explicit assertions about how men live or should live, but much of our literature leads up to or embodies such assertions. The objection to Johnson's view is not that it wrongly relates literature to life, but that it is too narrow in its conception of that relationship. All that has to be demanded of the generalisation is that in abstracting from experience it has not distorted or falsified; it should exhibit, in Johnson's own words, 'that comprehension and expanse of thought which at once fills the whole mind, and of which the first effect is sudden astonishment, and the second rational admiration'. This is what Johnson aimed at, and what he achieved very often. Moreover, the same fondness for generalisation which is involved in the polysyllabic diction led to memorable aphorisms, epigrams, brevities of all kinds, often expressed in the simplest language. *The Rambler No. 155* contains a passage which illustrates how the search for generalised truth leads Johnson first into a polysyllabic statement about flatterers, suddenly into a brilliant and pithy epigram, and then into an extended comment:

> He that shall solicit the favour of his patron by praising him for qualities which he can find in himself, will always be defeated by the more daring panegyrist who enriches him with adscititious excellence, and plunders the sages and heroes of antiquity for the decoration of his name. Just praise is only a debt, but flattery is a present. The acknowledgement of those virtues on which conscience

congratulates us is a tribute which we can at any time exact with confidence, but the celebration of those which we only feign or which we desire, without any vigorous endeavours to attain them, is received as a confession of sovereignty over regions that we never conquered, as a favourable decision of disputable claims, and is more welcome as it is more gratuitous.

It is the epigram which sticks in the mind—the function of such brevities was, according to Johnson, to contract 'the great rules of life into short sentences, which may be easily impressed on the memory, and taught by frequent recollection to recur habitually to the mind whenever occasion calls them into use' —but the insight condensed into eleven words is derived from the longer sentences in which it is framed.

The same passage also illustrates some of the features of balance, parallelism, and antithesis which are objected to by those who find Johnson's style over-manipulated or self-consciously rhetorical. In a sense it is certainly rhetorical in that it stems from the classical and medieval art of rhetoric according to which the writer, like the orator, should employ a whole battery of literary devices to persuade his audience; the modern preference is for a style which, like Dryden's, approximates to conversation rather than to oratory. But the difference is not really one of persuasiveness (the conversational style is merely a particular mode of persuasion); it arises from different but equally valid notions about art, on the one hand that art should conceal art, and on the other that, as art seeks to impose order on and perceive meaning in the chaos of experience, it should manifest such order and significance in every aspect of its execution. The heroic couplet, as perfected by Pope, is an expression of this second concept. By all the arts of rhetoric, including subtle variations of balance and antithesis, the poet controls his medium to suit his matter, and, by setting couplet against couplet, line against line, phrase against phrase, and word against word, not only gains point and memorability but also establishes relationships, adds meaning, and fully articulates his thought. As W. K. Wimsatt has shown, Johnson's style is almost a prose equivalent of the heroic couplet, and derives from its devices benefits very similar to those derived by Pope. To an ear trained as Johnson's was on the heroic couplet, one expression naturally called up other expressions related to it by parallel or contrast, and, as the thought became more complex, so the sentences blossomed into pairs and triplets of phrases and clauses, related to establish in full the articulation of the thought. Consequently, his sentences, however long and complex, rarely fail to be lucid. The following sentence from *The Rambler No. 39* (on 'The unhappiness of women whether single or married'), though of exceptional length (nearly two hundred words), complex in thought and syntax, and further complicated by a rather heavy irony, remains easy enough to follow:

If they refuse the society of men, and continue in that state which is reasonably supposed to place happiness most in their own power, they seldom give those that observe their conduct, or frequent their conversation, any exalted notions of the blessing of liberty; for whether it be that they are angry to see with what inconsiderate eagerness the rest of their sex rushes into slavery, or at the absurd vanity with which married ladies boast the change of their condition, and condemn the heroines who endeavour by their example to assert the natural liberty of their sex; or whether they are conscious that, like barren countries, they are free, only because they were never thought to deserve the trouble of a conquest, or imagine that their sincerity is not always without suspicion when they declare their contempt for men, it is certain that they generally appear to have some great and incessant cause of uneasiness, and that many of them have at last been persuaded by powerful rhetoricians to try the life which they had so long contemned, and put on the bridal ornaments at a time then they least became them.

The comparison of Johnson's prose with poetry was made by his contemporaries. Anna Seward, the poetess, who knew him well, declared:

Excepting his orthographic works, everything which Dr. Johnson wrote was poetry, whose essence consists not in numbers, or in jingle, but in the strength and glow of a fancy to which all the stores of nature and of art stand in prompt administration, and in an eloquence which conveys their blended illustrations in a language 'more tuneable than needs or rhyme or verse to add more harmony'.

Miss Seward recognises that the function of Johnson's rhetoric was to adorn the thought as well as articulate it, and she emphasises the quality of imagination which enriches so much of Johnson's prose. Metaphors, similes, and analogies came readily to Johnson's mind, though it is not always easy to distinguish between them because the metaphors and similes frequently serve the analogical function of explanation. In *The Idler No. 34*, where Johnson talks about 'parallels', 'imaginary similitudes', and 'metaphorical sense' without distinguishing between them, and illustrates them with an extended analogy between making punch and making conversation, he describes their practical use:

> To illustrate one thing by its resemblance to another has been always the most popular and efficacious art of instruction. There is, indeed, no other method of teaching that of which anyone is ignorant, but by means of something already known, and a mind so enlarged by contemplation and enquiry, that it has always many objects within its view, will seldom be long without some near and familiar image through which any easy transition may be made to truths more distant and obscure.

But his images and analogies rarely perform a simple instructive function. 'Sorrow is a kind of rust of the soul' works on the imagination and the emotions as well as on the understanding, and even the analogy between punch and conversation concludes with a sentence in which the humorous and ironic connotations of the words dominate the explanatory comparison:

> He only can please long, who, by tempering the acid of satire with the sugar of civility, and allaying the heat of wit with the frigidity of humble chat, can make the true punch of conversation; and, as that punch can be drunk in the greatest quantity which has the largest proportion of water, so that companion will be oftenest welcome whose talk flows out with inoffensive copiousness and unenvied insipidity.

It is not entirely accidental that both these illustrations come from the last sentences of an essay, for, although Johnson's mind was by nature and inclination prolific of imagery, he often deliberately conducts his argument towards a concluding image which will embody the gist of his observations and leave a vivid and lasting impression. Thus in *The Rambler No. 14*, where Johnson is explaining why people who seek the acquaintance of authors are frequently disappointed in them (because 'for many reasons a man writes much better than he lives'), he closes with an ornate and elaborate figure which sums up memorably the whole content of the essay:

A transition from an author's books to his conversation is too often like an entrance into a large city, after a distant prospect. Remotely, we see nothing but spires of temples and turrets of palaces, and imagine it the residence of splendour, grandeur and magnificence; but, when we have passed the gates, we find it perplexed with narrow passages, disgraced with despicable cottages, embarrassed with obstructions, and clouded with smoke.

Of no author is this less true than of Johnson himself. According to all accounts, he spoke as he wrote. A young lady who travelled with him in a coach remarked, 'Every sentence is an essay'; a gentleman who knew him said that 'he would take up a topic, and utter upon it a number of *The Rambler*'; and Mrs. Thrale reported that the style of *The Rambler* was 'so natural to him, and so much like his common mode of conversing'. This, above all, is what preserves his style against the criticisms which began while he was still alive and have continued ever since; it rings true as an expression of the man's character and habit of mind. His style is not a model that one would recommend to other writers; to write like him it is necessary to think and feel like him. The same could be said of many great writers.

Of course, as is true of any grand manner, the manner occasionally obtrudes, and sometimes swamps the content. There is a particular danger of this when one is writing, as Johnson usually was, in haste. He sat up all night to write forty-eight of the printed pages of the *Life of Savage*; the *Rambler* essays were written while the printers waited for copy; *Rasselas* occupied the evenings of one week; and Boswell tells an amusing story about the composition of the *Idler* essays:

Many of these excellent essays were written as hastily as an ordinary letter. Mr. Langton remembers Johnson, when on a visit at Oxford, asking him one evening how long it was till the post went out; and, on being told about half an hour, he exclaimed, 'Then we shall do very well.' He upon this instantly sat down and finished an *Idler*, which it was necessary should be in London the next day. Mr. Langton having signified a wish to read it, 'Sir,' said he, 'you shall not do more than I have done myself.' He then folded it up and sent it off.

Johnson's speed in composition may be attributed partly to his experience as a hack-writer, and partly to those powers of application to which he referred when he said that 'a man may write at any time, if he will set himself doggedly to it'. But this does not account for the quality of the *Ramblers*, which he was producing twice a week in the intervals of his labours on the dictionary. Boswell gives the only explanation:

It can be accounted for only in this way: that by reading and meditation, and a very close inspection of life, he had accumulated a great fund of miscellaneous knowledge, which, by a peculiar promptitude of mind, was ever ready at his call, and which he had constantly accustomed himself to clothe in the most apt and energetic expression.

Moreover, through his 'meditation' and 'close inspection of life' Johnson seems to have arrived at certain fundamental beliefs about life and morality which served as guides to his thought on a very wide range of subjects, and these recur again and again in his essays, whether he is dealing with some vast generalisation or telling a story. The story of Dick Shifter (*The Idler No. 71*) is a particular illustration of the notions discussed in general terms in *The Adventurer No. 126*; the reader who laughs at the absurdity of Will Marvel (*The Idler No. 49*) finds in the next essay that he has been laughing at his own absurdity and that of all men; and in *Rasselas* the themes of dozens of essays are illustrated and discussed in a story about an Abyssinian prince.

Central to all Johnson's thought is the conviction that 'life is everywhere a state, in which much is to be endured and little to be enjoyed', and that 'the cure for the greatest part of human miseries is not radical but palliative'. How far this conviction was influenced by his physical illness and his capacity for suffering is impossible to say. Anyone who had charged Johnson with neurotic distortion would have been accused of voluntary self-deception. He thought that any man who opened his eyes could see that the evils and misfortunes of life were intolerable and lasting, and its pleasures superficial and transient. He was a Christian pessimist who believed that man's desire for happiness was given him so that, finding no fulfilment in this world, it would turn his attention to the next, where it would be fulfilled to all eternity. Therefore, to Johnson, any attempt to imagine an escape into some sort of earthly happiness or to argue away or minimise man's suffering was not only mistaken but an interference with God's purpose.

As a corollary to this belief, Johnson resisted all attempts to decry harmless pleasures, since no matter how trivial and transient they might be, they were necessary to make life bearable and helped to fend off despair. Similarly he was 'always afraid of determining on the side of envy or cruelty', since to do so was, even if one found oneself on that side unintentionally or for plausible reasons, to increase the pain men had to endure. As a man and as a writer Johnson delighted in wit and humour. The tragic view of life did not entail gloomy resignation or apathy, but, on the contrary, a determination to get as much pleasure as possible out of life, both for himself and others, to compensate for its inevitable sorrows. Even in *Rasselas*, the theme of which is that man can never find happiness on earth, there is frequent laughter.

Thirdly, while he was always angered by anything which seemed to him to undermine moral standards or the authority of the Christian revelation, he was well aware that men could not live up to their own standards or religious beliefs. He was tolerant of human imperfections, provided that they were not presented as perfections. Mrs. Montagu was a lady whose literary efforts he had dismissed with contempt and with whom he quarrelled, but when the motives of her kindness were treated with sarcasm he defended her forcefully:

A literary lady of large fortune was mentioned, as one who did good to many, but by no means 'by stealth', and, instead of 'blushing to find it fame', acted evidently from vanity. JOHNSON: I have seen no beings who do as much good from benevolence, as she does, from whatever motive. If there are such under the earth or in the clouds, I wish they would come up or come down. . . . No, Sir, to act from pure benevolence is not possible for finite beings. Human benevolence is mingled with vanity, interest, or some other motive.

This tolerant recognition of human failings is very characteristic of Johnson and is one of the reasons why he is severe on
moralists who demand of men more than is in their power to
perform, or who, like the Stoics, refuse to allow for what is
inescapable in human nature.

Finally, since the great source of human unhappiness and
folly was self-delusion, the great precept 'which the wisdom
and virtue of all ages have concurred to enforce' was 'Know
thyself'. Three *Ramblers* (*Nos. 24, 28*, and *155*) deal directly
with this precept, and a very large number are related to it
more or less explicitly. Johnson goes so far as to describe it as
'a dictate, which, in the whole extent of its meaning, may be
said to comprise all the speculation requisite to a moral agent.
For what more can be necessary to the regulation of life than
the knowledge of our original, our end, our duties, and our
relation to other beings?' But this would be to require of man
more than he is capable of, since of these divisions of self-
knowledge 'some are too extensive for the powers of man,
and some require light from above'. Nevertheless, it was a
moral duty to attain to such a degree of self-knowledge as was
possible, and to this purpose Johnson repeatedly recommended
the practice, to which he adhered himself, of periodical reviews of one's nature and behaviour. The whole series of
moral essays, and particularly those in *The Rambler*, can be
seen as parts of Johnson's endeavour to promote self-knowledge
and dissipate self-delusion. 'He who thinks reasonably must
think morally.'

If these are the corner-stones of Johnson's morality, the
foundation of all is his Christian belief. In this he was content
to be orthodox and Anglican, largely it would seem on the
grounds that 'the state has a right to regulate the religion of
the people, who are the children of the state'. 'An obstinate
rationality' stood between him and Roman Catholicism, and
he suspected that those who laid claim to an 'inward light' or
to receiving direct communication from God were usually
deluded; but, although he vigorously defended the Church of
England as an institution, he was not intolerant in matters of
doctrine: 'For my part, Sir, I think all Christians, whether
Papists or Protestants, agree in the essential articles, and that
their differences are trivial, and rather political than religious.'
Throughout his life he was recurrently troubled by doubts,
but he remained convinced that all virtue depended on religion

for its authority and its motive. As he had prayed before beginning *The Rambler*, so, in the concluding number, he claimed that the 'professedly serious' essays, 'if I have been able to execute my own intentions, will be found exactly conformable to the precepts of Christianity, without any accommodation to the licentiousness and levity of the present age'.

All the periodical essays were produced during the eleven years between spring 1750 and spring 1760, and exhibit little change in Johnson's moral position. There is, however, considerable change in his tone and manner. *The Rambler* does contain light and amusing essays, but these are hardly typical; what made the bound volumes of the unsuccessful periodical sell so well, and what sent Boswell to cultivate an acquaintance with Johnson, was the profoundly sincere and serious attitude towards life, the 'art of thinking' applied to human behaviour, the earnest desire to enlighten and reform men, the splendid and sometimes sombre rhetoric—in all of which respects *The Rambler* is distinguished from its predecessors and its successors in periodical literature.

The twenty-nine essays contributed to Hawkesworth's periodical *The Adventurer* between March 1753 and March 1754 are somewhat longer than the *Rambler* essays, and, perhaps, a little more relaxed in style, but there is no essential difference. *The Idler* essays, however, were not published as separate works, but were contributions to a weekly newspaper, *The Universal Chronicle*, and, besides being shorter, are not so lofty in style, have fewer classical and more topical allusions, and include a higher proportion of essays designed principally to entertain. The 1750s were the years in which Johnson's literary reputation was made, and although success did not change his way of thinking, it is possible that it encouraged a sense of a more intimate relationship with his audience. Certainly from the middle 1750s the pithy and forceful elements in his style became more prevalent, and the long, periodic, and rhetorical sentences less frequent.

The review of Soame Jenyns's book, *A Free Enquiry into the Nature and Origin of Evil*, shows greater stylistic variety than anything Johnson had previously written. It was one of a number of reviews which he wrote in 1756 and 1757 for a periodical entitled *The Literary Magazine: or Universal Review*, and I can think of no review in the language to match its combination of logical argument and passionate conviction. Jenyns had offended by indulging in idle speculation about what could not be known and was of no relevance to human behaviour, and by concealing beneath vague or false abstractions the true condition of the poor and wretched. 'Life must be seen before it can be known': this was the principle of all worthwhile moral thinking, and neglect of it led, on the one hand, to callous indifference to suffering, and, on the other, to glib justification of oppression. The review is a thoroughly destructive analysis of Jenyns's argument, and a statement of the procedures incumbent on any moralist. As himself a persistent seeker of general truths, Johnson was well aware of the dangers of generalisation on insufficient knowledge and without constant reference to life; as a master of analogical illustration he was quick to perceive the absurd implications of an ill-chosen analogy; as a coherent reasoner he detected and exposed each false step in logic; and as a practical moralist he convicted the theoretical moralist of moral insensitivity and of failure to perceive the moral consequences of the positions he adopted.

3

RASSELAS

Rasselas, written nearly two years after the review, in 1759, is the only one of Johnson's moral writings comparable to it in variety of style and approach. There has been some argument about the exact circumstances in which it came to be written, but the main facts are beyond dispute. In January 1759 Johnson's mother was dying at Lichfield, where she was being attended by his step-daughter, Lucy Porter. Johnson seems to have been busy and yet to have been short of ready cash. He talked of the possibility of coming to Lichfield, and sent Lucy money and promised more. On 20 January he wrote to William Strahan, the publisher, reminding him of a story of which he had spoken on the previous night as being nearly ready for the press:

The title will be
The Choice of Life
or
The History of . . . Prince of Abyssinia.

The letter closed with a request for the payment in cash of thirty pounds of the price in a week's time when the manuscript would be delivered. This money was used to pay the expenses of Mrs. Johnson's funeral, which took place on 23 January.

He later told Sir Joshua Reynolds that he had written the book in the evenings of one week, although it is possible that he had thought about it earlier and had been impelled to write it rapidly by the pressing need for money. However, there is no doubt that the book was begun shortly before his mother's death and was finished hurriedly. Yet even in the first edition there are very few signs of haste; apart from a loose end about the treasure buried in the Abyssinian palace, and a few clumsily constructed sentences, *Rasselas* seems a carefully planned and highly finished work of art.

It certainly owed much of its immediate success to its fictional form. 'Oriental tales' had been popular since the translation of the *Arabian Nights' Tales* and the *Persian Tales* at the beginning of the century: Addison had used them in

The Spectator, and Johnson himself had written for *The Rambler* several moral tales set in the Near East, including the story of Seged, lord of Ethiopia, who, like Rasselas, vainly sought for happiness. Moreover, Johnson was writing at a time when the novels of Richardson and Fielding had created a great demand for long fictions.

Whether or not *Rasselas* is to be called a novel depends on what is understood by the term. If it means merely 'a prose fiction of some length', then the book is a novel. But if the term is reserved for prose fictions in which consistently portrayed characters are involved in a complex and developing action, then it will not fit *Rasselas*. On the whole it seems better to avoid the term, if only because its current use arouses expectations about the story and the people involved in it which Johnson's work does not and was not intended to satisfy. The unifying principle of *Rasselas* is an argument rather than a story, and its persons are representative points of view rather than fully presented characters. The argument is concerned with questions familiar to readers of Johnson's earlier writings: 'In what does happiness consist? How and where may it be found?'

The story begins in the Happy Valley because here is a place seemingly designed for happiness, an earthly paradise which includes all that is desirable and excludes all that is harmful. Ironically it is in fact designed as a place of imprisonment for princes of the blood-royal, presumably to prevent the formation of groups of supporters behind various claimants to the throne. A further irony is that it is only by making the place a prison that the seclusion necessary to keep it 'happy' can be preserved. A brief but balanced sentence points the irony: 'Thus every year produced new schemes of delight and new competitors for imprisonment.'

The artificiality of this attempt to create a 'valley of happiness' is, in itself, a comment on the difficulty of finding happiness in life; and the account of the valley raises the question of the validity of what has been created. Most of the princes seem content and show no desire to escape. Can they be said to have achieved happiness, and is Rasselas merely a malcontent? For the princes 'pleasure and repose' alternate; all their senses are gratified; but their satisfaction and 'their opinion of their own felicity' have to be encouraged by exaggerated reports of the disasters of the outside world and by songs in praise of the Happy Valley. When Rasselas addresses the animals, whose desires are 'corporal' and readily satisfied, and whose satisfactions are interspersed with sleep, he is, in effect, addressing the princes. If they are happy, their happiness 'is not the felicity of man'. Man has some hidden sense or some non-sensual desires which the Happy Valley does not satisfy, and which 'must be satisfied before he can be happy'.

This introduces a new irony, for, in the conversation with his old instructor, Rasselas blames his unhappiness on his not having anything to desire. Thus, very early in the story, the dilemma is established. Man by his nature is constantly motivated by the search for happiness. As long as there is something which he wants and does not have, he cannot be described as entirely happy; but, on the other hand, man is so constituted that he cannot be happy unless he has something to desire, something to pursue. Through Rasselas, Johnson is already defining happiness in such a way that, almost by definition, it is unattainable by man. The crowning paradox is produced by the old man's attempt at argument, for it leads to the suggestion that the sight of the world's miseries is necessary to human happiness.

At this point, everything in the story approximates to irony or paradox. Once Rasselas has reached a conclusion as to why he is unhappy, he ceases to be so, 'considering himself as master of a secret stock of happiness'. 'The desire of doing something', which has relieved his gloom, induces day-dreams in which he does nothing, and at last he realises that, although he has rejected the luxury of the feasts which pleased the other princes, he has instead 'sat feasting on intellectual luxury'. His self-reproach for idleness becomes another form of idleness, and, on the other hand, his determined search for a way to escape, which at first seems to supply him with 'a source of inexhaustible enquiry', ultimately produces, after the failure of the inventor, sadness and discontent.

Thus, in these early chapters of *Rasselas*, which are sometimes treated as though they merely provided an exotic starting-point for the real search, Johnson has already established some of the complexity of the problem of happiness and, in particular, its complication by the inconsistency and unpredictability of human nature. These last factors are immediately emphasised in the conversation with Imlac. Much of the comedy of his interruptions arises from the inability of Rasselas to recognise his own failings, as for instance when Imlac has to explain that 'Inconsistencies . . . cannot both be right, but, imputed to man, they may both be true'. In fact, what marks the superiority of Imlac's self-knowledge is that he can recognise absurdities in his own behaviour: that, once he had learned from his instructors what they had to teach, he found them no 'wiser or better than common men'; that the sea, which had at first seemed to set his soul free, very quickly became boring; that, like Rasselas in his day-dreams, he occupied himself with plans for dealing with situations which never occurred; that the Mogul who condescended to question him, though he said nothing of any account, seemed to him extraordinarily wise and good. Yet Imlac, too, has his weak spot: he can be realistic enough, when Rasselas enquires about the happiness of other nations, to say that there is so much unhappiness that few have time 'to estimate the comparative happiness of others'; but he forgets that he has listed precisely this task among the many others incumbent on a poet. Where his own profession is involved, Imlac can be, as even Rasselas perceives, as self-deluding and unrealistic as any other man. Chapter X is often quoted as evidence of Johnson's opinions on literary matters, and certainly in general terms it reflects those opinions; but it needs to be remembered that from the first sentence, where the veneration accorded to the poet is compared to that paid to 'the Angelic Nature', to the penultimate sentence where the poet is said to write 'as a being superior to time and place', Johnson is showing Imlac as carried away by an exaggerated fervour. Imlac is Johnson's mouthpiece, but here Johnson is laughing at himself. No man can be entirely free from self-deception, not even an author engaged in exposing it.

The prime function of the conversation with Imlac is to serve as a bridge between the isolated prince and the external world. Through it a double view of the world is presented; Imlac's experienced disillusion is contrasted with Rasselas's naïve hopefulness, which cannot understand how cruelty and injustice can survive in Abyssinia, cannot see how a man can want more money when he has already more than he dare make use of, believes that Imlac must have mistaken the motives of his travelling-companions, and is sure that there can be no malice or envy in the Happy Valley. But the most marked and fundamental contrast is between Imlac's assertion that in life 'much is to be endured and little to be enjoyed' and Rasselas's conviction that, if he could choose his way of life, he could 'fill every day with pleasure'. As in the section on the poet, it should not be too readily assumed that Imlac is meant to be entirely right and Rasselas entirely wrong. Imlac warns Rasselas that if he does escape to the outer world he will often wish to be back in the Happy Valley, but this is only the converse of Imlac's own position, and of his wish to warn those who try to enter the valley. However little enjoyment there may be outside, Imlac in captivity is sorrowful to think 'that none of my pleasures can be again enjoyed'. It is dangerous to regard Imlac as a character in a novel whose remarks can be taken merely as products of his situation, temperament, and mood; on the other hand, it is equally dangerous to regard him as the author's spokesman, exempted from the irony which plays round all the other figures. Imlac's comment on life is one which Johnson himself had often made, but he also recognised in himself and others the ineradicable hope expressed by Rasselas. Both sides of the picture are united by the unnamed person (certainly a spokesman for the author) who comments sympathetically on the story of the hermit:

'For the hope of happiness', says he, 'is so strongly impressed that the longest experience is not able to efface it. Of the present state, whatever it be, we feel, and are forced to confess, the misery, yet, when the same state is again at a distance, imagination paints it as desirable.'

This applies equally well to Rasselas and to Imlac; and it is therefore better to regard the dialogue between them as being between two essential, if inconsistent, elements in human nature, rather than as between wisdom and simplicity. It is the alternation of hope and disillusion which leads to 'the conclusion in which nothing is concluded'.

Before the search proper starts, Johnson introduces two ideas which question the validity of such a search at all. Rasselas's first impression in society is that everyone is happy, excepting himself; to this Imlac replies that we are always ready to believe that others possess happiness because it supports our hope of attaining it ourselves. This readiness is exhibited by Rasselas throughout the book, and it makes the failure of his attempt to find a happy man all the more pointed. Secondly, Rasselas argues that, even if perfect happiness cannot be achieved, different ways of life must be relatively more or less

C

happy, and therefore examination of them will enable us to choose 'the least evil'. Imlac's answer is that good and evil in life are so confused and inter-related, and so dependent on chance or particular circumstances, that before any valid grounds for choice could be determined the whole of life would have been taken up in the enquiry. The efficacy of the projected search has already been questioned; here Imlac is suggesting that the quest for earthly happiness is itself a waste of life, a suggestion which becomes important towards the end of the book.

The search begins with a definition of its object: 'Happiness . . . must be something solid and permanent, without fear and without uncertainty.' So defined, it is a state which even the most optimistic eye cannot perceive in life. The definition ensures the failure of the search before it has properly begun, and it might be argued that it is only by demanding such extravagant terms that Johnson is able to show that man cannot know happiness in this world. Johnson's reply would presumably be that these terms represent the state to which man aspires. He is not denying that men find brief experiences of happiness, but, having found them, they want them to continue and they fear that they will end. Indeed, as Nekayah says in Chapter XXXVI, 'happiness is itself the cause of misery'. The conclusion to which Johnson is working is a religious one. Rasselas has observed that all the desires of the animals have their proper satisfactions; man, however, has this aspiration towards a state which is evidently not attainable on earth. Johnson's belief is that the Creator who planted in man the aspiration will in the after-life provide its satisfaction, and that the existence of an aspiration for a state manifestly not attainable in this world is itself both an evidence of another world and a promise that man shall know it. The terms of the definition of happiness are a necessary consequence of this belief.

It is not surprising that the party finds no way of life which comes near to satisfying the definition. The recipes for happiness offered by the two philosophers are either impracticable or meaningless; the young are involved in trivial and transient pleasures, the old possessed with regrets and self-reproach; the shepherds are ignorant and brutish, the learned troubled with delusions of grandeur; public life and private life are both filled with envy and scheming; rich and poor alike share

anxieties and fears; the hermit is desolate and the ruler surrounded with conspirators; marriage is full of pains and celibacy without pleasures; even the monuments of the past tell
of 'the insufficiency of human enjoyments'.

The pleasures that men do find are far from the 'permanence'
of happiness because they are all dependent on 'novelty'.
This dependence is almost a subsidiary theme in the book.
The men allowed into the Happy Valley had to be able 'to add
novelty to luxury'; Rasselas regrets the loss of childhood because then nature always had something new to show; the
hermit's cell soon lost 'the pleasure of novelty'; when, after
the debate on marriage, Rasselas is almost discouraged, Imlac
says that he is confining himself to a city which 'can now afford
few novelties'; the Pyramids reveal the folly of supposing that
anyone 'can feed the appetite of novelty with successive gratifications'; and, towards the end of the book, Nekayah makes
the theme explicit:

> Such . . . is the state of life, that none are happy but by the
> anticipation of change: the change itself is nothing; when
> we have made it, the next wish is to change again.

The difference between the happiness sought for and the
happiness found is the difference between permanence and
novelty, between the eternal and the temporal. To look for
what is timeless in a world of time is to waste time. Imlac
makes precisely this point before introducing the subject of
the Pyramids: 'It seems to me . . . that while you are making
the choice of life, you neglect to live.' The old man's regrets
are for 'much time squandered upon trifles, and more lost in
idleness and vacancy'. The episode in the catacombs, with the
resulting attempts to prove the immateriality and immortality
of the soul, serves to remind Rasselas of the promise without
which the prospect of death would be gloomy, to warn him to
'remember the shortness of our present state', and to suggest
that some of the dead were 'snatched away, while they were
busy, like us, in the choice of life'. This is the culmination of
Johnson's argument—that for men the choice of life matters
less than 'the choice of eternity'.

To describe the argument of *Rasselas* as gloomy is a half-
truth. To Johnson himself, and to anyone who shares his
belief in immortality, the short life in which much is to be

endured will be followed by an eternity of happiness, and the absence of happiness from this world is a guarantee of its presence in the next. It may be a tragic view of life, but it is certainly not a tragic view of human destiny.

The conduct of the story is even less gloomy than the argument. Compared with some of the more sombre *Rambler* essays, *Rasselas* is lively in presentation and often witty or humorous. Johnson is amused, not angered, by human folly. He laughs at the satisfaction Rasselas derives from the eloquent recital of his miseries; at the old instructor whose arguments produce a conclusion opposite to what he intended; at the fantasy about a virgin orphan and the consequent four months spent 'in resolving to lose no more time in idle resolves'; at the preacher of non-attachment who responds with 'joy and wonder' to a gift of gold, the hermit with a buried treasure, and the unintelligible philosopher who 'departed with the air of a man that had co-operated with the present system'; at Nekayah's reluctant abandonment of 'the duty of periodical affliction'; and, finally, at the new dreams that fasten on the minds of the travellers in the last chapter. These are only a few of the many touches of humour; one is reminded of Johnson's old college-friend who said, 'You are a philosopher, Dr. Johnson. I have tried too in my time to be a philosopher; but, I don't know how, cheerfulness was always breaking in.' The two men had more in common than the friend (or Boswell) realised.

The humour was a necessary counter-balance to the element of melancholy in Johnson's disposition and in his character as a moralist. The endeavour of *Rasselas* to dispel flattering delusions inevitably meant an emphasis on those aspects of life to which men closed their eyes, but the treatment prevents the disillusion from being depressing. Moreover, human grief is shown to be as transient and as much governed by self-delusion as human happiness.

Few people today share Johnson's view of life, although some authors (Samuel Beckett, for instance) come close to his vision of 'the vanity of human wishes' and of what Beckett has called 'our pernicious and incurable optimism'. But to derive pleasure and profit from *Rasselas*, it is not necessary to accept Johnson's religion or his belief that this life is only a preparation for immortality: the book's value comes from the quality of the mind at work on every page, scrutinising and assessing whatever is constant in human nature and behaviour, and expressing its observations and conclusions with force and eloquence. As Johnson claimed in *The Idler No. 59*:

> He that writes upon general principles, or delivers universal truths, may hope to be read long, because his work will be equally useful at all times and in every country, but he cannot expect it to be received with eagerness, or to spread with rapidity, because desire can have no particular stimulation; that which is to be loved long must be loved with reason rather than with passion. He that lays out his labours upon temporary subjects easily finds readers, and quickly loses them; for what should make the book valued when its subject is no more?

The success of *Rasselas* both in Great Britain and in Europe was very rapid, despite the curious similarities with Voltaire's *Candide*, which appeared in the same year. Johnson observed that, 'if they had not been published so closely one after the other that there was not time for imitation, it would have been in vain to deny that the scheme of that which came latest was taken from the other'. Both authors had used a travel-fiction to attack the belief of the Leibnizian Optimists that 'all is for the best in the best of all possible worlds', and there are accidental resemblances in the plan and conduct of the stories, but the spirit and manner of the two authors is so entirely different that, even if there had been evidence that one had read the other's work before beginning his own, it would hardly have impaired his claim to originality. For Johnson, *Rasselas* marks the culmination and, in effect, the end of his specifically moral writings, for, although the *Idler* essays continued to appear until April 1760, his subsequent work was primarily critical and, to a much smaller extent, political.

4

LATER CAREER

Johnson had, of course, been a critic since the 1730s, and, besides writing various articles, reviews, and short literary biographies for various magazines, had included many important critical papers in his periodical essays. But he had long had in mind a much bigger literary undertaking.

As early as 1745, at the time of the *Miscellaneous Observations on the Tragedy of Macbeth*, he had put out *Proposals for a New Edition of Shakespeare*, but nothing came of them. In 1756, with the fame of the *Dictionary* and *The Rambler* to support them, new proposals were issued for an edition promised by the end of 1757. Subscriptions were received, but Johnson seems to have lacked enthusiasm for the labours of editing. The long delay in the appearance of the promised volumes occasioned many attacks such as that of Charles Churchill, who, in 1762, complained,

> He for subscribers baits his hook,
> And takes their cash—but where's the book?

At last, in 1765, the edition appeared, and was an immediate success, although the quality of Johnson's editing of the text is far inferior to that of the critical penetration shown in the 'Preface' and the notes, which set a new standard in the criticism of Shakespeare. To some aspects of Shakespeare's genius Johnson seems curiously blind, but in general the intelligence and insight are superb, and matched by Johnson's finest eloquence.

The same qualities are shown in Johnson's major critical work, and probably his greatest work of any kind, *The Lives of the Poets*. These appeared in two instalments in 1779 and 1781 as biographical and critical introductions to the works of the English poets (roughly between Milton and Gray), published by a consortium of London booksellers. Some of his judgements are unsympathetic and some intentionally provoking, though it has often been said that it is more profitable to quarrel with Johnson than to agree with another critic. He is always interesting; there is always observation and thought behind every sentence; if he is occasionally prejudiced against an author, he is often moved to splendid and penetrating enthusiasm, sometimes for the same author. As in his moral writings, one does not have to agree with his conclusions in order to be delighted and instructed by the spectacle of this powerful and lively mind, considering poets and their works and reaching for general truths about literature and about life. For Johnson the moralist is still very much present in Johnson the critic; he is always asking of the poem, 'Is human life and human nature really like that?', and of the poet, 'What have you to contribute to man's understanding of himself, of his fellow-men, of his environment, and of his duties and responsibilities to man and to God?' This moral preoccupation is sometimes responsible for critical failings, especially where it seems to demand some explicit moral teaching, but more often it is the source of Johnson's deepest perceptions and most convincing judgements. For him literature was just one of many human activities, though a very important one, and as such it was subject to the same moral criteria as every other form of man's behaviour. It is a view which has its dangers, not always avoided by Johnson, but it is ultimately less damaging to literature and art in general than the view that they exist in some sphere where life has no place and is an irrelevance.

About the political pamphlets—*The False Alarm* (1770), *Thoughts on the Late Transactions Respecting the Falkland Islands* (1771), *The Patriot* (1774), and *Taxation No Tyranny* (1775)—it is not necessary to say anything here; the last is the most vigorous and the most prejudiced, but none is of importance in Johnson's literary achievement. But his life between 1760 and his death on 13 December 1784 cannot be summed up by his literary output, for it was during these years that he became the dominant figure in the literary life of London and the central character in a book as original and distinguished as his own greatest works.

As I have said, at the time when he was writing *Rasselas* Johnson was still not free from money troubles. But in 1762, through the influence of some friends, he was awarded a pension of £300 a year by the government. It was not an easy thing for a man to accept who, in the *Dictionary*, had defined 'pension' as 'an allowance made to anyone without an equivalent. In England it is generally understood to mean pay given to a state hireling for treason to his country.' However, he was assured that this pension was granted for what he had done, and not for anything he was expected to do for the government. The money gave Johnson more leisure for what had always been his favourite occupation—talking with his friends. In the late 'fifties and early 'sixties he was making many new friends, among them such men as Dr. Burney, Joshua Reynolds, Edmund Burke, Oliver Goldsmith, and Topham Beauclerk, who, if they could not equal Johnson in conversation and argument, could bring out the best in him. Of Burke Johnson once said when he was ill, 'That fellow calls forth all my powers. Were I to see Burke now it would kill me.'

In May 1763 a young Scotsman, James Boswell, made the acquaintance of Johnson, and pursued the acquaintance so energetically that in August, when he had to leave England to study law in Holland, Johnson insisted on accompanying him as far as Harwich. Thus, from the beginning the relationship was not that of tyrant and sycophant, but of a strange but affectionate friendship. Boswell is no longer regarded as a foolish hanger-on who by some extraordinary accident wrote the greatest biography in the language. He was a man of many talents, many follies, and some vices, and a connoisseur of great men, especially men of great intellectual power. He was never afraid of appearing foolish if by doing so he could set Johnson's mind and tongue working on some issue which he thought might produce new wisdom or new verbal fireworks, and thus he not only recorded what Johnson said, but provoked and assisted it. In a sense the composition of the biography began while the two men were together. The contrast between their minds and characters played its part in holding them together, and is exemplified in the two books which appeared after their joint visit to Scotland—Johnson's *Journey to the Western Islands of Scotland* (1775), dignified, eloquent, thoughtful, always moving from particular observations to generalised truths about man and society, and Boswell's *Journal of a Tour to the Hebrides, with Samuel Johnson, LL.D.* (1776), lively, full of detailed observation and incident, and as much about his companion as about their tour.

The portrait of Johnson in the *Life* is beyond praise; it preserves the man as no other man, much less any other author, has been preserved, and, without hiding his failings, displays those 'talents, acquirements and virtues' which, Boswell concluded, 'were so extraordinary, that the more his character is considered, the more he will be regarded by the present age, and by posterity, with admiration and reverence'.

It says a great deal for the strength of the impression made by Johnson that in all the accounts by those who knew him— people as different in temperament from Boswell and from each other as Sir John Hawkins, Mrs. Thrale, and Fanny Burney—there is the same basic image of his manner and his extraordinary talents and humanity. Some he offended, others saw only the kinder side of his character, but in all essential respects their accounts of him tally or complement each other. Such apparent inconsistencies as there are stem, for the most part, from the complexity of his nature, and from the difficulty for those who shared one part of his life to understand the other parts. The same man who dominated the intellectuals of the Literary Club relaxed in the comfortable surroundings of the Thrales' home at Streatham, and returned at week-ends to the house which he shared with the learned but sometimes peevish blind woman, Miss Williams; the surly Dr. Levett, an unlicensed doctor to the poor; his negro servant, Francis Barber; and, later, two more difficult women, the widowed Mrs. Desmoulins and 'Poll' Carmichael. It was not an easy household; apart from its members' individual peculiarities, they were, as Johnson reported, ill-mixed: 'Williams hates everybody. Levett hates Desmoulins and does not love Williams. Desmoulins hates them both. Poll loves none of them.' No doubt Johnson took these people into his home partly through a sense of Christian duty, though most men would have found some less exhausting form of charity. But at the height of his intellectual and social eminence he may also have felt a need for contact with a harder, less sophisticated level of society. Curiously, the elegant Mrs. Thrale seems to have perceived this aspect of him better than anyone else. She wrote:

Dr. Johnson knew how to be merry with mean people too, as well as to be sad with them; he loved the lower ranks of humanity with a real affection: and though his talents and learning kept him always in the sphere of upper life, yet he never lost sight of the time when he and they shared pain and pleasure in common.

In the margin of her copy of Boswell's *Life*, she wrote against a passage in one of Johnson's letters referring to an old school-friend, 'Ever sighing for the tea and bread and butter of life, when satiated with the turtle and burgundy of it.'

Mrs. Thrale also supplies a story which sums up many of Johnson's chief characteristics as a moralist—his readiness to measure moral theorisings against life, his sense of the wretchedness of life and the need for small alleviations, the clarity of his moral perceptions, his compassion, and his fear of 'determining on the side of envy or cruelty'. In theory he believed that money given to beggars could more profitably be employed in paying those who worked for their living, and yet he gave freely to beggars. In answer to the objection that such charity was spent on gin and tobacco, Johnson answered:

> And why should they be denied such sweeteners of their existence? . . . It is surely very savage to refuse them every possible avenue to pleasure, reckoned too coarse for our own acceptance. Life is a pill which none of us can bear to swallow without gilding; yet for the poor we delight in stripping it still barer, and are not ashamed to show even visible displeasure if ever the bitter taste is taken from their mouths.

THE HISTORY OF RASSELAS,
PRINCE OF ABYSSINIA

CHAPTER I

Description of a palace in a valley

Ye who listen with credulity to the whispers of fancy, and pursue with eagerness the phantoms of hope; who expect that age will perform the promises of youth, and that the deficiencies of the present day will be supplied by the morrow; attend to the history of Rasselas prince of Abyssinia.

Rasselas was the fourth son of the mighty emperor in whose dominions the Father of waters begins his course, whose bounty pours down the streams of plenty, and scatters over half the world the harvests of Egypt.

According to the custom which has descended from age to age among the monarchs of the torrid zone, he was confined in a private palace, with the other sons and daughters of Abyssinian royalty, till the order of succession should call him to the throne.

The place which the wisdom or policy of antiquity had destined for the residence of the Abyssinian princes was a spacious valley in the kingdom of Amhara, surrounded on every side by mountains, of which the summits overhang the middle part. The only passage by which it could be entered was a cavern that passed under a rock, of which it has long been disputed whether it was the work of nature or of human industry. The outlet of the cavern was concealed by a thick wood, and the mouth which opened into the valley was closed with gates of iron, forged by the artificers of ancient days, so massy that no man could, without the help of engines, open or shut them.

From the mountains on every side, rivulets descended that

filled all the valley with verdure and fertility, and formed a lake in the middle inhabited by fish of every species, and frequented by every fowl whom nature has taught to dip the wing in water. This lake discharged its superfluities by a stream which entered a dark cleft of the mountain on the northern side, and fell with dreadful noise from precipice to precipice till it was heard no more.

The sides of the mountains were covered with trees, the banks of the brooks were diversified with flowers; every blast shook spices from the rocks, and every month dropped fruits upon the ground. All animals that bite the grass, or browse the shrub, whether wild or tame, wandered in this extensive circuit, secured from beasts of prey by the mountains which confined them. On one part were flocks and herds feeding in the pastures, on another all the beasts of chase frisking in the lawns; the sprightly kid was bounding on the rocks, the subtle monkey frolicking in the trees, and the solemn elephant reposing in the shade. All the diversities of the world were brought together, the blessings of nature were collected, and its evils extracted and excluded.

The valley, wide and fruitful, supplied its inhabitants with the necessaries of life, and all delights and superfluities were added at the annual visit which the emperor paid his children, when the iron gate was opened to the sound of music; and during eight days everyone that resided in the valley was required to propose whatever might contribute to make seclusion pleasant, to fill up the vacancies of attention, and lessen the tediousness of time. Every desire was immediately granted. All the artificers of pleasure were called to gladden the festivity; the musicians exerted the power of harmony, and the dancers showed their activity before the princes, in hope that they should pass their lives in this blissful captivity, to which these only were admitted whose performance was thought able to add novelty to luxury. Such was the appearance of security and delight which this retirement afforded, that they to whom it was new always desired that it might be perpetual; and, as those on whom the iron gate had once closed were never suffered to return, the effect of longer experience could not be known. Thus every year produced new schemes of delight and new competitors for imprisonment.

The palace stood on an eminence raised about thirty paces above the surface of the lake. It was divided into many squares or courts, built with greater or less magnificence according to the rank of those for whom they were designed. The roofs were turned into arches of massy stone joined with a cement that grew harder by time, and the building stood from century to century, deriding the solstitial rains and equinoctial hurricanes, without need of reparation.

This house, which was so large as to be fully known to none but some ancient officers who successively inherited the secrets of the place, was built as if Suspicion herself had dictated the plan. To every room there was an open and secret passage; every square had a communication with the rest, either from the upper stories by private galleries, or by subterranean passages from the lower apartments. Many of the columns had unsuspected cavities in which successive monarchs reposited their treasures. They then closed up the opening with marble, which was never to be removed but in the utmost exigencies of the kingdom, and recorded their accumulations in a book which was itself concealed in a tower not entered but by the emperor, attended by the prince who stood next in succession.

CHAPTER II

The discontent of Rasselas in the Happy Valley

Here the sons and daughters of Abyssinia lived only to know the soft vicissitudes of pleasure and repose, attended by all that were skilful to delight, and gratified with whatever the senses can enjoy. They wandered in gardens of fragrance, and slept in the fortresses of security. Every art was practised to make them pleased with their own condition. The sages who instructed them told them of nothing but the miseries of public life, and described all beyond the mountains as regions of calamity, where discord was always raging, and where man preyed upon man.

To heighten their opinion of their own felicity, they were daily entertained with songs, the subject of which was the Happy Valley. Their appetites were excited by frequent enumerations of different enjoyments, and revelry and merriment was the business of every hour from the dawn of morning to the close of even.

These methods were generally successful; few of the princes had ever wished to enlarge their bounds, but passed their lives in full conviction that they had all within their reach that art or nature could bestow, and pitied those whom fate had excluded from this seat of tranquillity, as the sport of chance and the slaves of misery.

Thus they rose in the morning, and lay down at night, pleased with each other and with themselves; all but Rasselas, who, in the twenty-sixth year of his age, began to withdraw himself from their pastimes and assemblies, and to delight in solitary walks and silent meditation. He often sat before tables covered with luxury, and forgot to taste the dainties that were placed before him: he rose abruptly in the midst of the song, and hastily retired beyond the sound of music. His attendants observed the change and endeavoured to renew his love of pleasure: he neglected their endeavours, repulsed their invitations, and spent day after day on the banks of rivulets sheltered with trees, where he sometimes listened to the birds in the branches, sometimes observed the fish playing in the stream, and anon cast his eyes upon the pastures and mountains filled with animals, of which some were biting the herbage, and some sleeping among the bushes.

This singularity of his humour made him much observed. One of the sages, in whose conversation he had formerly delighted, followed him secretly, in hope of discovering the cause of his disquiet. Rasselas, who knew not that anyone was near him, having for some time fixed his eyes upon the goats that were browsing among the rocks, began to compare their condition with his own.

'What', said he, 'makes the difference between man and all

the rest of the animal creation? Every beast that strays beside me has the same corporal necessities with myself; he is hungry and crops the grass, he is thirsty and drinks the stream; his thirst and hunger are appeased, he is satisfied and sleeps; he rises again and is hungry, he is again fed and is at rest. I am hungry and thirsty like him, but when thirst and hunger cease I am not at rest; I am, like him, pained with want, but am not, like him, satisfied with fullness. The intermediate hours are tedious and gloomy; I long again to be hungry that I may again quicken my attention. The birds peck the berries or the corn, and fly away to the groves where they sit in seeming happiness on the branches, and waste their lives in tuning one unvaried series of sounds. I likewise can call the lutanist and the singer, but the sounds that pleased me yesterday weary me today, and will grow yet more wearisome tomorrow. I can discover within me no power of perception which is not glutted with its proper pleasure, yet I do not feel myself delighted. Man has surely some latent sense for which this place affords no gratification, or he has some desires distinct from sense which must be satisfied before he can be happy.'

After this he lifted up his head, and, seeing the moon rising, walked towards the palace. As he passed through the fields, and saw the animals around him, 'Ye', said he, 'are happy, and need not envy me that walk thus among you, burthened with myself; nor do I, ye gentle beings, envy your felicity; for it is not the felicity of man. I have many distresses from which ye are free; I fear pain when I do not feel it; I sometimes shrink at evils recollected, and sometimes start at evils anticipated: surely the equity of providence has balanced peculiar sufferings with peculiar enjoyments.'

With observations like these the prince amused himself as he returned, uttering them with a plaintive voice, yet with a look that discovered him to feel some complacence in his own perspicacity, and to receive some solace of the miseries of life from consciousness of the delicacy with which he felt and the eloquence with which he bewailed them. He mingled cheerfully in the diversions of the evening, and all rejoiced to find that his heart was lightened.

CHAPTER III

The wants of him that wants nothing

On the next day his old instructor, imagining that he had now made himself acquainted with his disease of mind, was in hope of curing it by counsel, and officiously sought an opportunity of conference, which the prince, having long considered him as one whose intellects were exhausted, was not very willing to afford: 'Why', said he, 'does this man thus intrude upon me? Shall I be never suffered to forget those lectures which pleased only while they were new, and to become new again must be forgotten?' He then walked into the wood, and composed himself to his usual meditations, when, before his thoughts had taken any settled form, he perceived his pursuer at his side, and was at first prompted by his impatience to go hastily away; but, being unwilling to offend a man whom he had once reverenced and still loved, he invited him to sit down with him on the bank.

The old man, thus encouraged, began to lament the change which had been lately observed in the prince, and to enquire why he so often retired from the pleasures of the palace to loneliness and silence. 'I fly from pleasure,' said the prince, 'because pleasure has ceased to please; I am lonely because I am miserable, and am unwilling to cloud with my presence the happiness of others.' 'You, Sir,' said the sage, 'are the first who has complained of misery in the Happy Valley. I hope to convince you that your complaints have no real cause. You are here in full possession of all that the emperor of Abyssinia can bestow; here is neither labour to be endured nor danger to be dreaded, yet here is all that labour or danger can procure. Look round and tell me which of your wants is without supply: if you want nothing, how are you unhappy?'

'That I want nothing,' said the prince, 'or that I know not what I want, is the cause of my complaint; if I had any known want, I should have a certain wish; that wish would excite endeavour, and I should not then repine to see the sun move so slowly towards the western mountain, or lament when the day breaks and sleep will no longer hide me from myself. When I see the kids and the lambs chasing one another, I fancy that I should be happy if I had something to pursue. But, possessing all that I can want, I find one day and one hour exactly like another, except that the latter is still more tedious than the former. Let your experience inform me how the day may now seem as short as in my childhood, while nature was yet fresh, and every moment showed me what I never had observed before. I have already enjoyed too much; give me something to desire.'

The old man was surprised at this new species of affliction, and knew not what to reply, yet was unwilling to be silent. 'Sir,' said he, 'if you had seen the miseries of the world, you would know how to value your present state.' 'Now', said the prince, 'you have given me something to desire; I shall long to see the miseries of the world, since the sight of them is necessary to happiness.'

CHAPTER IV

The prince continues to grieve and muse

At this time the sound of music proclaimed the hour of repast, and the conversation was concluded. The old man went away sufficiently discontented to find that his reasonings had produced the only conclusion which they were intended to prevent. But in the decline of life shame and grief are of short duration; whether it be that we bear easily what we have borne long, or that, finding ourselves in age less regarded, we less regard others; or that we look with slight regard upon afflictions to which we know that the hand of death is about to put an end.

The prince, whose views were extended to a wider space, could not speedily quiet his emotions. He had been before terrified at the length of life which nature promised him, because he considered that in a long time much must be endured; he now rejoiced in his youth, because in many years much might be done.

D

This first beam of hope that had been ever darted into his mind rekindled youth in his cheeks, and doubled the lustre of his eyes. He was fired with the desire of doing something, though he knew not yet with distinctness either end or means.

He was now no longer gloomy and unsocial; but, considering himself as master of a secret stock of happiness which he could enjoy only by concealing it, he affected to be busy in all schemes of diversion, and endeavoured to make others pleased with the state of which he himself was weary. But pleasures never can be so multiplied or continued as not to leave much of life unemployed; there were many hours, both of the night and day, which he could spend without suspicion in solitary thought. The load of life was much lightened: he went eagerly into the assemblies, because he supposed the frequency of his presence necessary to the success of his purposes; he retired gladly to privacy, because he had now a subject of thought.

His chief amusement was to picture to himself that world which he had never seen; to place himself in various conditions; to be entangled in imaginary difficulties, and to be engaged in wild adventures: but his benevolence always terminated his projects in the relief of distress, the detection of fraud, the defeat of oppression, and the diffusion of happiness.

Thus passed twenty months of the life of Rasselas. He busied himself so intensely in visionary bustle that he forgot his real solitude; and, amidst hourly preparations for the various incidents of human affairs, neglected to consider by what means he should mingle with mankind.

One day, as he was sitting on a bank, he feigned to himself an orphan virgin robbed of her little portion by a treacherous lover, and crying after him for restitution and redress. So strongly was the image impressed upon his mind, that he started up in the maid's defence, and run forward to seize the plunderer with all the eagerness of real pursuit. Fear naturally quickens the flight of guilt. Rasselas could not catch the fugitive with his utmost efforts; but, resolving to weary by perseverance him whom he could not surpass in speed, he pressed on till the foot of the mountain stopped his course.

Here he recollected himself, and smiled at his own useless impetuosity. Then raising his eyes to the mountain, 'This', said he, 'is the fatal obstacle that hinders at once the enjoyment of pleasure and the exercise of virtue. How long is it that my hopes and wishes have flown beyond this boundary of my life, which yet I never have attempted to surmount!'

Struck with this reflection, he sat down to muse, and remembered that, since he first resolved to escape from his confinement, the sun had passed twice over him in his annual course. He now felt a degree of regret with which he had never been before acquainted. He considered how much might have been done in the time which had passed and left nothing real behind it. He compared twenty months with the life of man. 'In life', said he, 'is not to be counted the ignorance of infancy, or imbecility of age. We are long before we are able to think, and we soon cease from the power of acting. The true period of human existence may be reasonably estimated as forty years, of which I have mused away the four and twentieth part. What I have lost was certain, for I have certainly possessed it; but of twenty months to come who can assure me?'

The consciousness of his own folly pierced him deeply, and he was long before he could be reconciled to himself. 'The rest of my time', said he, 'has been lost by the crime or folly of my ancestors and the absurd institutions of my country; I remember it with disgust, but without remorse: but the months that have passed since new light darted into my soul, since I formed a scheme of reasonable felicity, have been squandered by my own fault. I have lost that which can never be restored: I have seen the sun rise and set for twenty months, an idle gazer on the light of heaven. In this time the birds have left the nest of their mother, and committed themselves to the woods and to the skies: the kid has forsaken the teat, and learned by degrees to climb the rocks in quest of independent sustenance. I only have made no advances, but am still helpless and ignorant. The moon by more than twenty changes admonished me of the flux of life; the stream that rolled before my feet upbraided my inactivity. I sat feasting on intellectual luxury, regardless alike of the examples of the earth and the instructions of the planets. Twenty months are passed; who shall restore them?'

These sorrowful meditations fastened upon his mind; he passed four months in resolving to lose no more time in idle resolves, and was awakened to more vigorous exertion by hearing a maid, who had broken a porcelain cup, remark that what cannot be repaired is not to be regretted.

This was obvious; and Rasselas reproached himself that he had not discovered it, having not known, or not considered, how many useful hints are obtained by chance, and how often the mind, hurried by her own ardour to distant views, neglects the truths that lie open before her. He, for a few hours, regretted his regret, and from that time bent his whole mind upon the means of escaping from the valley of happiness.

CHAPTER V

The prince meditates his escape

He now found that it would be very difficult to effect that which it was very easy to suppose effected. When he looked round about him, he saw himself confined by the bars of nature, which had never yet been broken, and by the gate, through which none that once had passed it were ever able to return. He was now impatient as an eagle in a grate. He passed week after week in clambering the mountains to see if there was any aperture which the bushes might conceal, but found all the summits inaccessible by their prominence. The iron gate he despaired to open; for it was not only secured with all the power of art, but was always watched by successive sentinels, and was by its position exposed to the perpetual observation of all the inhabitants.

He then examined the cavern through which the waters of the lake were discharged; and, looking down at a time when the sun shone strongly upon its mouth, he discovered it to be full of broken rocks, which, though they permitted the stream to flow through many narrow passages, would stop any body of solid bulk. He returned discouraged and dejected; but, having now known the blessing of hope, resolved never to despair.

In these fruitless searches he spent ten months. The time, however, passed cheerfully away: in the morning he rose with new hope, in the evening applauded his own diligence, and in the night slept sound after his fatigue. He met a thousand amusements which beguiled his labour and diversified his thoughts. He discerned the various instincts of animals and properties of plants, and found the place replete with wonders, of which he purposed to solace himself with the contemplation, if he should never be able to accomplish his flight, rejoicing that his endeavours, though yet unsuccessful, had supplied him with a source of inexhaustible enquiry.

But his original curiosity was not yet abated; he resolved to obtain some knowledge of the ways of men. His wish still continued, but his hope grew less. He ceased to survey any longer the walls of his prison, and spared to search by new toils for interstices which he knew could not be found, yet determined to keep his design always in view and lay hold on any expedient that time should offer.

CHAPTER VI

A dissertation on the art of flying

Among the artists that had been allured into the Happy Valley, to labour for the accommodation and pleasure of its inhabitants, was a man eminent for his knowledge of the mechanic powers, who had contrived many engines both of use and recreation. By a wheel, which the stream turned, he forced the water into a tower, whence it was distributed to all the apartments of the palace. He erected a pavilion in the garden, around which he kept the air always cool by artificial showers. One of the groves, appropriated to the ladies, was ventilated by fans, to which the rivulet that run through it gave a constant motion; and instruments of soft music were placed at proper distances, of which some played by the impulse of the wind, and some by the power of the stream.

This artist was sometimes visited by Rasselas, who was pleased with every kind of knowledge, imagining that the time would come when all his acquisitions should be of use to him in the open world. He came one day to amuse himself in his usual manner, and found the master busy in building a sailing chariot: he saw that the design was practicable upon a level surface, and with expressions of great esteem solicited its completion. The workman was pleased to find himself so much regarded by the prince, and resolved to gain yet higher honours. 'Sir,' said he, 'you have seen but a small part of what the mechanic sciences can perform. I have been long of opinion that, instead of the tardy conveyance of ships and chariots, man might use the swifter migration of wings; that the fields of air are open to knowledge, and that only ignorance and idleness need crawl upon the ground.'

This hint rekindled the prince's desire of passing the mountains, and having seen what the mechanist had already performed, he was willing to fancy that he could do more; yet resolved to enquire further before he suffered hope to afflict him by disappointment. 'I am afraid', said he to the artist, 'that your imagination prevails over your skill, and that you now tell me rather what you wish than what you know. Every animal has his element assigned him; the birds have the air, and man and beasts the earth.' 'So', replied the mechanist, 'fishes have the water, in which yet beasts can swim by nature, and men by art. He that can swim needs not despair to fly: to swim is to fly in a grosser fluid, and to fly is to swim in a subtler. We are only to proportion our power of resistance to the different density of the matter through which we are to pass. You will be necessarily upborne by the air, if you can renew any impulse upon it faster than the air can recede from the pressure.'

'But the exercise of swimming', said the prince, 'is very laborious; the strongest limbs are soon wearied; I am afraid the act of flying will be yet more violent, and wings will be of no great use unless we can fly further than we can swim.'

'The labour of rising from the ground', said the artist, 'will be great, as we see it in the heavier domestic fowls; but, as we mount higher, the earth's attraction and the body's gravity will be gradually diminished, till we shall arrive at a region where the man will float in the air without any tendency to fall: no care will then be necessary but to move forwards, which the gentlest impulse will effect. You, Sir, whose curiosity is so extensive, will easily conceive with what pleasure a philosopher, furnished with wings and hovering in the sky, would see the earth, and all its inhabitants, rolling beneath him, and presenting to him successively, by its diurnal motion, all the countries within the same parallel. How must it amuse the pendant spectator to see the moving scene of land and ocean, cities and deserts! To survey with equal security the marts of trade, and the fields of battle; mountains infested by barbarians, and fruitful regions gladdened by plenty, and lulled by peace! How easily shall we then trace the Nile through all his passage; pass over to distant regions, and examine the face of nature from one extremity of the earth to the other!'

'All this', said the prince, 'is much to be desired, but I am afraid that no man will be able to breathe in these regions of speculation and tranquillity. I have been told that respiration is difficult upon lofty mountains, yet from these precipices, though so high as to produce great tenuity of the air, it is very easy to fall: and I suspect that from any height where life can be supported there may be danger of too quick descent.'

'Nothing', replied the artist, 'will ever be attempted, if all possible objections must be first overcome. If you will favour my project, I will try the first flight at my own hazard. I have considered the structure of all volant animals, and find the folding continuity of the bat's wings most easily accommodated to the human form. Upon this model I shall begin my task tomorrow, and in a year expect to tower into the air beyond the malice or pursuit of man. But I will work only on this condition, that the art shall not be divulged, and that you shall not require me to make wings for any but ourselves.'

'Why', said Rasselas, 'should you envy others so great an advantage? All skill ought to be exerted for universal good;

every man has owed much to others, and ought to repay the
kindness that he has received.'

'If men were all virtuous,' returned the artist, 'I should with
great alacrity teach them all to fly. But what would be the
security of the good, if the bad could at pleasure invade them
from the sky? Against an army sailing through the clouds,
neither walls, nor mountains, nor seas could afford any security.
A flight of northern savages might hover in the wind, and light
at once with irresistible violence upon the capital of a fruitful
region that was rolling under them. Even this valley, the retreat of princes, the abode of happiness, might be violated by
the sudden descent of some of the naked nations that swarm
on the coast of the southern sea.'

The prince promised secrecy, and waited for the performance, not wholly hopeless of success. He visited the work from
time to time, observed its progress, and remarked the in-
genious contrivances to facilitate motion, and unite levity with
strength. The artist was every day more certain that he should
leave vultures and eagles behind him, and the contagion of his
confidence seized upon the prince.

In a year the wings were finished, and, on a morning appointed, the maker appeared furnished for flight on a little
promontory: he waved his pinions awhile to gather air, then
leaped from his stand, and in an instant dropped into the lake.
His wings, which were of no use in the air, sustained him in
the water, and the prince drew him to land, half dead with
terror and vexation.

CHAPTER VII

The prince finds a man of learning

The prince was not much afflicted by this disaster, having
suffered himself to hope for a happier event only because he
had no other means of escape in view. He still persisted in his
design to leave the Happy Valley by the first opportunity.

His imagination was now at a stand; he had no prospect of

entering into the world, and, notwithstanding all his endeavours to support himself, discontent by degrees preyed upon him, and he began again to lose his thoughts in sadness, when the rainy season, which in these countries is periodical, made it inconvenient to wander in the woods.

The rain continued longer and with more violence than had been ever known: the clouds broke on the surrounding mountains, and the torrents streamed into the plain on every side, till the cavern was too narrow to discharge the water. The lake overflowed its banks, and all the level of the valley was covered with the inundation. The eminence, on which the palace was built, and some other spots of rising ground were all that the eye could now discover. The herds and flocks left the pastures, and both the wild beasts and the tame retreated to the mountains.

This inundation confined all the princes to domestic amusements, and the attention of Rasselas was particularly seized by a poem which Imlac recited upon the various conditions of humanity. He commanded the poet to attend him in his apartment and recite his verses a second time; then, entering into familiar talk, he thought himself happy in having found a man who knew the world so well, and could so skilfully paint the scenes of life. He asked a thousand questions about things, to which, though common to all other mortals, his confinement from childhood had kept him a stranger. The poet pitied his ignorance, and loved his curiosity, and entertained him from day to day with novelty and instruction, so that the prince regretted the necessity of sleep, and longed till the morning should renew his pleasure.

As they were sitting together, the prince commanded Imlac to relate his history, and to tell by what accident he was forced, or by what motive induced, to close his life in the Happy Valley. As he was going to begin his narrative, Rasselas was called to a concert, and obliged to restrain his curiosity till the evening.

CHAPTER VIII

The history of Imlac

The close of the day is, in the regions of the torrid zone, the only season of diversion and entertainment, and it was therefore midnight before the music ceased, and the princesses retired. Rasselas then called for his companion and required him to begin the story of his life.

'Sir,' said Imlac, 'my history will not be long: the life that is devoted to knowledge passes silently away, and is very little diversified by events. To talk in public, to think in solitude, to read and to hear, to enquire, and answer enquiries, is the business of a scholar. He wanders about the world without pomp or terror, and is neither known nor valued but by men like himself.

'I was born in the kingdom of Goiama, at no great distance from the fountain of the Nile. My father was a wealthy merchant, who traded between the inland countries of Afric and the ports of the Red Sea. He was honest, frugal and diligent, but of mean sentiments and narrow comprehension: he desired only to be rich, and to conceal his riches, lest he should be spoiled by the governors of the province.'

'Surely,' said the prince, 'my father must be negligent of his charge, if any man in his dominions dares take that which belongs to another. Does he not know that kings are accountable for injustice permitted as well as done? If I were emperor, not the meanest of my subjects should be oppressed with impunity. My blood boils when I am told that a merchant durst not enjoy his honest gains for fear of losing [them] by the rapacity of power. Name the governor who robbed the people, that I may declare his crimes to the emperor.'

'Sir,' said Imlac, 'your ardour is the natural effect of virtue animated by youth: the time will come when you will acquit your father, and perhaps hear with less impatience of the governor. Oppression is, in the Abyssinian dominions, neither frequent nor tolerated; but no form of government has been yet discovered by which cruelty can be wholly prevented.

Subordination supposes power on one part and subjection on the other; and if power be in the hands of men, it will sometimes be abused. The vigilance of the supreme magistrate may do much, but much will still remain undone. He can never know all the crimes that are committed, and can seldom punish all that he knows.'

'This', said the prince, 'I do not understand, but I had rather hear thee than dispute. Continue thy narration.'

'My father', proceeded Imlac, 'originally intended that I should have no other education than such as might qualify me for commerce; and, discovering in me great strength of memory and quickness of apprehension, often declared his hope that I should be some time the richest man in Abyssinia.'

'Why', said the prince, 'did thy father desire the increase of his wealth, when it was already greater than he durst discover or enjoy? I am unwilling to doubt thy veracity, yet inconsistencies cannot both be true.'

'Inconsistencies', answered Imlac, 'cannot both be right, but, imputed to man, they may both be true. Yet diversity is not inconsistency. My father might expect a time of greater security. However, some desire is necessary to keep life in motion, and he whose real wants are supplied must admit those of fancy.'

'This', said the prince, 'I can in some measure conceive. I repent that I interrupted thee.'

'With this hope', proceeded Imlac, 'he sent me to school; but, when I had once found the delight of knowledge, and felt the pleasure of intelligence and the pride of invention, I began silently to despise riches, and determined to disappoint the purpose of my father, whose grossness of conception raised my pity. I was twenty years old before his tenderness would expose me to the fatigue of travel, in which time I had been instructed, by successive masters, in all the literature of my native country. As every hour taught me something new, I lived in a continual course of gratifications; but, as I advanced towards manhood, I lost much of the reverence with which I had been used to look on my instructors; because, when the lesson was ended, I did not find them wiser or better than common men.

'At length my father resolved to initiate me in commerce, and, opening one of his subterranean treasuries, counted out ten thousand pieces of gold. "This, young man," said he, "is the stock with which you must negotiate. I began with less than the fifth part, and you see how diligence and parsimony have increased it. This is your own to waste or to improve. If you squander it by negligence or caprice, you must wait for my death before you will be rich: if, in four years, you double your stock, we will thenceforward let subordination cease, and live together as friends and partners; for he shall always be equal with me, who is equally skilled in the art of growing rich."

'We laid our money upon camels, concealed in bales of cheap goods, and travelled to the shore of the Red Sea. When I cast my eye on the expanse of waters my heart bounded like that of a prisoner escaped. I felt an unextinguishable curiosity kindle in my mind, and resolved to snatch this opportunity of seeing the manners of other nations, and of learning sciences unknown in Abyssinia.

'I remembered that my father had obliged me to the improvement of my stock, not by a promise which I ought not to violate, but by a penalty which I was at liberty to incur; and therefore determined to gratify my predominant desire, and, by drinking at the fountains of knowledge, to quench the thirst of curiosity.

'As I was supposed to trade without connection with my father, it was easy for me to become acquainted with the master of a ship, and procure a passage to some other country. I had no motives of choice to regulate my voyage; it was sufficient for me that, wherever I wandered, I should see a country which I had not seen before. I therefore entered a ship bound for Surat, having left a letter for my father declaring my intention.

CHAPTER IX

The history of Imlac continued

'When I first entered upon the world of waters, and lost sight of land, I looked round about me with pleasing terror, and, thinking my soul enlarged by the boundless prospect, imagined that I could gaze round for ever without satiety; but, in a short time, I grew weary of looking on barren uniformity, where I could only see again what I had already seen. I then descended into the ship, and doubted for a while whether all my future pleasures would not end like this in disgust and disappointment. "Yet, surely," said I, "the ocean and the land are very different; the only variety of water is rest and motion, but the earth has mountains and valleys, deserts and cities: it is inhabited by men of different customs and contrary opinions; and I may hope to find variety in life, though I should miss it in nature."

'With this hope I quieted my mind; and amused myself during the voyage sometimes by learning from the sailors the art of navigation, which I have never practised, and sometimes by forming schemes for my conduct in different situations, in not one of which I have been ever placed.

'I was almost weary of my naval amusements when we landed safely at Surat. I secured my money, and, purchasing some commodities for show, joined myself to a caravan that was passing into the inland country. My companions, for some reason or other, conjecturing that I was rich, and, by my enquiries and admiration, finding that I was ignorant, considered me as a novice whom they had a right to cheat, and who was to learn at the usual expense the art of fraud. They exposed me to the theft of servants and the exaction of officers, and saw me plundered upon false pretences, without any advantage to themselves, but that of rejoicing in the superiority of their own knowledge.'

'Stop a moment,' said the prince. 'Is there such depravity in man, as that he should injure another without benefit to himself? I can easily conceive that all are pleased with superiority;

but your ignorance was merely accidental, which, being neither your crime nor your folly, could afford them no reason to applaud themselves; and the knowledge which they had, and which you wanted, they might as effectually have shown by warning you as betraying you.'

'Pride', said Imlac, 'is seldom delicate; it will please itself with very mean advantages; and envy feels not its own happiness, but when it may be compared with the misery of others. They were my enemies because they thought me rich, and my oppressors because they delighted to find me weak.'

'Proceed,' said the prince. 'I doubt not of the facts which you relate, but imagine that you impute them to mistaken motives.'

'In this company', said Imlac, 'I arrived at Agra, the capital of Indostan, the city in which the great Mogul commonly resides. I applied myself to the language of the country, and in a few months was able to converse with the learned men, some of whom I found morose and reserved, and others easy and communicative; some were unwilling to teach another what they had with difficulty learned themselves, and some showed that the end of their studies was to gain the dignity of instructing.

'To the tutor of the young princes I recommended myself so much that I was presented to the emperor as a man of uncommon knowledge. The emperor asked me many questions concerning my country and my travels, and, though I cannot now recollect anything that he uttered above the power of a common man, he dismissed me astonished at his wisdom, and enamoured of his goodness.

'My credit was now so high, that the merchants, with whom I had travelled, applied to me for recommendations to the ladies of the court. I was surprised at their confidence of solicitation, and gently reproached them with their practices on the road. They heard me with cold indifference, and showed no tokens of shame or sorrow.

'They then urged their request with the offer of a bribe; but what I would not do for kindness I would not do for money, and refused them, not because they had injured me, but because I would not enable them to injure others; for I knew they would have made use of my credit to cheat those who should buy their wares.

'Having resided at Agra till there was no more to be learned, I travelled into Persia, where I saw many remains of ancient magnificence, and observed many new accommodations of life. The Persians are a nation eminently social, and their assemblies afforded me daily opportunities of remarking characters and manners, and of tracing human nature through all its variations.

'From Persia I passed into Arabia, where I saw a nation at once pastoral and warlike; who live without any settled habitation; whose only wealth is their flocks and herds; and who have yet carried on, through all ages, an hereditary war with all mankind, though they neither covet nor envy their possessions.

CHAPTER X

Imlac's history continued. A dissertation upon poetry

'Wherever I went, I found that poetry was considered as the highest learning, and regarded with a veneration somewhat approaching to that which man would pay to the Angelic Nature. And it yet fills me with wonder, that, in almost all countries, the most ancient poets are considered as the best: whether it be that every other kind of knowledge is an acquisition gradually attained, and poetry is a gift conferred at once; or that the first poetry of every nation surprised them as a novelty, and retained the credit by consent which it received by accident at first: or whether the province of poetry is to describe nature and passion, which are always the same, and the first writers took possession of the most striking objects for description and the most probable occurrences for fiction, and left nothing to those that followed them but transcription of the same events, and new combinations of the same images —whatever be the reason, it is commonly observed that the early writers are in possession of nature, and their followers of art: that the first excel in strength and invention, and the latter in elegance and refinement.

'I was desirous to add my name to this illustrious fraternity. I read all the poets of Persia and Arabia, and was able to repeat by memory the volumes that are suspended in the mosque of Mecca. But I soon found that no man was ever great by imitation. My desire of excellence impelled me to transfer my attention to nature and to life. Nature was to be my subject, and men to be my auditors: I could never describe what I had not seen: I could not hope to move those with delight or terror, whose interests and opinions I did not understand.

'Being now resolved to be a poet, I saw everything with a new purpose; my sphere of attention was suddenly magnified; no kind of knowledge was to be overlooked. I ranged mountains and deserts for images and resemblances, and pictured upon my mind every tree of the forest and flower of the valley. I observed with equal care the crags of the rock and the pinnacles of the palace. Sometimes I wandered along the mazes of the rivulet, and sometimes watched the changes of the summer clouds. To a poet nothing can be useless. Whatever is beautiful, and whatever is dreadful, must be familiar to his imagination: he must be conversant with all that is awfully vast or elegantly little. The plants of the garden, the animals of the wood, the minerals of the earth, and meteors of the sky must all concur to store his mind with inexhaustible variety: for every idea is useful for the enforcement or decoration of moral or religious truth; and he who knows most will have most power of diversifying his scenes, and of gratifying his reader with remote allusions and unexpected instruction.

'All the appearances of nature I was therefore careful to study, and every country which I have surveyed has contributed something to my poetical powers.'

'In so wide a survey,' said the prince, 'you must surely have left much unobserved. I have lived, till now, within the circuit of these mountains, and yet cannot walk abroad without the sight of something which I had never beheld before, or never heeded.'

'The business of a poet', said Imlac, 'is to examine not the individual but the species; to remark general properties and large appearances: he does not number the streaks of the tulip, or describe the different shades in the verdure of the forest. He is to exhibit in his portraits of nature such prominent and striking features, as recall the original to every mind; and must neglect the minuter discriminations, which one may have remarked and another have neglected, for those characteristics which are alike obvious to vigilance and carelessness.

'But the knowledge of nature is only half the task of a poet; he must be acquainted likewise with all the modes of life. His character requires that he estimate the happiness and misery of every condition; observe the power of all the passions in all their combinations, and trace the changes of the human mind as they are modified by various institutions and accidental influences of climate or custom, from the sprightliness of infancy to the despondence of decrepitude. He must divest himself of the prejudices of his age or country; he must consider right and wrong in their abstracted and invariable state; he must disregard present laws and opinions, and rise to general and transcendental truths, which will always be the same; he must therefore content himself with the slow progress of his name, contemn the applause of his own time, and commit his claims to the justice of posterity. He must write as the interpreter of nature, and the legislator of mankind, and consider himself as presiding over the thoughts and manners of successive generations, as a being superior to time and place. His labour is not yet at an end: he must know many languages and many sciences; and, that his style may be worthy of his thoughts, must, by incessant practice, familiarise to himself every delicacy of speech and grace of harmony.'

E

CHAPTER XI

Imlac's narrative continued. A hint on pilgrimage

Imlac now felt the enthusiastic fit, and was proceeding to aggrandise his own profession, when the prince cried out, 'Enough! Thou hast convinced me that no human being can ever be a poet. Proceed now with thy narration.'

'To be a poet', said Imlac, 'is indeed very difficult.' 'So difficult,' returned the prince, 'that I will at present hear no more of his labours. Tell me whither you went when you had seen Persia.'

'From Persia', said the poet, 'I travelled through Syria, and for three years resided in Palestine, where I conversed with great numbers of the northern and western nations of Europe, the nations which are now in possession of all power and all knowledge, whose armies are irresistible, and whose fleets command the remotest parts of the globe. When I compared these men with the natives of our own kingdom and those that surround us, they appeared almost another order of beings. In their countries it is difficult to wish for anything that may not be obtained: a thousand arts, of which we never heard, are continually labouring for their convenience and pleasure; and whatever their own climate has denied them is supplied by their commerce.'

'By what means', said the prince, 'are the Europeans thus powerful? Or why, since they can so easily visit Asia and Africa for trade or conquest, cannot the Asiatics and Africans invade their coasts, plant colonies in their ports, and give laws to their natural princes? The same wind that carries them back would bring us thither.'

'They are more powerful, Sir, than we,' answered Imlac, 'because they are wiser; knowledge will always predominate over ignorance, as man governs the other animals. But why their knowledge is more than ours, I know not what reason can be given, but the unsearchable will of the Supreme Being.'

'When', said the prince with a sigh, 'shall I be able to visit Palestine, and mingle with this mighty confluence of nations?

Till that happy moment shall arrive, let me fill up the time with such representations as thou canst give me. I am not ignorant of the motive that assembles such numbers in that place, and cannot but consider it as the centre of wisdom and piety, to which the best and wisest men of every land must be continually resorting.'

'There are some nations', said Imlac, 'that send few visitants to Palestine; for many numerous and learned sects in Europe concur to censure pilgrimage as superstitious, or deride it as ridiculous.'

'You know', said the prince, 'how little my life has made me acquainted with diversity of opinions: it will be too long to hear the arguments on both sides; you, that have considered them, tell me the result.'

'Pilgrimage,' said Imlac, 'like many other acts of piety, may be reasonable or superstitious, according to the principles upon which it is performed. Long journeys in search of truth are not commanded. Truth, such as is necessary to the regulation of life, is always found where it is honestly sought. Change of place is no natural cause of the increase of piety, for it inevitably produces dissipation of mind. Yet, since men go every day to view the places where great actions have been performed and return with stronger impressions of the event, curiosity of the same kind may naturally dispose us to view that country whence our religion had its beginning; and I believe no man surveys those awful scenes without some confirmation of holy resolutions. That the Supreme Being may be more easily propitiated in one place than in another is the dream of idle superstition; but that some places may operate upon our own minds in an uncommon manner is an opinion which hourly experience will justify. He who supposes that his vices may be more successfully combated in Palestine will, perhaps, find himself mistaken, yet he may go thither without folly: he who thinks they will be more freely pardoned dishonours at once his reason and religion.'

'These', said the prince, 'are European distinctions. I will consider them another time. What have you found to be the effect of knowledge? Are those nations happier than we?'

'There is so much infelicity', said the poet, 'in the world, that scarce any man has leisure from his own distresses to estimate the comparative happiness of others. Knowledge is certainly one of the means of pleasure, as is confessed by the natural desire which every mind feels of increasing its ideas. Ignorance is mere privation, by which nothing can be produced: it is a vacuity in which the soul sits motionless and torpid for want of attraction; and, without knowing why, we always rejoice when we learn, and grieve when we forget. I am therefore inclined to conclude that, if nothing counteracts the natural consequence of learning, we grow more happy as our minds take a wider range.

'In enumerating the particular comforts of life we shall find many advantages on the side of the Europeans. They cure wounds and diseases with which we languish and perish. We suffer inclemencies of weather which they can obviate. They have engines for the despatch of many laborious works, which we must perform by manual industry. There is such communication between distant places that one friend can hardly be said to be absent from another. Their policy removes all public inconveniences: they have roads cut through their mountains, and bridges laid upon their rivers. And, if we descend to the privacies of life, their habitations are more commodious, and their possessions are more secure.'

'They are surely happy,' said the prince, 'who have all these conveniences, of which I envy none so much as the facility with which separated friends interchange their thoughts.'

'The Europeans', answered Imlac, 'are less unhappy than we, but they are not happy. Human life is everywhere a state in which much is to be endured, and little to be enjoyed.'

CHAPTER XII

The story of Imlac continued

'I am not yet willing', said the prince, 'to suppose that happiness is so parsimoniously distributed to mortals, nor can believe but that, if I had the choice of life, I should be able to fill every day with pleasure. I would injure no man, and should provoke no resentment: I would relieve every distress, and should enjoy the benedictions of gratitude. I would choose my friends among the wise, and my wife among the virtuous; and therefore should be in no danger from treachery or unkindness. My children should, by my care, be learned and pious, and would repay to my age what their childhood had received. What would dare to molest him who might call on every side to thousands enriched by his bounty, or assisted by his power? And why should not life glide quietly away in the soft reciprocation of protection and reverence? All this may be done without the help of European refinements, which appear by their effects to be rather specious than useful. Let us leave them and pursue our journey.'

'From Palestine', said Imlac, 'I passed through many regions of Asia, in the more civilized kingdoms as a trader, and among the barbarians of the mountains as a pilgrim. At last I began to long for my native country, that I might repose after my travels and fatigues in the places where I had spent my earliest years, and gladden my old companions with the recital of my adventures. Often did I figure to myself those with whom I had sported away the gay hours of dawning life sitting round me in its evening, wondering at my tales and listening to my counsels.

'When this thought had taken possession of my mind, I considered every moment as wasted which did not bring me nearer to Abyssinia. I hastened into Egypt, and, notwithstanding my impatience, was detained ten months in the contemplation of its ancient magnificence, and in enquiries after the remains of its ancient learning. I found in Cairo a mixture of all nations, some brought thither by the love of knowledge, some by the hope of gain, and many by the desire of living after their own manner without observation and of lying hid in the obscurity of multitudes: for, in a city populous as Cairo, it is possible to obtain at the same time the gratifications of society and the secrecy of solitude.

'From Cairo I travelled to Suez and embarked on the Red Sea, passing along the coast till I arrived at the port from

which I had departed twenty years before. Here I joined
myself to a caravan and re-entered my native country.

'I now expected the caresses of my kinsmen and the con-
gratulations of my friends, and was not without hope that my
father, whatever value he had set upon riches, would own
with gladness and pride a son who was able to add to the
felicity and honour of the nation. But I was soon convinced
that my thoughts were vain. My father had been dead four-
teen years, having divided his wealth among my brothers, who
were removed to some other provinces. Of my companions
the greater part was in the grave; of the rest some could with
difficulty remember me, and some considered me as one corrupted by foreign manners.

'A man used to vicissitudes is not easily dejected. I forgot
after a time my disappointment, and endeavoured to recommend myself to the nobles of the kingdom: they admitted me
to their tables, heard my story, and dismissed me. I opened
a school, and was prohibited to teach. I then resolved to sit
down in the quiet of domestic life, and addressed a lady that
was fond of my conversation, but rejected my suit because my
father was a merchant.

'Wearied at last with solicitation and repulses, I resolved
to hide myself for ever from the world, and depend no longer
on the opinion or caprice of others. I waited for the time when
the gate of the Happy Valley should open, that I might bid
farewell to hope and fear: the day came; my performance was
distinguished with favour, and I resigned myself with joy to
perpetual confinement.'

'Hast thou here found happiness at last?' said Rasselas. 'Tell
me without reserve; art thou content with thy condition? Or
dost thou wish to be again wandering and enquiring? All the
inhabitants of this valley celebrate their lot, and, at the annual
visit of the emperor, invite others to partake of their felicity.'

'Great prince,' said Imlac, 'I shall speak the truth: I know
not one of all your attendants who does not lament the hour
when he entered this retreat. I am less unhappy than the rest,
because I have a mind replete with images, which I can vary
and combine at pleasure. I can amuse my solitude by the

renovation of the knowledge which begins to fade from my memory, and with the recollection of the accidents of my past life. Yet all this ends in the sorrowful consideration that my acquirements are now useless and that none of my pleasures can be again enjoyed. The rest, whose minds have no impression but of the present moment, are either corroded by malignant passions or sit stupid in the gloom of perpetual vacancy.'

'What passions can infest those', said the prince, 'who have no rivals? We are in a place where impotence precludes malice, and where all envy is repressed by community of enjoyments.'

'There may be community', said Imlac, 'of material possessions, but there can never be community of love or of esteem. It must happen that one will please more than another; he that knows himself despised will always be envious, and still more envious and malevolent if he is condemned to live in the presence of those who despise him. The invitations by which they allure others to a state which they feel to be wretched proceed from the natural malignity of hopeless misery. They are weary of themselves and of each other, and expect to find relief in new companions. They envy the liberty which their folly has forfeited, and would gladly see all mankind imprisoned like themselves.

'From this crime, however, I am wholly free. No man can say that he is wretched by my persuasion. I look with pity on the crowds who are annually soliciting admission to captivity, and wish that it were lawful for me to warn them of their danger.'

'My dear Imlac,' said the prince. 'I will open to thee my whole heart, that I have long meditated an escape from the Happy Valley. I have examined the mountains on every side, but find myself insuperably barred: teach me the way to break my prison; thou shalt be the companion of my flight, the guide of my rambles, the partner of my fortune, and my sole director in the *choice of life*.'

'Sir,' answered the poet, 'your escape will be difficult, and, perhaps, you may soon repent your curiosity. The world, which you figure to yourself smooth and quiet as the lake in the valley, you will find a sea foaming with tempests and boiling with whirlpools: you will be sometimes overwhelmed by the waves of violence, and sometimes dashed against the rocks of treachery. Amidst wrongs and frauds, competitions and anxieties, you will wish a thousand times for these seats of quiet, and willingly quit hope to be free from fear.'

'Do not seek to deter me from my purpose,' said the prince. 'I am impatient to see what thou hast seen; and, since thou art thyself weary of the valley, it is evident that thy former state was better than this. Whatever be the consequence of my experiment, I am resolved to judge with my own eyes of the various conditions of men, and then to make deliberately my *choice of life.*'

'I am afraid', said Imlac, 'you are hindered by stronger restraints than my persuasions; yet, if your determination is fixed, I do not counsel you to despair. Few things are impossible to diligence and skill.'

CHAPTER XIII

Rasselas discovers the means of escape

The prince now dismissed his favourite to rest, but the narrative of wonders and novelties filled his mind with perturbation. He revolved all that he had heard, and prepared innumerable questions for the morning.

Much of his uneasiness was now removed. He had a friend to whom he could impart his thoughts, and whose experience could assist him in his designs. His heart was no longer condemned to swell with silent vexation. He thought that even the Happy Valley might be endured with such a companion, and that, if they could range the world together, he should have nothing further to desire.

In a few days the water was discharged, and the ground dried. The prince and Imlac then walked out together to converse without the notice of the rest. The prince, whose thoughts were always on the wing, as he passed by the gate, said, with a countenance of sorrow, 'Why art thou so strong, and why is man so weak?'

'Man is not weak,' answered his companion. 'Knowledge is more than equivalent to force. The master of mechanics laughs at strength. I can burst the gate, but cannot do it secretly. Some other expedient must be tried.'

As they were walking on the side of the mountain they observed that the conies, which the rain had driven from their burrows, had taken shelter among the bushes, and formed holes behind them, tending upwards in an oblique line. 'It has been the opinion of antiquity,' said Imlac, 'that human reason borrowed many arts from the instinct of animals; let us, therefore, not think ourselves degraded by learning from the coney. We may escape by piercing the mountain in the same direction. We will begin where the summit hangs over the middle part, and labour upward till we shall issue out beyond the prominence.'

The eyes of the prince, when he heard this proposal, sparkled with joy. The execution was easy, and the success certain.

No time was now lost. They hastened early in the morning to choose a place proper for their mine. They clambered with great fatigue among crags and brambles, and returned without having discovered any part that favoured their design. The second and the third day were spent in the same manner, and with the same frustration. But on the fourth they found a small cavern, concealed by a thicket, where they resolved to make their experiment.

Imlac procured instruments proper to hew stone and remove earth, and they fell to their work on the next day with more eagerness than vigour. They were presently exhausted by their efforts, and sat down to pant upon the grass. The prince, for a moment, appeared to be discouraged. 'Sir,' said his companion, 'practice will enable us to continue our labour for a longer time; mark, however, how far we have advanced, and you will find that our toil will some time have an end. Great works are performed, not by strength, but perseverance: yonder palace was raised by single stones, yet you see its height and spaciousness. He that shall walk with vigour three hours a day will pass in seven years a space equal to the circumference of the globe.'

They returned to their labour day after day, and, in a short time, found a fissure in the rock which enabled them to pass far with very little obstruction. This Rasselas considered as a good omen. 'Do not disturb your mind', said Imlac, 'with other hopes or fears than reason may suggest: if you are pleased with prognostics of good, you will be terrified likewise with tokens of evil, and your whole life will be a prey to superstition. Whatever facilitates our work is more than an omen, it is a cause of success. This is one of those pleasing surprises which often happen to active resolution. Many things difficult to design prove easy to performance.'

CHAPTER XIV

Rasselas and Imlac receive an unexpected visit

They had now wrought their way to the middle, and solaced their labour with the approach of liberty, when the prince, coming down to refresh himself with air, found his sister Nekayah standing before the mouth of the cavity. He started and stood confused, afraid to tell his design, and yet hopeless to conceal it. A few moments determined him to repose on her fidelity, and secure her secrecy by a declaration without reserve.

'Do not imagine', said the princess, 'that I came hither as a spy: I had often observed from my window that you and Imlac directed your walk every day towards the same point, but I did not suppose you had any better reason for the preference than a cooler shade, or more fragrant bank, nor followed you with any other design than to partake of your conversation. Since then not suspicion but fondness has detected you, let me not lose the advantage of my discovery. I am equally weary of confinement with yourself, and not less desirous of knowing what is done or suffered in the world.

Permit me to fly with you from this tasteless tranquillity, which will yet grow more loathsome when you have left me. You may deny me to accompany you, but cannot hinder me from following.'

The prince, who loved Nekayah above his other sisters, had no inclination to refuse her request, and grieved that he had lost an opportunity of showing his confidence by a voluntary communication. It was therefore agreed that she should leave the valley with them, and that, in the meantime, she should watch lest any other straggler should, by chance or curiosity, follow them to the mountain.

At length their labour was at an end; they saw light beyond the prominence, and, issuing to the top of the mountain, beheld the Nile, yet a narrow current, wandering beneath them.

The prince looked round with rapture, anticipated all the pleasures of travel, and in thought was already transported beyond his father's dominions. Imlac, though very joyful at his escape, had less expectation of pleasure in the world, which he had before tried, and of which he had been weary.

Rasselas was so much delighted with a wider horizon that he could not soon be persuaded to return into the valley. He informed his sister that the way was open, and that nothing now remained but to prepare for their departure.

CHAPTER XV

The prince and princess leave the valley, and see many wonders

The prince and princess had jewels sufficient to make them rich whenever they came into a place of commerce, which, by Imlac's direction, they hid in their clothes, and, on the night of the next full moon, all left the valley. The princess was followed only by a single favourite, who did not know whither she was going.

They clambered through the cavity, and began to go down on the other side. The princess and her maid turned their eyes towards every part, and, seeing nothing to bound their prospect, considered themselves as in danger of being lost in a dreary vacuity. They stopped and trembled. 'I am almost afraid', said the princess, 'to begin a journey of which I cannot perceive an end, and to venture into this immense plain where I may be approached on every side by men whom I never saw.' The prince felt nearly the same emotions, though he thought it more manly to conceal them.

Imlac smiled at their terrors, and encouraged them to proceed, but the princess continued irresolute till she had been imperceptibly drawn forward too far to return.

In the morning they found some shepherds in the field, who set milk and fruits before them. The princess wondered that she did not see a palace ready for her reception and a table spread with delicacies; but, being faint and hungry, she drank the milk and ate the fruits, and thought them of a higher flavour than the products of the valley.

They travelled forward by easy journeys, being all unaccustomed to toil or difficulty, and knowing that, though they might be missed, they could not be pursued. In a few days they came into a more populous region, where Imlac was diverted with the admiration which his companions expressed at the diversity of manners, stations, and employments.

Their dress was such as might not bring upon them the suspicion of having anything to conceal, yet the prince, wherever he came, expected to be obeyed, and the princess was frighted, because those that came into her presence did not prostrate themselves before her. Imlac was forced to observe them with great vigilance, lest they should betray their rank by their unusual behaviour, and detained them several weeks in the first village to accustom them to the sight of common mortals.

By degrees the royal wanderers were taught to understand that they had for a time laid aside their dignity, and were to expect only such regard as liberality and courtesy could procure. And Imlac, having by many admonitions prepared them to endure the tumults of a port and the ruggedness of the commercial race, brought them down to the sea-coast.

The prince and his sister, to whom everything was new, were gratified equally at all places, and therefore remained for some months at the port without any inclination to pass further. Imlac was content with their stay, because he did not think it safe to expose them, unpractised in the world, to the hazards of a foreign country.

At last he began to fear lest they should be discovered, and proposed to fix a day for their departure. They had no pretensions to judge for themselves, and referred the whole scheme to his direction. He therefore took passage in a ship to Suez, and, when the time came, with great difficulty prevailed on the princess to enter the vessel. They had a quick and prosperous voyage, and from Suez travelled by land to Cairo.

CHAPTER XVI

They enter Cairo, and find every man happy

As they approached the city, which filled the strangers with astonishment, 'This', said Imlac to the prince, 'is the place where travellers and merchants assemble from all the corners of the earth. You will here find men of every character and every occupation. Commerce is here honourable: I will act as a merchant, and you shall live as strangers, who have no other end of travel than curiosity; it will soon be observed that we are rich; our reputation will procure us access to all whom we shall desire to know; you will see all the conditions of humanity, and enable yourself at leisure to make your *choice of life*.'

They now entered the town, stunned by the noise and offended by the crowds. Instruction had not yet so prevailed over habit but that they wondered to see themselves pass undistinguished along the street, and met by the lowest of the people without reverence or notice. The princess could not at first bear the thought of being levelled with the vulgar, and, for some days, continued in her chamber, where she was served by her favourite as in the palace of the valley.

Imlac, who understood traffic, sold part of the jewels the next day, and hired a house, which he adorned with such magnificence that he was immediately considered as a merchant of great wealth. His politeness attracted many acquaintance, and his generosity made him courted by many dependants. His table was crowded by men of every nation, who all admired his knowledge and solicited his favour. His companions, not being able to mix in the conversation, could make no discovery of their ignorance or surprise, and were gradually initiated in the world as they gained knowledge of the language.

The prince had, by frequent lectures, been taught the use and nature of money; but the ladies could not for a long time comprehend what the merchants did with small pieces of gold and silver, or why things of so little use should be received as equivalent to the necessaries of life.

They studied the language two years, while Imlac was preparing to set before them the various ranks and conditions of mankind. He grew acquainted with all who had anything uncommon in their fortune or conduct. He frequented the voluptuous and the frugal, the idle and the busy, the merchants and the men of learning.

The prince, being now able to converse with fluency, and having learned the caution necessary to be observed in his intercourse with strangers, began to accompany Imlac to places of resort and to enter into all assemblies, that he might make his *choice of life*.

For some time he thought choice needless, because all appeared to him equally happy. Wherever he went he met gaiety and kindness, and heard the song of joy or the laugh of carelessness. He began to believe that the world overflowed with universal plenty, and that nothing was withheld either from want or merit; that every hand showered liberality, and every heart melted with benevolence. 'And who then', says he, 'will be suffered to be wretched?'

Imlac permitted the pleasing delusion, and was unwilling to crush the hope of inexperience; till one day, having sat a while silent, 'I know not', said the prince, 'what can be the reason that I am more unhappy than any of our friends. I see them perpetually and unalterably cheerful, but feel my own mind restless and uneasy. I am unsatisfied with those pleasures which I seem most to court; I live in the crowds of jollity, not so much to enjoy company as to shun myself, and am only loud and merry to conceal my sadness.'

'Every man', said Imlac, 'may, by examining his own mind, guess what passes in the minds of others: when you feel that your own gaiety is counterfeit, it may justly lead you to suspect that of your companions not to be sincere. Envy is commonly reciprocal. We are long before we are convinced that happiness is never to be found, and each believes it possessed by others, to keep alive the hope of obtaining it for himself. In the assembly where you passed the last night, there appeared such sprightliness of air and volatility of fancy as might have suited beings of an higher order, formed to inhabit serener regions inaccessible to care or sorrow: yet, believe me, prince, there was not one who did not dread the moment when solitude should deliver him to the tyranny of reflection.'

'This', said the prince, 'may be true of others, since it is true of me; yet, whatever be the general infelicity of man, one condition is more happy than another, and wisdom surely directs us to take the least evil in the *choice of life*.'

'The causes of good and evil', answered Imlac, 'are so various and uncertain, so often entangled with each other, so diversified by various relations, and so much subject to accidents which cannot be foreseen, that he who would fix his condition upon incontestable reasons of preference must live and die enquiring and deliberating.'

'But, surely,' said Rasselas, 'the wise men, to whom we listen with reverence and wonder, chose that mode of life for themselves which they thought most likely to make them happy.'

'Very few', said the poet, 'live by choice. Every man is placed in his present condition by causes which acted without his foresight, and with which he did not always willingly cooperate; and therefore you will rarely meet one who does not think the lot of his neighbour better than his own.'

'I am pleased to think,' said the prince, 'that my birth has given me at least one advantage over others, by enabling me to determine for myself. I have here the world before me; I will review it at leisure: surely happiness is somewhere to be found.'

CHAPTER XVII

The prince associates with young men of spirit and gaiety

Rasselas rose next day and resolved to begin his experiments upon life. 'Youth', cried he, 'is the time of gladness: I will join myself to the young men, whose only business is to gratify their desires, and whose time is all spent in a succession of enjoyments.'

To such societies he was readily admitted, but a few days brought him back weary and disgusted. Their mirth was without images, their laughter without motive; their pleasures were gross and sensual, in which the mind had no part; their conduct was at once wild and mean; they laughed at order and at law, but the frown of power dejected and the eye of wisdom abashed them.

The prince soon concluded that he should never be happy in a course of life of which he was ashamed. He thought it unsuitable to a reasonable being to act without a plan, and to be sad or cheerful only by chance. 'Happiness', said he, 'must be something solid and permanent, without fear and without uncertainty.'

But his young companions had gained so much of his regard by their frankness and courtesy that he could not leave them without warning and remonstrance. 'My friends,' said he, 'I have seriously considered our manners and our prospects, and find that we have mistaken our own interest. The first years of man must make provision for the last. He that never thinks never can be wise. Perpetual levity must end in ignorance; and intemperance, though it may fire the spirits for an hour, will make life short or miserable. Let us consider that youth is of no long duration, and that in maturer age, when the enchantments of fancy shall cease and phantoms of delight dance no more about us, we shall have no comforts but the esteem of wise men and the means of doing good. Let us, therefore, stop, while to stop is in our power: let us live as men who are sometime to grow old, and to whom it will be the most dreadful of all evils not to count their past years but by follies, and to be reminded of their former luxuriance of health only by the maladies which riot has produced.'

They stared awhile in silence one upon another, and at last drove him away by a general chorus of continued laughter.

The consciousness that his sentiments were just and his intentions kind was scarcely sufficient to support him against the horror of derision. But he recovered his tranquillity, and pursued his search.

CHAPTER XVIII

The prince finds a wise and happy man

As he was one day walking in the street, he saw a spacious building which all were, by the open doors, invited to enter: he followed the stream of people, and found it a hall or school of declamation, in which professors read lectures to their auditory. He fixed his eye upon a sage raised above the rest, who discoursed with great energy on the government of the passions. His look was venerable, his action graceful, his pronunciation clear, and his diction elegant. He showed, with great strength of sentiment and variety of illustration, that human nature is degraded and debased when the lower faculties predominate over the higher; that when fancy, the parent of passion, usurps the dominion of the mind, nothing ensues but the natural effect of unlawful government—perturbation and confusion; that she betrays the fortresses of the intellect to rebels, and excites her children to sedition against reason their lawful sovereign. He compared reason to the sun, of which the light is constant, uniform, and lasting; and fancy to a meteor, of bright but transitory lustre, irregular in its motion and delusive in its direction.

F

He then communicated the various precepts given from time to time for the conquest of passion, and displayed the happiness of those who had obtained the important victory, after which man is no longer the slave of fear nor the fool of hope; is no more emaciated by envy, inflamed by anger, emasculated by tenderness, or depressed by grief; but walks on calmly through the tumults or the privacies of life, as the sun pursues alike his course through the calm or the stormy sky.

He enumerated many examples of heroes, immovable by pain or pleasure, who looked with indifference on those modes or accidents to which the vulgar give the names of good and evil. He exhorted his hearers to lay aside their prejudices, and arm themselves against the shafts of malice or misfortune by invulnerable patience, concluding that this state only was happiness and that this happiness was in everyone's power.

Rasselas listened to him with the veneration due to the instructions of a superior being, and, waiting for him at the door, humbly implored the liberty of visiting so great a master of true wisdom. The lecturer hesitated a moment, when Rasselas put a purse of gold into his hand, which he received with a mixture of joy and wonder.

'I have found', said the prince at his return to Imlac, 'a man who can teach all that is necessary to be known, who, from the unshaken throne of rational fortitude, looks down on the scenes of life changing beneath him. He speaks, and attention watches his lips. He reasons, and conviction closes his periods. This man shall be my future guide: I will learn his doctrines, and imitate his life.'

'Be not too hasty', said Imlac, 'to trust, or to admire, the teachers of morality: they discourse like angels, but they live like men.'

Rasselas, who could not conceive how any man could reason so forcibly without feeling the cogency of his own arguments, paid his visit in a few days, and was denied admission. He had now learned the power of money, and made his way by a piece of gold to the inner apartment, where he found the philosopher in a room half-darkened, with his eyes misty and his face pale. 'Sir,' said he, 'you are come at a time when all human friendship is useless; what I suffer cannot be remedied, what I have lost cannot be supplied. My daughter, my only daughter, from whose tenderness I expected all the comforts of my age, died last night of a fever. My views, my purposes, my hopes are at an end: I am now a lonely being disunited from society.'

'Sir,' said the prince, 'mortality is an event by which a wise man can never be surprised: we know that death is always near, and it should therefore always be expected.' 'Young man,' answered the philosopher, 'you speak like one that has never felt the pangs of separation.' 'Have you then forgot the precepts', said Rasselas, 'which you so powerfully enforced? Has wisdom no strength to arm the heart against calamity? Consider, that external things are naturally variable, but truth and reason are always the same.' 'What comfort', said the mourner, 'can truth and reason afford me? Of what effect are they now, but to tell me that my daughter will not be restored?'

The prince, whose humanity would not suffer him to insult misery with reproof, went away convinced of the emptiness of rhetorical sound, and the inefficacy of polished periods and studied sentences.

CHAPTER XIX

A glimpse of pastoral life

He was still eager upon the same enquiry, and, having heard of a hermit that lived near the lowest cataract of the Nile and filled the whole country with the fame of his sanctity, resolved to visit his retreat, and enquire whether that felicity, which public life could not afford, was to be found in solitude, and whether a man, whose age and virtue made him venerable, could teach any peculiar art of shunning evils or enduring them.

Imlac and the princess agreed to accompany him, and, after the necessary preparations, they began their journey. Their way lay through fields, where shepherds tended their flocks and the lambs were playing upon the pasture. 'This', said the poet, 'is the life which has been often celebrated for its innocence and quiet: let us pass the heat of the day among the shepherds' tents, and know whether all our searches are not to terminate in pastoral simplicity.'

The proposal pleased them, and they induced the shepherds, by small presents and familiar questions, to tell their opinion of their own state: they were so rude and ignorant, so little able to compare the good with the evil of the occupation, and so indistinct in their narratives and descriptions, that very little could be learned from them. But it was evident that their hearts were cankered with discontent; that they considered themselves as condemned to labour for the luxury of the rich, and looked up with stupid malevolence toward those that were placed above them.

The princess pronounced with vehemence that she would never suffer these envious savages to be her companions, and that she should not soon be desirous of seeing any more specimens of rustic happiness; but could not believe that all the accounts of primeval pleasures were fabulous, and was yet in doubt whether life had anything that could be justly preferred to the placid gratifications of fields and woods. She hoped that the time would come, when, with a few virtuous and elegant companions, she should gather flowers planted by her own hand, fondle the lambs of her own ewe, and listen, without care, among brooks and breezes, to one of her maidens reading in the shade.

CHAPTER XX

The danger of prosperity

On the next day they continued their journey, till the heat compelled them to look round for shelter. At a small distance they saw a thick wood, which they no sooner entered than they perceived that they were approaching the habitations of men.

The shrubs were diligently cut away to open walks where the shades were darkest; the boughs of opposite trees were artificially interwoven; seats of flowery turf were raised in vacant spaces, and a rivulet, that wantoned along the side of a winding path, had its banks sometimes opened into small basins, and its stream sometimes obstructed by little mounds of stone heaped together to increase its murmurs.

They passed slowly through the wood, delighted with such unexpected accommodations, and entertained each other with conjecturing what, or who, he could be, that, in those rude and unfrequented regions, had leisure and art for such harmless luxury.

As they advanced they heard the sound of music, and saw youths and virgins dancing in the grove; and, going still further, beheld a stately palace built upon a hill surrounded with woods. The laws of eastern hospitality allowed them to enter, and the master welcomed them like a man liberal and wealthy.

He was skilful enough in appearances soon to discern that they were no common guests, and spread his table with magnificence. The eloquence of Imlac caught his attention, and the lofty courtesy of the princess excited his respect. When they offered to depart he entreated their stay, and was the next day still more unwilling to dismiss them than before. They were easily persuaded to stop, and civility grew up in time to freedom and confidence.

The prince now saw all the domestics cheerful, and all the face of nature smiling round the place, and could not forbear to hope that he should find here what he was seeking; but, when he was congratulating the master upon his possessions, he answered with a sigh, 'My condition has indeed the appearance of happiness, but appearances are delusive. My prosperity puts my life in danger; the Bassa of Egypt is my enemy, incensed only by my wealth and popularity. I have been hitherto protected against him by the princes of the country; but, as the favour of the great is uncertain, I know not how soon my defenders may be persuaded to share the plunder with the Bassa. I have sent my treasures into a distant country,

and, upon the first alarm, am prepared to follow them. Then
will my enemies riot in my mansion, and enjoy the gardens
which I have planted.'

They all joined in lamenting his danger and deprecating
his exile, and the princess was so much disturbed with the
tumult of grief and indignation that she retired to her apartment. They continued with their kind inviter a few days longer,
and then went forward to find the hermit.

CHAPTER XXI

The happiness of solitude. The hermit's history

They came on the third day, by the direction of the peasants,
to the hermit's cell: it was a cavern in the side of a mountain,
overshadowed with palm-trees, at such a distance from the
cataract that nothing more was heard than a gentle uniform
murmur, such as composed the mind to pensive meditation,
especially when it was assisted by the wind whistling among
the branches. The first rude essay of nature had been so much
improved by human labour that the cave contained several
apartments, appropriated to different uses, and often afforded
lodging to travellers whom darkness or tempests happened to
overtake.

The hermit sat on a bench at the door to enjoy the coolness of the evening. On one side lay a book with pens and
papers, on the other mechanical instruments of various kinds.
As they approached him unregarded, the princess observed
that he had not the countenance of a man that had found, or
could teach, the way to happiness.

They saluted him with great respect, which he repaid like
a man not unaccustomed to the forms of courts. 'My children',
said he, 'if you have lost your way, you shall be willingly supplied with such conveniences for the night as this cavern will
afford. I have all that nature requires, and you will not expect
delicacies in a hermit's cell.'

They thanked him, and, entering, were pleased with the

neatness and regularity of the place. The hermit set flesh and wine before them, though he fed only upon fruits and water. His discourse was cheerful without levity, and pious without enthusiasm. He soon gained the esteem of his guests, and the princess repented of her hasty censure.

At last Imlac began thus: 'I do not now wonder that your reputation is so far extended; we have heard at Cairo of your wisdom, and came hither to implore your direction for this young man and maiden in the *choice of life.*'

'To him that lives well,' answered the hermit, 'every form of life is good; nor can I give any other rule for choice than to remove from all apparent evil.'

'He will remove most certainly from evil,' said the prince, 'who shall devote himself to that solitude which you have recommended by your example.'

'I have indeed lived fifteen years in solitude,' said the hermit, 'but have no desire that my example should gain any imitators. In my youth I professed arms, and was raised by degrees to the highest military rank. I have traversed wide countries at the head of my troops, and seen many battles and sieges. At last, being disgusted by the preferment of a younger officer, and finding my vigour beginning to decay, I resolved to close my life in peace, having found the world full of snares, discord, and misery. I had once escaped from the pursuit of the enemy by the shelter of this cavern, and therefore chose it for my final residence. I employed artificers to form it into chambers, and stored it with all that I was likely to want.

'For some time after my retreat, I rejoiced like a tempest-beaten sailor at his entrance into the harbour, being delighted with the sudden change of the noise and hurry of war to stillness and repose. When the pleasure of novelty went away, I employed my hours in examining the plants which grow in the valley and the minerals which I collected from the rocks. But that enquiry is now grown tasteless and irksome. I have been for some time unsettled and distracted: my mind is disturbed with a thousand perplexities of doubt and vanities of imagination which hourly prevail upon me, because I have no opportunities of relaxation or diversion. I am sometimes ashamed

to think that I could not secure myself from vice but by
retiring from the practice of virtue, and begin to suspect that
I was rather impelled by resentment, than led by devotion,
into solitude. My fancy riots in scenes of folly, and I lament
that I have lost so much and have gained so little. In solitude,
if I escape the example of bad men, I want likewise the counsel
and conversation of the good. I have been long comparing
the evils with the advantages of society, and resolve to return
into the world tomorrow. The life of a solitary man will be
certainly miserable, but not certainly devout.'

They heard his resolution with surprise, but, after a short
pause, offered to conduct him to Cairo. He dug up a considerable treasure which he had hid among the rocks, and accompanied them to the city, on which, as he approached it, he
gazed with rapture.

CHAPTER XXII

The happiness of a life led according to nature

Rasselas went often to an assembly of learned men, who met
at stated times to unbend their minds and compare their
opinions. Their manners were somewhat coarse, but their conversation was instructive, and their disputations acute, though
sometimes too violent, and often continued till neither controvertist remembered upon what question they began. Some
faults were almost general among them: everyone was desirous
to dictate to the rest, and everyone was pleased to hear the
genius or knowledge of another depreciated.

In this assembly Rasselas was relating his interview with
the hermit, and the wonder with which he heard him censure
a course of life which he had so deliberately chosen and so
laudably followed. The sentiments of the hearers were various.
Some were of opinion that the folly of his choice had been
justly punished by condemnation to perpetual perseverance.
One of the youngest among them, with great vehemence, pronounced him an hypocrite. Some talked of the right of society

to the labour of individuals, and considered retirement as a desertion of duty. Others readily allowed that there was a time when the claims of the public were satisfied, and when a man might properly sequester himself, to review his life and purify his heart.

One, who appeared more affected with the narrative than the rest, thought it likely that the hermit would, in a few years, go back to his retreat, and, perhaps, if shame did not restrain or death intercept him, return once more from his retreat into the world: 'For the hope of happiness', says he, 'is so strongly impressed that the longest experience is not able to efface it. Of the present state, whatever it be, we feel, and are forced to confess, the misery, yet, when the same state is again at a distance, imagination paints it as desirable. But the time will surely come when desire will be no longer our torment, and no man shall be wretched but by his own fault.'

'This', said a philosopher, who had heard him with tokens of great impatience, 'is the present condition of a wise man. The time is already come when none are wretched but by their own fault. Nothing is more idle than to enquire after happiness, which nature has kindly placed within our reach. The way to be happy is to live according to nature, in obedience to that universal and unalterable law with which every heart is originally impressed; which is not written on it by precept, but engraven by destiny; not instilled by education, but infused at our nativity. He that lives according to nature will suffer nothing from the delusions of hope or importunities of desire: he will receive and reject with equability of temper; and act or suffer as the reason of things shall alternately prescribe. Other men may amuse themselves with subtle definitions, or intricate ratiocination. Let them learn to be wise by easier means: let them observe the hind of the forest and the linnet of the grove: let them consider the life of animals, whose motions are regulated by instinct; they obey their guide and are happy. Let us therefore, at length, cease to dispute, and learn to live; throw away the encumbrance of precepts, which they who utter them with so much pride and pomp do not understand, and carry with us this simple and intelligible maxim: that deviation from nature is deviation from happiness.'

When he had spoken, he looked round him with a placid air, and enjoyed the consciousness of his own beneficence. 'Sir,' said the prince, with great modesty, 'as I, like all the rest of mankind, am desirous of felicity, my closest attention has been fixed upon your discourse: I doubt not the truth of a position which a man so learned has so confidently advanced. Let me only know what it is to live according to nature.'

'When I find young men so humble and so docile,' said the philosopher, 'I can deny them no information which my studies have enabled me to afford. To live according to nature is to act always with due regard to the fitness arising from the relations and qualities of causes and effects; to concur with the great and unchangeable scheme of universal felicity; to co-operate with the general disposition and tendency of the present system of things.'

The prince soon found that this was one of the sages whom he should understand less as he heard him longer. He therefore bowed and was silent, and the philosopher, supposing him satisfied and the rest vanquished, rose up and departed with the air of a man that had co-operated with the present system.

CHAPTER XXIII

The prince and his sister divide between them the work of observation

Rasselas returned home full of reflections, doubtful how to direct his future steps. Of the way to happiness he found the learned and simple equally ignorant; but, as he was yet young, he flattered himself that he had time remaining for more experiments and further enquiries. He communicated to Imlac his observations and his doubts, but was answered by him with new doubts, and remarks that gave him no comfort. He therefore discoursed more frequently and freely with his sister, who had yet the same hope with himself, and always assisted him to give some reason why, though he had been hitherto frustrated, he might succeed at last.

'We have hitherto', said she, 'known but little of the world: we have never yet been either great or mean. In our own country, though we had royalty, we had no power, and in this we have not yet seen the private recesses of domestic peace. Imlac favours not our search, lest we should in time find him mistaken. We will divide the task between us: you shall try what is to be found in the splendour of courts, and I will range the shades of humbler life. Perhaps command and authority may be the supreme blessings, as they afford most opportunities of doing good: or, perhaps, what this world can give may be found in the modest habitations of middle fortune, too low for great designs and too high for penury and distress.'

CHAPTER XXIV

The prince examines the happiness of high stations

Rasselas applauded the design, and appeared next day with a splendid retinue at the court of the Bassa. He was soon distinguished for his magnificence, and admitted, as a prince whose curiosity had brought him from distant countries, to an intimacy with the great officers and frequent conversation with the Bassa himself.

He was at first inclined to believe that the man must be pleased with his own condition whom all approached with reverence and heard with obedience, and who had the power to extend his edicts to a whole kingdom. 'There can be no pleasure', said he, 'equal to that of feeling at once the joy of thousands all made happy by wise administration. Yet, since by the law of subordination this sublime delight can be in one nation but the lot of one, it is surely reasonable to think there is some satisfaction more popular and accessible, and that millions can hardly be subjected to the will of a single man only to fill his particular breast with incommunicable content.'

These thoughts were often in his mind, and he found no

solution of the difficulty. But as presents and civilities gained
him more familiarity, he found that almost every man that
stood high in employment hated all the rest, and was hated
by them, and that their lives were a continual succession of
plots and detections, stratagems and escapes, faction and
treachery. Many of those who surrounded the Bassa were sent
only to watch and report his conduct; every tongue was
muttering censure and every eye was searching for a fault.

At last the letters of revocation arrived; the Bassa was carried
in chains to Constantinople, and his name was mentioned no
more.

'What are we now to think of the prerogatives of power?'
said Rasselas to his sister. 'Is it without any efficacy to good?
Or is the subordinate degree only dangerous, and the supreme
safe and glorious? Is the Sultan the only happy man in his
dominions? Or is the Sultan himself subject to the torments
of suspicion and the dread of enemies?'

In a short time the second Bassa was deposed. The Sultan
that had advanced him was murdered by the Janissaries, and
his successor had other views and different favourites.

CHAPTER XXV

The princess pursues her enquiry with more diligence
than success

The princess, in the meantime, insinuated herself into many
families; for there are few doors through which liberality,
joined with good humour, cannot find its way. The daughters
of many houses were airy and cheerful, but Nekayah had been
too long accustomed to the conversation of Imlac and her
brother to be much pleased with childish levity and prattle
which had no meaning. She found their thoughts narrow, their
wishes low, and their merriment often artificial. Their pleasures, poor as they were, could not be preserved pure, but were
embittered by petty competitions and worthless emulation.
They were always jealous of the beauty of each other—of a

quality to which solicitude can add nothing, and from which detraction can take nothing away. Many were in love with triflers like themselves, and many fancied that they were in love when in truth they were only idle. Their affection was seldom fixed on sense or virtue, and therefore seldom ended but in vexation. Their grief, however, like their joy, was transient; everything floated in their mind unconnected with the past or future, so that one desire easily gave way to another, as a second stone cast into the water effaces and confounds the circles of the first.

With these girls she played as with inoffensive animals, and found them proud of her countenance and weary of her company.

But her purpose was to examine more deeply, and her affability easily persuaded the hearts that were swelling with sorrow to discharge their secrets in her ear: and those whom hope flattered, or prosperity delighted, often courted her to partake their pleasures.

The princess and her brother commonly met in the evening in a private summer-house on the bank of the Nile, and related to each other the occurrences of the day. As they were sitting together, the princess cast her eyes upon the river that flowed before her. 'Answer,' said she, 'great father of waters, thou that rollest thy floods through eighty nations, to the invocations of the daughter of thy native king. Tell me if thou waterest, through all thy course, a single habitation from which thou dost not hear the murmurs of complaint.'

'You are then', said Rasselas, 'not more successful in private houses than I have been in courts.' 'I have, since the last partition of our provinces,' said the princess, 'enabled myself to enter familiarly into many families where there was the fairest show of prosperity and peace, and know not one house that is not haunted by some fiend that destroys its quiet.

'I did not seek ease among the poor, because I concluded that there it could not be found. But I saw many poor whom I had supposed to live in affluence. Poverty has, in large cities, very different appearances: it is often concealed in splendour, and often in extravagance. It is the care of a very great part

of mankind to conceal their indigence from the rest: they
support themselves by temporary expedients, and every day
is lost in contriving for the morrow.

'This, however, was an evil, which, though frequent, I saw
with less pain because I could relieve it. Yet some have refused
my bounties, more offended with my quickness to detect their
wants than pleased with my readiness to succour them: and
others, whose exigencies compelled them to admit my kindness,
have never been able to forgive their benefactress. Many, however, have been sincerely grateful without the ostentation of
gratitude or the hope of other favours.'

CHAPTER XXVI

The princess continues her remarks upon private life

Nekayah, perceiving her brother's attention fixed, proceeded
in her narrative.

'In families where there is or is not poverty there is commonly discord: if a kingdom be, as Imlac tells us, a great
family, a family likewise is a little kingdom, torn with factions
and exposed to revolutions. An unpractised observer expects
the love of parents and children to be constant and equal; but
this kindness seldom continues beyond the years of infancy: in
a short time the children become rivals to their parents. Benefits are allayed by reproaches, and gratitude debased by envy.

'Parents and children seldom act in concert: each child endeavours to appropriate the esteem or fondness of the parents,
and the parents, with yet less temptation, betray each other to
their children; thus some place their confidence in the father,
and some in the mother, and, by degrees, the house is filled
with artifices and feuds.

'The opinions of children and parents, of the young and the
old, are naturally opposite, by the contrary effects of hope and
despondence, of expectation and experience, without crime or
folly on either side. The colours of life in youth and age appear
different, as the face of nature in spring and winter. And how

can children credit the assertions of parents, which their own eyes show them to be false?

'Few parents act in such a manner as much to enforce their maxims by the credit of their lives. The old man trusts wholly to slow contrivance and gradual progression: the youth expects to force his way by genius, vigour, and precipitance. The old man pays regard to riches, and the youth reverences virtue. The old man deifies prudence: the youth commits himself to magnanimity and chance. The young man, who intends no ill, believes that none is intended, and therefore acts with openness and candour: but his father, having suffered the injuries of fraud, is impelled to suspect and too often allured to practise it. Age looks with anger on the temerity of youth, and youth with contempt on the scrupulosity of age. Thus parents and children, for the greatest part, live on to love less and less: and, if those whom nature has thus closely united are the torments of each other, where shall we look for tenderness and consolation?

'Surely,' said the prince, 'you must have been unfortunate in your choice of acquaintance: I am unwilling to believe that the most tender of all relations is thus impeded in its effects by natural necessity.'

'Domestic discord', answered she, 'is not inevitably and fatally necessary, but yet is not easily avoided. We seldom see that a whole family is virtuous: the good and evil cannot well agree; and the evil can yet less agree with one another: even the virtuous fall sometimes to variance, when their virtues are of different kinds and tending to extremes. In general, those parents have most reverence who most deserve it: for he that lives well cannot be despised.

'Many other evils infest private life. Some are the slaves of servants whom they have trusted with their affairs. Some are kept in continual anxiety to the caprice of rich relations, whom they cannot please, and dare not offend. Some husbands are imperious, and some wives perverse: and, as it is always more easy to do evil than good, though the wisdom or virtue of one can very rarely make many happy, the folly or vice of one may often make many miserable.'

'If such be the general effect of marriage,' said the prince,

'I shall, for the future, think it dangerous to connect my interest with that of another, lest I should be unhappy by my partner's fault.'

'I have met', said the princess, 'with many who live single for that reason; but I never found that their prudence ought to raise envy. They dream away their time without friendship, without fondness, and are driven to rid themselves of the day, for which they have no use, by childish amusements, or vicious delights. They act as beings under the constant sense of some known inferiority, that fills their minds with rancour and their tongues with censure. They are peevish at home, and malevolent abroad; and, as the outlaws of human nature, make it their business and their pleasure to disturb that society which debars them from its privileges. To live without feeling or exciting sympathy, to be fortunate without adding to the felicity of others or afflicted without tasting the balm of pity, is a state more gloomy than solitude: it is not retreat but exclusion from mankind. Marriage has many pains, but celibacy has no pleasures.'

'What then is to be done?' said Rasselas. 'The more we enquire, the less we can resolve. Surely he is most likely to please himself that has no other inclination to regard.'

CHAPTER XXVII

Disquisition upon greatness

The conversation had a short pause. The prince, having considered his sister's observations, told her that she had surveyed life with prejudice, and supposed misery where she did not find it. 'Your narrative', says he, 'throws yet a darker gloom upon the prospects of futurity: the predictions of Imlac were but faint sketches of the evils painted by Nekayah. I have been lately convinced that quiet is not the daughter of grandeur or of power: that her presence is not to be bought by wealth, nor enforced by conquest. It is evident that as any man acts in a wider compass he must be more exposed to opposition from

enmity, or miscarriage from chance; whoever has many to
please or to govern must use the ministry of many agents, some
of whom will be wicked, and some ignorant; by some he will be
misled, and by others betrayed. If he gratifies one he will offend
another: those that are not favoured will think themselves
injured; and, since favours can be conferred but upon few, the
greater number will be always discontented.'

'The discontent,' said the princess, 'which is thus unreasonable, I hope that I shall always have spirit to despise, and you
power to repress.'

'Discontent', answered Rasselas, 'will not always be without
reason under the most just or vigilant administration of public affairs. None, however attentive, can always discover that
merit which indigence or faction may happen to obscure; and
none, however powerful, can always reward it. Yet he that sees
inferior desert advanced above him will naturally impute that
preference to partiality or caprice; and, indeed, it can scarcely
be hoped that any man, however magnanimous by nature or
exalted by condition, will be able to persist for ever in fixed
and inexorable justice of distribution: he will sometimes indulge his own affections, and sometimes those of his favourites;
he will permit some to please him who can never serve him;
he will discover in those whom he loves qualities which in
reality they do not possess; and to those from whom he receives
pleasure he will in his turn endeavour to give it. Thus will
recommendations sometimes prevail which were purchased by
money, or by the more destructive bribery of flattery and
servility.

'He that has much to do will do something wrong, and of
that wrong must suffer the consequences; and, if it were possible that he should always act rightly, yet, when such numbers
are to judge of his conduct, the bad will censure and obstruct
him by malevolence, and the good sometimes by mistake.

'The highest stations cannot therefore hope to be the abodes
of happiness, which I would willingly believe to have fled from
thrones and palaces to seats of humble privacy and placid obscurity. For what can hinder the satisfaction, or intercept
the expectations, of him whose abilities are adequate to his

G

employments, who sees with his own eyes the whole circuit of
his influence, who chooses by his own knowledge all whom he
trusts, and whom none are tempted to deceive by hope or fear?
Surely he has nothing to do but to love and to be loved, to be
virtuous and to be happy.'

'Whether perfect happiness would be procured by perfect
goodness', said Nekayah, 'this world will never afford an opportunity of deciding. But this, at least, may be maintained, that
we do not always find visible happiness in proportion to visible
virtue. All natural and almost all political evils are incident
alike to the bad and good: they are confounded in the misery of
a famine and not much distinguished in the fury of a faction;
they sink together in a tempest, and are driven together from
their country by invaders. All that virtue can afford is quietness
of conscience, a steady prospect of a happier state; this may
enable us to endure calamity with patience; but remember
that patience must suppose pain.'

CHAPTER XXVIII

Rasselas and Nekayah continue their conversation

'Dear princess,' said Rasselas, 'you fall into the common errors
of exaggeratory declamation, by producing, in a familiar disquisition, examples of national calamities and scenes of extensive misery, which are found in books rather than in the
world, and which, as they are horrid, are ordained to be rare.
Let us not imagine evils which we do not feel, nor injure life
by misrepresentations. I cannot bear that querulous eloquence
which threatens every city with a siege like that of Jerusalem,
that makes famine attend on every flight of locusts, and sus-
pends pestilence on the wing of every blast that issues from the
south.

'On necessary and inevitable evils, which overwhelm kingdoms at once, all disputation is vain: when they happen they
must be endured. But it is evident that these bursts of universal
distress are more dreaded than felt: thousands and ten

thousands flourish in youth, and wither in age, without the knowledge of any other than domestic evils, and share the same pleasures and vexations whether their kings are mild or cruel, whether the armies of their country pursue their enemies, or retreat before them. While courts are disturbed with intestine competitions, and ambassadors are negotiating in foreign countries, the smith still plies his anvil, and the husbandman drives his plough forward; the necessaries of life are required and obtained, and the successive business of the seasons continues to make its wonted revolutions.

'Let us cease to consider what, perhaps, may never happen, and what, when it shall happen, will laugh at human speculation. We will not endeavour to modify the motions of the elements or to fix the destiny of kingdoms. It is our business to consider what beings like us may perform; each labouring for his own happiness by promoting within his circle, however narrow, the happiness of others.

'Marriage is evidently the dictate of nature; men and women were made to be companions of each other, and therefore I cannot be persuaded but that marriage is one of the means of happiness.'

'I know not', said the princess,' whether marriage be more than one of the innumerable modes of human misery. When I see and reckon the various forms of connubial infelicity, the unexpected causes of lasting discord, the diversities of temper, the oppositions of opinion, the rude collisions of contrary desire where both are urged by violent impulses, the obstinate contests of disagreeing virtues where both are supported by consciousness of good intention, I am sometimes disposed to think with the severer casuists of most nations that marriage is rather permitted than approved, and that none, but by the instigation of a passion too much indulged, entangle themselves with indissoluble compacts.'

'You seem to forget', replied Rasselas, 'that you have, even now, represented celibacy as less happy than marriage. Both conditions may be bad, but they cannot both be worst. Thus it happens when wrong opinions are entertained, that they mutually destroy each other, and leave the mind open to truth.'

'I did not expect', answered the princess, 'to hear that imputed to falsehood which is the consequence only of frailty. To the mind, as to the eye, it is difficult to compare with exactness objects vast in their extent and various in their parts. Where we see or conceive the whole at once we readily note the discriminations and decide the preference: but of two systems, of which neither can be surveyed by any human being in its full compass of magnitude and multiplicity of complication, where is the wonder, that, judging of the whole by parts, I am affected by one or the other as either presses on my memory or fancy? We differ from ourselves, just as we differ from each other, when we see only part of the question, as in the multifarious relations of politics and morality: but when we perceive the whole at once, as in numerical computations, all agree in one judgement, and none ever varies his opinion.'

'Let us not add', said the prince, 'to the other evils of life the bitterness of controversy, nor endeavour to vie with each other in subtleties of argument. We are employed in a search, of which both are equally to enjoy the success or suffer by the miscarriage. It is therefore fit that we assist each other. You surely conclude too hastily from the infelicity of marriage against its institution. Will not the misery of life prove equally that life cannot be the gift of heaven? The world must be peopled by marriage, or peopled without it.'

'How the world is to be peopled', returned Nekayah, 'is not my care, and needs not be yours. I see no danger that the present generation should omit to leave successors behind them: we are not now enquiring for the world, but for ourselves.'

CHAPTER XXIX

The debate on marriage continued

'The good of the whole', says Rasselas, 'is the same with the good of all its parts. If marriage be best for mankind it must be evidently best for individuals, or a permanent and necessary duty must be the cause of evil, and some must be inevitably sacrificed to the convenience of others. In the estimate which you have made of the two states, it appears that the incommodities of a single life are, in a great measure, necessary and certain, but those of the conjugal state accidental and avoidable.

'I cannot forbear to flatter myself that prudence and benevolence will make marriage happy. The general folly of mankind is the cause of general complaint. What can be expected but disappointment and repentance from a choice made in the immaturity of youth, in the ardour of desire, without judgement, without foresight, without enquiry after conformity of opinions, similarity of manners, rectitude of judgement, or purity of sentiment?

'Such is the common process of marriage. A youth and maiden meeting by chance, or brought together by artifice, exchange glances, reciprocate civilities, go home, and dream of one another. Having little to divert attention or diversify thought, they find themselves uneasy when they are apart, and therefore conclude that they shall be happy together. They marry, and discover what nothing but voluntary blindness had before concealed; they wear out life in altercations, and charge nature with cruelty.

'From those early marriages proceeds likewise the rivalry of parents and children: the son is eager to enjoy the world before the father is willing to forsake it, and there is hardly room at once for two generations. The daughter begins to bloom before the mother can be content to fade, and neither can forbear to wish for the absence of the other.

'Surely all these evils may be avoided by that deliberation and delay which prudence prescribes to irrevocable choice. In the variety and jollity of youthful pleasures life may be well enough supported without the help of a partner. Longer time will increase experience, and wider views will allow better opportunities of enquiry and selection: one advantage, at least, will be certain; the parents will be visibly older than their children.'

'What reason cannot collect,' said Nekayah, 'and what experiment has not yet taught, can be known only from the report of others. I have been told that late marriages are not eminently happy. This is a question too important to be neglected, and I have often proposed it to those whose accuracy of remark and comprehensiveness of knowledge made their suffrages worthy of regard. They have generally determined that it is dangerous for a man and woman to suspend their fate upon each other at a time when opinions are fixed and habits are established, when friendships have been contracted on both sides, when life has been planned into method, and the mind has long enjoyed the contemplation of its own prospects.

'It is scarcely possible that two travelling through the world under the conduct of chance should have been both directed to the same path, and it will not often happen that either will quit the track which custom has made pleasing. When the desultory levity of youth has settled into regularity, it is soon succeeded by pride ashamed to yield, or obstinacy delighting to contend. And even though mutual esteem produces mutual desire to please, time itself, as it modifies unchangeably the external mien, determines likewise the direction of the passions, and gives an inflexible rigidity to the manners. Long customs are not easily broken: he that attempts to change the course of his own life very often labours in vain; and how shall we do that for others which we are seldom able to do for ourselves?'

'But, surely,' interposed the prince, 'you suppose the chief motive of choice forgotten or neglected. Whenever I shall seek a wife, it shall be my first question whether she be willing to be led by reason.'

'Thus it is', said Nekayah, 'that philosophers are deceived. There are a thousand familiar disputes which reason never can decide, questions that elude investigation and make logic ridiculous, cases where something must be done and where little can be said. Consider the state of mankind, and enquire how few can be supposed to act upon any occasions, whether small or great, with all the reasons of action present to their minds. Wretched would be the pair above all names of wretchedness, who should be doomed to adjust by reason every morning all the minute detail of a domestic day.

'Those who marry at an advanced age will probably escape

the encroachments of their children; but, in diminution of this advantage, they will be likely to leave them, ignorant and helpless, to a guardian's mercy: or, if that should not happen, they must at least go out of the world before they see those whom they love best either wise or great.

'From their children, if they have less to fear, they have less also to hope, and they lose, without equivalent, the joys of early love, and the convenience of uniting with manners pliant and minds susceptible of new impressions, which might wear away their dissimilitudes by long cohabitation, as soft bodies, by continual attrition, conform their surfaces to each other.

'I believe it will be found that those who marry late are best pleased with their children, and those who marry early with their partners.'

'The union of these two affections', said Rasselas, 'would produce all that could be wished. Perhaps there is a time when marriage might unite them, a time neither too early for the father, nor too late for the husband.'

'Every hour', answered the princess, 'confirms my prejudice in favour of the position so often uttered by the mouth of Imlac, "That nature sets her gifts on the right hand and on the left." Those conditions which flatter hope and attract desire are so constituted, that, as we approach one, we recede from another. There are goods so opposed that we cannot seize both, but, by too much prudence, may pass between them at too great a distance to reach either. This is often the fate of long consideration; he does nothing who endeavours to do more than is allowed to humanity. Flatter not yourself with contrarieties of pleasure. Of the blessings set before you make your choice, and be content. No man can taste the fruits of autumn while he is delighting his scent with the flowers of the spring: no man can, at the same time, fill his cup from the source and from the mouth of the Nile.'

CHAPTER XXX

Imlac enters, and changes the conversation

Here Imlac entered, and interrupted them. His look was clouded with thought. 'Imlac,' said Rasselas, 'I have been taking from the princess the dismal history of private life, and am almost discouraged from further search.'

'It seems to me,' said Imlac, 'that while you are making the *choice of life* you neglect to live. You wander about a single city, which, however large and diversified, can now afford few novelties, and forget that you are in a country, famous among the earliest monarchies for the power and wisdom of its inhabitants; a country where the sciences first dawned that illuminate the world, and beyond which the arts cannot be traced of civil society or domestic life.

'The old Egyptians have left behind them monuments of industry and power before which all European magnificence is confessed to fade away. The ruins of their architecture are the schools of modern builders, and from the wonders which time has spared we may conjecture, though uncertainly, what it has destroyed.'

'My curiosity', said Rasselas, 'does not very strongly lead me to survey piles of stone or mounds of earth; my business is with man. I came hither not to measure fragments of temples or trace choked aqueducts, but to look upon the various scenes of the present world.'

'The things that are now before us', said the princess, 'necessarily require attention, and sufficiently deserve it. What have I to do with the heroes or the monuments of ancient times, with times which never can return, and heroes whose form of life was different from all that the present condition of mankind requires or allows?'

'To know anything,' returned the poet, 'we must know its effects; to see men we must see their works, that we may learn what reason has dictated, or passion has incited, and find what are the most powerful motives of action. To judge rightly of the present we must oppose it to the past; for all judgement is comparative, and of the future nothing can be known. The truth is that no mind is much employed upon the present: recollection and anticipation fill up almost all our moments. Our passions are joy and grief, love and hatred, hope and fear. Of joy and grief the past is the object, and the future of hope and fear; even love and hatred respect the past, for the cause must have been before the effect.

'The present state of things is the consequence of the former, and it is natural to enquire what were the sources of the good that we enjoy, or of the evil that we suffer. If we act only for ourselves, to neglect the study of history is not prudent: if we are entrusted with the care of others, it is not just. Ignorance, when it is voluntary, is criminal; and he may properly be charged with evil who refused to learn how he might prevent it.

'There is no part of history so generally useful as that which relates the progress of the human mind, the gradual improvement of reason, the successive advances of science, the vicissitudes of learning and ignorance, which are the light and darkness of thinking beings, the extinction and resuscitation of arts, and all the revolutions of the intellectual world. If accounts of battles and invasions are peculiarly the business of princes, the useful or elegant arts are not to be neglected; those who have kingdoms to govern have understandings to cultivate.

'Example is always more efficacious than precept. A soldier is formed in war, and a painter must copy pictures. In this, contemplative life has the advantage: great actions are seldom seen, but the labours of art are always at hand for those who desire to know what art has been able to perform.

'When the eye or the imagination is struck with any uncommon work the next transition of an active mind is to the means by which it was performed. Here begins the true use of such contemplation; we enlarge our comprehension by new ideas, and perhaps recover some art lost to mankind, or learn what is less perfectly known in our own country. At least we compare our own with former times, and either rejoice at our improvements, or, what is the first motion towards good, discover our defects.'

'I am willing', said the prince, 'to see all that can deserve my search.' 'And I', said the princess, 'shall rejoice to learn something of the manners of antiquity.'

'The most pompous monument of Egyptian greatness, and one of the most bulky works of manual industry,' said Imlac, 'are the Pyramids, fabrics raised before the time of history, and of which the earliest narratives afford us only uncertain traditions. Of these the greatest is still standing, very little injured by time.'

'Let us visit them tomorrow,' said Nekayah. 'I have often heard of the Pyramids, and shall not rest till I have seen them within and without with my own eyes.'

CHAPTER XXXI

They visit the Pyramids

The resolution being thus taken, they set out the next day. They laid tents upon their camels, being resolved to stay among the Pyramids till their curiosity was fully satisfied. They travelled gently, turned aside to everything remarkable, stopped from time to time and conversed with the inhabitants, and observed the various appearances of towns, ruined and inhabited, of wild and cultivated nature.

When they came to the Great Pyramid they were astonished at the extent of the base and the height of the top. Imlac explained to them the principles upon which the pyramidal form was chosen for a fabric intended to co-extend its duration with that of the world: he showed that its gradual diminution gave it such stability as defeated all the common attacks of the elements, and could scarcely be overthrown by earthquakes themselves, the least resistible of natural violence. A concussion that should shatter the Pyramid would threaten the dissolution of the continent.

They measured all its dimensions, and pitched their tents at its foot. Next day they prepared to enter its interior apartments, and, having hired the common guides, climbed up to the first passage, when the favourite of the princess, looking into the cavity, stepped back and trembled. 'Pekuah,' said the princess, 'of what art thou afraid?' 'Of the narrow entrance,' answered the lady, 'and of the dreadful gloom. I dare not enter a place which must surely be inhabited by unquiet souls. The original possessors of these dreadful vaults will start up before us, and, perhaps, shut us up for ever.' She spoke, and threw her arms round the neck of her mistress.

'If all your fear be of apparitions,' said the prince, 'I will promise you safety: there is no danger from the dead; he that is once buried will be seen no more.'

'That the dead are seen no more,' said Imlac, 'I will not undertake to maintain against the concurrent and unvaried testimony of all ages and of all nations. There is no people, rude or learned, among whom apparitions of the dead are not related and believed. This opinion, which, perhaps, prevails as far as human nature is diffused, could become universal only by its truth: those that never heard of one another would not have agreed in a tale which nothing but experience can make credible. That it is doubted by single cavillers can very little weaken the general evidence, and some who deny it with their tongues confess it by their fears.

'Yet I do not mean to add new terrors to those which have already seized upon Pekuah. There can be no reason why spectres should haunt the Pyramid more than other places, or why they should have power or will to hurt innocence and purity. Our entrance is no violation of their privileges; we can take nothing from them; how then can we offend them?'

'My dear Pekuah,' said the princess, 'I will always go before you, and Imlac shall follow you. Remember that you are the companion of the princess of Abyssinia.'

'If the princess is pleased that her servant should die,' returned the lady, 'let her command some death less dreadful than enclosure in this horrid cavern. You know I dare not disobey you: I must go if you command me; but, if I once enter, I never shall come back.'

The princess saw that her fear was too strong for expostulation or reproof, and, embracing her, told her that she should stay in the tent till their return.' Pekuah was yet not satisfied, but entreated the princess not to pursue so dreadful a purpose as that of entering the recesses of the Pyramid. 'Though I cannot teach courage,' said Nekayah, 'I must not learn cowardice, nor leave at last undone what I came hither only to do.'

CHAPTER XXXII

They enter the Pyramid

Pekuah descended to the tents, and the rest entered the Pyramid: they passed through the galleries, surveyed the vaults of marble, and examined the chest in which the body of the founder is supposed to have been reposited. They then sat down in one of the most spacious chambers to rest awhile before they attempted to return.

'We have now', said Imlac, 'gratified our minds with an exact view of the greatest work of man, except the wall of China.

'Of the wall it is very easy to assign the motives. It secured a wealthy and timorous nation from the incursions of barbarians, whose unskilfulness in arts made it easier for them to supply their wants by rapine than by industry, and who from time to time poured in upon the habitations of peaceful commerce, as vultures descend upon domestic fowl. Their celerity and fierceness made the wall necessary, and their ignorance made it efficacious.

'But for the Pyramids no reason has ever been given adequate to the cost and labour of the work. The narrowness of the chambers proves that it could afford no retreat from enemies, and treasures might have been reposited at far less expense with equal security. It seems to have been erected only in compliance with that hunger of imagination which preys incessantly upon life and must be always appeased by some employment. Those who have already all that they can enjoy must enlarge their desires. He that has built for use till use is supplied, must begin to build for vanity, and extend his plan to the utmost power of human performance, that he may not be soon reduced to form another wish.

'I consider this mighty structure as a monument of the insufficiency of human enjoyments. A king, whose power is unlimited and whose treasures surmount all real and imaginary wants, is compelled to solace, by the erection of a Pyramid, the satiety of dominion and tastelessness of pleasures, and to amuse the tediousness of declining life by seeing thousands labouring without end, and one stone, for no purpose, laid upon another. Whoever thou art, that, not content with a moderate condition, imaginest happiness in royal magnificence, and dreamest that command or riches can feed the appetite of novelty with successive gratifications, survey the Pyramids, and confess thy folly!'

CHAPTER XXXIII

The princess meets with an unexpected misfortune

They rose up, and returned through the cavity at which they had entered, and the princess prepared for her favourite a long narrative of dark labyrinths and costly rooms, and of the different impressions which the varieties of the way had made upon her. But, when they came to their train, they found everyone silent and dejected: the men discovered shame and fear in their countenances, and the women were weeping in the tents.

What had happened they did not try to conjecture, but immediately enquired. 'You had scarcely entered into the Pyramid,' said one of the attendants, 'when a troop of Arabs rushed upon us: we were too few to resist them, and too slow to escape. They were about to search the tents, set us on our camels, and drive us along before them, when the approach of some Turkish horsemen put them to flight; but they seized the lady Pekuah with her two maids, and carried them away: the Turks are now pursuing them by our instigation, but I fear they will not be able to overtake them.'

The princess was overpowered with surprise and grief. Rasselas, in the first heat of his resentment, ordered his servants to follow him, and prepared to pursue the robbers with his sabre in his hand. 'Sir,' said Imlac, 'what can you hope from violence or valour? The Arabs are mounted on horses trained to battle and retreat; we have only beasts of burden. By leaving our present station we may lose the princess, but cannot hope to regain Pekuah.'

In a short time the Turks returned, having not been able to reach the enemy. The princess burst out into new lamentations, and Rasselas could scarcely forbear to reproach them with cowardice; but Imlac was of opinion that the escape of the Arabs was no addition to their misfortune, for, perhaps, they would have killed their captives rather than have resigned them.

CHAPTER XXXIV

They return to Cairo without Pekuah

There was nothing to be hoped from longer stay. They returned to Cairo repenting of their curiosity, censuring the negligence of the government, lamenting their own rashness which had neglected to procure a guard, imagining many expedients by which the loss of Pekuah might have been prevented, and resolving to do something for her recovery, though none could find anything proper to be done.

Nekayah retired to her chamber, where her women attempted to comfort her, by telling her that all had their troubles, and that lady Pekuah had enjoyed much happiness in the world for a long time, and might reasonably expect a change of fortune. They hoped that some good would befall her wheresoever she was, and that their mistress would find another friend who might supply her place.

The princess made them no answer, and they continued the form of condolence, not much grieved in their hearts that the favourite was lost.

Next day the prince presented to the Bassa a memorial of the wrong which he had suffered and a petition for redress. The Bassa threatened to punish the robbers, but did not attempt to catch them, nor, indeed, could any account or description be given by which he might direct the pursuit.

It soon appeared that nothing would be done by authority. Governors, being accustomed to hear of more crimes than they can punish and more wrongs than they can redress, set themselves at ease by indiscriminate negligence, and presently forget the request when they lose sight of the petitioner.

Imlac then endeavoured to gain some intelligence by private agents. He found many who pretended to an exact knowledge of all the haunts of the Arabs and to regular correspondence with their chiefs, and who readily undertook the recovery of Pekuah. Of these, some were furnished with money for their journey, and came back no more; some were liberally paid for accounts which a few days discovered to be false. But the princess would not suffer any means, however improbable, to be left untried. While she was doing something, she kept her hope alive. As one expedient failed, another was suggested; when one messenger returned unsuccessful, another was despatched to a different quarter.

Two months had now passed, and of Pekuah nothing had been heard; the hopes which they had endeavoured to raise in each other grew more languid, and the princess, when she saw nothing more to be tried, sunk down inconsolable in hopeless dejection. A thousand times she reproached herself with the easy compliance by which she permitted her favourite to stay behind her. 'Had not my fondness', said she, 'lessened my authority, Pekuah had not dared to talk of her terrors. She ought to have feared me more than spectres. A severe look would have overpowered her; a peremptory command would have compelled obedience. Why did foolish indulgence prevail upon me? Why did I not speak and refuse to hear?'

'Great princess,' said Imlac, 'do not reproach yourself for your virtue, or consider that as blamable by which evil has accidentally been caused. Your tenderness for the timidity of Pekuah was generous and kind. When we act according to our

duty, we commit the event to him by whose laws our actions
are governed, and who will suffer none to be finally punished
for obedience. When, in prospect of some good, whether
natural or moral, we break the rules prescribed us, we withdraw from the direction of superior wisdom, and take all consequences upon ourselves. Man cannot so far know the connection
of causes and events as that he may venture to do wrong in
order to do right. When we pursue our end by lawful means,
we may always console our miscarriage by the hope of future
recompense. When we consult only our own policy, and attempt
to find a nearer way to good by overleaping the settled boundaries of right and wrong, we cannot be happy even by success,
because we cannot escape the consciousness of our fault; but,
if we miscarry, the disappointment is irremediably embittered.
How comfortless is the sorrow of him who feels at once the
pangs of guilt and the vexation of calamity which guilt has
brought upon him?

'Consider, princess, what would have been your condition,
if the lady Pekuah had entreated to accompany you, and, being
compelled to stay in the tents, had been carried away; or how
would you have borne the thought, if you had forced her into
the Pyramid, and she had died before you in agonies of terror.'

'Had either happened,' said Nekayah, 'I could not have endured life till now: I should have been tortured to madness
by the remembrance of such cruelty, or must have pined away
in abhorrence of myself.'

'This at least', said Imlac, 'is the present reward of virtuous
conduct, that no unlucky consequence can oblige us to repent
it.'

CHAPTER XXXV

The princess continues to lament Pekuah

Nekayah, being thus reconciled to herself, found that no evil
is unsupportable but that which is accompanied with consciousness of wrong. She was, from that time, delivered from
the violence of tempestuous sorrow, and sunk into silent pen-

siveness and gloomy tranquillity. She sat from morning to evening recollecting all that had been done or said by her Pekuah, treasured up with care every trifle on which Pekuah had set an accidental value, and which might recall to mind any little incident or careless conversation. The sentiments of her whom she now expected to see no more were treasured up in her memory as rules of life, and she deliberated to no other end than to conjecture on any occasion what would have been the opinion and counsel of Pekuah.

The women by whom she was attended knew nothing of her real condition, and therefore she could not talk to them but with caution and reserve. She began to remit her curiosity, having no great care to collect notions which she had no convenience of uttering. Rasselas endeavoured first to comfort and afterwards to divert her; he hired musicians, to whom she seemed to listen but did not hear them, and procured masters to instruct her in various arts, whose lectures, when they visited her again, were again to be repeated. She had lost her taste of pleasure and her ambition of excellence. And her mind, though forced into short excursions, always recurred to the image of her friend.

Imlac was every morning earnestly enjoined to renew his enquiries, and was asked every night whether he had yet heard of Pekuah, till, not being able to return the princess the answer that she desired, he was less and less willing to come into her presence. She observed his backwardness, and commanded him to attend her. 'You are not', said she, 'to confound impatience with resentment, or to suppose that I charge you with negligence because I repine at your unsuccessfulness. I do not much wonder at your absence; I know that the unhappy are never pleasing, and that all naturally avoid the contagion of misery. To hear complaints is wearisome alike to the wretched and the happy; for who would cloud by adventitious grief the short gleams of gaiety which life allows us? Or who that is struggling under his own evils will add to them the miseries of another?

'The time is at hand when none shall be disturbed any longer by the sighs of Nekayah: my search after happiness is

H

now at an end. I am resolved to retire from the world with all
its flatteries and deceits, and will hide myself in solitude, without any other care than to compose my thoughts and regulate
my hours by a constant succession of innocent occupations, till,
with a mind purified from all earthly desires, I shall enter into
that state to which all are hastening, and in which I hope again
to enjoy the friendship of Pekuah.'

'Do not entangle your mind', said Imlac, 'by irrevocable
determinations, nor increase the burthen of life by a voluntary
accumulation of misery: the weariness of retirement will continue or increase when the loss of Pekuah is forgotten. That
you have been deprived of one pleasure is no very good
reason for rejection of the rest.'

'Since Pekuah was taken from me,' said the princess, 'I have
no pleasure to reject or to retain. She that has no one to love
or trust has little to hope. She wants the radical principle of
happiness. We may, perhaps, allow that what satisfaction this
world can afford must arise from the conjunction of wealth,
knowledge and goodness: wealth is nothing but as it is bestowed, and knowledge nothing but as it is communicated.
Goodness affords the only comfort which can be enjoyed without a partner, and goodness may be practised in retirement.'

'How far solitude may admit goodness or advance it, I shall
not', replied Imlac, 'dispute at present. Remember the confession of the pious hermit. You will wish to return into the
world, when the image of your companion has left your
thoughts.' 'That time', said Nekayah, 'will never come. The
generous frankness, the modest obsequiousness, and the faith-
ful secrecy of my dear Pekuah, will always be more missed, as I
shall live longer to see vice and folly.'

'The state of a mind oppressed with a sudden calamity', said
Imlac, 'is like that of the fabulous inhabitants of the new-
created earth, who, when the first night came upon them, supposed that day never would return. When the clouds of sorrow
gather over us, we see nothing beyond them, nor can imagine
how they will be dispelled: yet a new day succeeded to the
night, and sorrow is never long without a dawn of ease. But
they who restrain themselves from receiving comfort do as

the savages would have done, had they put out their eyes when it was dark. Our minds, like our bodies, are in continual flux; something is hourly lost, and something acquired. To lose much at once is inconvenient to either, but while the vital powers remain uninjured, nature will find the means of reparation. Distance has the same effect on the mind as on the eye, and while we glide along the stream of time, whatever we leave behind us is always lessening, and that which we approach increasing in magnitude. Do not suffer life to stagnate; it will grow muddy for want of motion: commit yourself again to the current of the world; Pekuah will vanish by degrees; you will meet in your way some other favourite, or learn to diffuse yourself in general conversation.'

'At least,' said the prince, 'do not despair before all remedies have been tried: the enquiry after the unfortunate lady is still continued, and shall be carried on with yet greater diligence, on condition that you will promise to wait a year for the event, without any unalterable resolution.'

Nekayah thought this a reasonable demand, and made the promise to her brother, who had been advised by Imlac to require it. Imlac had, indeed, no great hope of regaining Pekuah, but he supposed that, if he could secure the interval of a year, the princess would be then in no danger of a cloister.

CHAPTER XXXVI

Pekuah is still remembered by the princess

Nekayah, seeing that nothing was omitted for the recovery of her favourite, and having, by her promise, set her intention of retirement at a distance, began imperceptibly to return to common cares and common pleasures. She rejoiced without her own consent at the suspension of her sorrows, and sometimes caught herself with indignation in the act of turning away her mind from the remembrance of her whom yet she resolved never to forget.

She then appointed a certain hour of the day for meditation

on the merits and fondness of Pekuah, and for some weeks retired constantly at the time fixed, and returned with her eyes
swollen and her countenance clouded. By degrees she grew
less scrupulous, and suffered any important and pressing avocation to delay the tribute of daily tears. She then yielded to
less occasions, sometimes forgot what she was indeed afraid to
remember, and, at last, wholly released herself from the duty of
periodical affliction.

Her real love of Pekuah was yet not diminished. A thousand
occurrences brought her back to memory, and a thousand
wants, which nothing but the confidence of friendship can
supply, made her frequently regretted. She, therefore, solicited
Imlac never to desist from enquiry, and to leave no art of
intelligence untried, that, at least, she might have the comfort
of knowing that she did not suffer by negligence or sluggish-
ness. 'Yet what', said she, 'is to be expected from our pursuit of
happiness, when we find the state of life to be such that happiness itself is the cause of misery? Why should we endeavour
to attain that of which the possession cannot be secured? I
shall henceforward fear to yield my heart to excellence, however bright, or to fondness, however tender, lest I should lose
again what I have lost in Pekuah.'

CHAPTER XXXVII

The princess hears news of Pekuah

In seven months, one of the messengers, who had been sent
away upon the day when the promise was drawn from the
princess, returned, after many unsuccessful rambles, from the
borders of Nubia, with an account that Pekuah was in the hands
of an Arab chief who possessed a castle or fortress on the
extremity of Egypt. The Arab, whose revenue was plunder,
was willing to restore her, with her two attendants, for two
hundred ounces of gold.

The price was no subject of debate. The princess was in
ecstasies when she heard that her favourite was alive and

might so cheaply be ransomed. She could not think of delaying for a moment Pekuah's happiness or her own, but entreated her brother to send back the messenger with the sum required. Imlac, being consulted, was not very confident of the veracity of the relater, and was still more doubtful of the Arab's faith, who might, if he were too liberally trusted, detain at once the money and the captives. He thought it dangerous to put themselves in the power of the Arab by going into his district, and could not expect that the Arab would so much expose himself as to come into the lower country, where he might be seized by the forces of the Bassa.

It is difficult to negotiate where neither will trust. But Imlac, after some deliberation, directed the messenger to propose that Pekuah should be conducted by ten horsemen to the monastery of St. Anthony, which is situated in the deserts of Upper Egypt, where she should be met by the same number and her ransom should be paid.

That no time might be lost, as they expected that the proposal would not be refused, they immediately began their journey to the monastery; and, when they arrived, Imlac went forward with the former messenger to the Arab's fortress. Rasselas was desirous to go with them, but neither his sister nor Imlac would consent. The Arab, according to the custom of his nation, observed the laws of hospitality with great exactness to those who put themselves into his power, and, in a few days, brought Pekuah with her maids, by easy journeys, to their place appointed, where he received the stipulated price, and, with great respect, restored her to liberty and her friends, and undertook to conduct them back towards Cairo beyond all danger of robbery or violence.

The princess and her favourite embraced each other with transport too violent to be expressed, and went out together to pour the tears of tenderness in secret, and exchange professions of kindness and gratitude. After a few hours they returned into the refectory of the convent, where, in the presence of the prior and his brethren, the prince required of Pekuah the history of her adventures.

CHAPTER XXXVIII

The adventures of the lady Pekuah

'At what time, and in what manner, I was forced away,' said Pekuah, 'your servants have told you. The suddenness of the event struck me with surprise, and I was at first rather stupefied than agitated with any passion of either fear or sorrow. My confusion was increased by the speed and tumult of our flight while we were followed by the Turks, who, as it seemed, soon despaired to overtake us, or were afraid of those whom they made a show of menacing.

'When the Arabs saw themselves out of danger they slackened their course, and, as I was less harassed by external violence, I began to feel more uneasiness in my mind. After some time we stopped near a spring shaded with trees in a pleasant meadow, where we were set upon the ground and offered such refreshments as our masters were partaking. I was suffered to sit with my maids apart from the rest, and none attempted to comfort or insult us. Here I first began to feel the full weight of my misery. The girls sat weeping in silence, and from time to time looked up to me for succour. I knew not to what condition we were doomed, nor could conjecture where would be the place of our captivity, or whence to draw any hope of deliverance. I was in the hands of robbers and savages, and had no reason to suppose that their pity was more than their justice, or that they would forbear the gratification of any ardour of desire or caprice of cruelty. I, however, kissed my maids, and endeavoured to pacify them by remarking that we were yet treated with decency, and that, since we were now carried beyond pursuit, there was no danger of violence to our lives.

'When we were to be set again on horseback, my maids clung round me and refused to be parted, but I commanded them not to irritate those who had us in their power. We travelled the remaining part of the day through an unfrequented and pathless country, and came by moonlight to the side of a hill, where the rest of the troop was stationed. Their tents were pitched, and their fires kindled, and our chief was welcomed as a man much beloved by his dependants.

'We were received into a large tent, where we found women who had attended their husbands in the expedition. They set before us the supper which they had provided, and I ate it rather to encourage my maids than to comply with any appetite of my own. When the meat was taken away they spread the carpets for repose. I was weary, and hoped to find in sleep that remission of distress which nature seldom denies. Ordering myself therefore to be undressed, I observed that the women looked very earnestly upon me, not expecting, I supposed, to see me so submissively attended. When my upper vest was taken off, they were apparently struck with the splendour of my clothes, and one of them timorously laid her hand upon the embroidery. She then went out, and, in a short time, came back with another woman, who seemed to be of higher rank and greater authority. She did, at her entrance, the usual act of reverence, and, taking me by the hand, placed me in a smaller tent, spread with finer carpets, where I spent the night quietly with my maids.

'In the morning, as I was sitting on the grass, the chief of the troop came towards me. I rose up to receive him, and he bowed with great respect. "Illustrious lady," said he, "my fortune is better than I had presumed to hope; I am told by my women that I have a princess in my camp." "Sir," answered I, "your women have deceived themselves and you; I am not a princess, but an unhappy stranger who intended soon to have left this country, in which I am now to be imprisoned for ever." "Whoever, or whencesoever, you are," returned the Arab, "your dress, and that of your servants, show your rank to be high and your wealth to be great. Why should you, who can so easily procure your ransom, think yourself in danger of perpetual captivity? The purpose of my incursions is to increase my riches, or, more properly, to gather tribute. The sons of Ishmael are the natural and hereditary lords of this part of the continent, which is usurped by late invaders and low-born tyrants, from whom we are compelled to take by the sword what is denied to justice.

The violence of war admits no distinction; the lance that is lifted at guilt and power will sometimes fall on innocence and gentleness."

'"How little", said I, "did I expect that yesterday it should have fallen upon me."

'"Misfortunes", answered the Arab, "should always be expected. If the eye of hostility could have learned to spare, excellence like yours had been exempt from injury. But the angels of affliction spread their toils alike for the virtuous and the wicked, for the mighty and the mean. Do not be disconsolate; I am not one of the lawless and cruel rovers of the desert; I know the rules of civil life: I will fix your ransom, give a passport to your messenger, and perform my stipulation with nice punctuality."

'You will easily believe that I was pleased with his courtesy; and, finding that his predominant passion was desire of money, I began now to think my danger less, for I knew that no sum would be thought too great for the release of Pekuah. I told him that he should have no reason to charge me with ingratitude if I was used with kindness, and that any ransom, which could be expected for a maid of common rank, would be paid, but that he must not persist to rate me as a princess. He said he would consider what he should demand, and then, smiling, bowed and retired.

'Soon after the women came about me, each contending to be more officious than the other, and my maids themselves were served with reverence. We travelled onward by short journeys. On the fourth day the chief told me that my ransom must be two hundred ounces of gold, which I not only promised him, but told him that I would add fifty more, if I and my maids were honourably treated.

'I never knew the power of gold before. From that time I was the leader of the troop. The march of every day was longer or shorter as I commanded, and the tents were pitched where I chose to rest. We now had camels and other conveniences for travel, my own women were always at my side, and I amused myself with observing the manners of the vagrant nations, and with viewing remains of ancient edifices with which these deserted countries appear to have been, in some distant age, lavishly embellished.

'The chief of the band was a man far from illiterate: he was able to travel by the stars or the compass, and had marked in his erratic expeditions such places as are most worthy the notice of a passenger. He observed to me that buildings are always best preserved in places little frequented and difficult of access: for, when once a country declines from its primitive splendour, the more inhabitants are left, the quicker ruin will be made. Walls supply stones more easily than quarries, and palaces and temples will be demolished to make stables of granite, and cottages of porphyry.

CHAPTER XXXIX

The adventures of Pekuah continued

'We wandered about in this manner for some weeks, whether, as our chief pretended, for my gratification, or, as I rather suspected, for some convenience of his own. I endeavoured to appear contented where sullenness and resentment would have been of no use, and that endeavour conduced much to the calmness of my mind; but my heart was always with Nekayah, and the troubles of the night much overbalanced the amusements of the day. My women, who threw all their cares upon their mistress, set their minds at ease from the time when they saw me treated with respect, and gave themselves up to the incidental alleviations of our fatigue without solicitude or sorrow. I was pleased with their pleasure, and animated with their confidence. My condition had lost much of its terror since I found that the Arab ranged the country merely to get riches. Avarice is an uniform and tractable vice: other intellectual distempers are different in different constitutions of mind; that which soothes the pride of one will offend the pride of another; but to the favour of the covetous there is a ready way — bring money and nothing is denied.

'At last we came to the dwelling of our chief, a strong and spacious house, built with stone in an island of the Nile, which lies, as I was told, under the tropic. "Lady," said the Arab, "you shall rest a few weeks after your journey in this place, where you are to consider yourself as sovereign. My occupation is war: I have therefore chosen this obscure residence, from which I can issue unexpected and to which I can retire unpursued. You may now repose in security: here are few pleasures, but here is no danger." He then led me into the inner apartments, and, seating me in the place of honour, bowed to the ground. His women, who considered me as a rival, looked on me with malignity; but, being soon informed that I was a great lady detained only for my ransom, they began to vie with each other in obsequiousness and reverence.

'Being again comforted with new assurances of speedy liberty, I was for some days diverted from impatience by the novelty of the place. The turrets overlooked the country to a great distance and afforded a view of many windings of the stream. In the day I wandered from one place to another as the course of the sun varied the splendour of the prospect, and saw many things which I had never seen before. The crocodiles and river-horses were common in this unpeopled region, and I often looked upon them with terror, though I knew that they could not hurt me. For some time I expected to see mermaids and tritons, which, as Imlac has told me, the European travellers have stationed in the Nile, but no such beings ever appeared, and the Arab, when I enquired after them, laughed at my credulity.

'At night the Arab always attended me to a tower set apart for celestial observations, where he endeavoured to teach me the names and courses of the stars. I had no great inclination to this study, but an appearance of attention was necessary to please my instructor who valued himself for his skill, and, in a little while, I found some employment requisite to beguile the tediousness of time which was to be passed always amidst the same objects. I was weary of looking in the morning on things from which I had turned away weary in the evening: I therefore was at last willing to observe the stars rather than do nothing, but could not always compose my thoughts, and was very often thinking on Nekayah when others imagined me contemplating the sky. Soon after, the Arab went upon another expedition, and then my only pleasure was to talk with my maids about the accident by which we were carried away, and the happiness that we should all enjoy at the end of our captivity.'

'There were women in your Arab's fortress,' said the princess. 'Why did you not make them your companions, enjoy their conversation, and partake their diversions? In a place where they found business or amusement, why should you alone sit corroded with idle melancholy? Or why could not you bear for a few months that condition to which they were condemned for life?'

'The diversions of the women', answered Pekuah, 'were only childish play, by which the mind accustomed to stronger operations could not be kept busy. I could do all which they delighted in doing by powers merely sensitive, while my intellectual faculties were flown to Cairo. They ran from room to room as a bird hops from wire to wire in his cage. They danced for the sake of motion, as lambs frisk in a meadow. One sometimes pretended to be hurt that the rest might be alarmed, or hid herself that another might seek her. Part of their time passed in watching the progress of light bodies that floated on the river, and part in marking the various forms into which clouds broke in the sky.

'Their business was only needlework, in which I and my maids sometimes helped them; but you know that the mind will easily straggle from the fingers, nor will you suspect that captivity and absence from Nekayah could be much solaced by silken flowers.

'Nor was much satisfaction to be hoped from their conversation: for of what could they be expected to talk? They had seen nothing; for they had lived from early youth in that narrow spot: of what they had not seen they could have no knowledge, for they could not read. They had no ideas but of the few things that were within their view, and had hardly names for anything but their clothes and their food. As I bore a superior character, I was often called to terminate their quarrels, which I decided as equitably as I could. If it could have amused me to hear the complaints of each against the rest, I might have been often detained by long stories, but the motives of their animosity were so small that I could not listen long without intercepting the tale.'

'How', said Rasselas, 'can the Arab, whom you represented as a man of more than common accomplishments, take any pleasure in his seraglio, when it is filled only with women like these? Are they exquisitely beautiful?'

'They do not', said Pekuah, 'want that unaffecting and ignoble beauty which may subsist without sprightliness or sublimity, without energy of thought or dignity of virtue. But to a man like the Arab such beauty was only a flower casually plucked and carelessly thrown away. Whatever pleasures he might find among them, they were not those of friendship or society. When they were playing about him he looked on them with inattentive superiority: when they vied for his regard he sometimes turned away disgusted. As they had no knowledge, their talk could take nothing from the tediousness of life; as they had no choice, their fondness, or appearance of fondness, excited in him neither pride nor gratitude; he was not exalted in his own esteem by the smiles of a woman who saw no other man, nor was much obliged by that regard of which he could never know the sincerity, and which he might often perceive to be exerted not so much to delight him as to pain a rival. That which he gave, and they received, as love was only a careless distribution of superfluous time, such love as man can bestow upon that which he despises, such as has neither hope nor fear, neither joy nor sorrow.'

'You have reason, lady, to think yourself happy,' said Imlac, 'that you have been thus easily dismissed. How could a mind, hungry for knowledge, be willing, in an intellectual famine, to lose such a banquet as Pekuah's conversation?'

'I am inclined to believe', answered Pekuah, 'that he was for some time in suspense; for, notwithstanding his promise, whenever I proposed to despatch a messenger to Cairo, he found some excuse for delay. While I was detained in his house he made many incursions into the neighbouring countries, and, perhaps, he would have refused to discharge me, had his plunder been equal to his wishes. He returned always courteous, related his adventures, delighted to hear my observations, and endeavoured to advance my acquaintance with the stars. When I importuned him to send away my letters, he soothed me with professions of honour and sincerity; and, when I could be no longer decently denied, put his troop again in motion, and left me to govern in his absence. I was much afflicted by this studied procrastination, and was sometimes afraid that I should be forgotten; that you would leave Cairo, and I must end my days in an island of the Nile.

'I grew at last hopeless and dejected, and cared so little to entertain him that he for a while more frequently talked with my maids. That he should fall in love with them, or with me, might have been equally fatal, and I was not much pleased with the growing friendship. My anxiety was not long; for, as I recovered some degree of cheerfulness, he returned to me, and I could not forbear to despise my former uneasiness.

'He still delayed to send for my ransom, and would, perhaps, never have determined, had not your agent found his way to him. The gold, which he would not fetch, he could not reject when it was offered. He hastened to prepare for our journey hither like a man delivered from the pain of an intestine conflict. I took leave of my companions in the house, who dismissed me with cold indifference.'

Nekayah, having heard her favourite's relation, rose and embraced her, and Rasselas gave her an hundred ounces of gold, which she presented to the Arab for the fifty that were promised.

CHAPTER XL

The history of a man of learning

They returned to Cairo, and were so well pleased at finding themselves together that none of them went much abroad. The prince began to love learning, and one day declared to Imlac that he intended to devote himself to science and pass the rest of his days in literary solitude.

'Before you make your final choice,' answered Imlac, 'you ought to examine its hazards, and converse with some of those who are grown old in the company of themselves. I have just left the observatory of one of the most learned astronomers in the world, who has spent forty years in unwearied attention to the motions and appearances of the celestial bodies, and has drawn out his soul in endless calculations. He admits a few friends once a month to hear his deductions and enjoy his discoveries. I was introduced as a man of knowledge worthy of his notice. Men of various ideas and fluent conversation are commonly welcome to those whose thoughts have been long fixed upon a single point, and who find the images of other things stealing away. I delighted him with my remarks; he smiled at the narrative of my travels, and was glad to forget the constellations, and descend for a moment into the lower world.

'On the next day of vacation I renewed my visit, and was so fortunate as to please him again. He relaxed from that time the severity of his rule, and permitted me to enter at my own choice. I found him always busy, and always glad to be relieved. As each knew much which the other was desirous of learning, we exchanged our notions with great delight. I perceived that I had every day more of his confidence, and always found new cause of admiration in the profundity of his mind. His comprehension is vast, his memory capacious and retentive, his discourse is methodical, and his expression clear.

'His integrity and benevolence are equal to his learning. His deepest researches and most favourite studies are willingly interrupted for any opportunity of doing good by his counsel or his riches. To his closest retreat, at his most busy moments, all are admitted that want his assistance: "For though I exclude idleness and pleasure, I will never", says he, "bar my doors against charity. To man is permitted the contemplation of the skies, but the practice of virtue is commanded."'

'Surely,' said the princess, 'this man is happy.'

'I visited him', said Imlac, 'with more and more frequency, and was every time more enamoured of his conversation: he was sublime without haughtiness, courteous without formality, and communicative without ostentation. I was at first, Madam, of your opinion, thought him the happiest of mankind, and often congratulated him on the blessing that he enjoyed. He seemed to hear nothing with indifference but the praises of his condition, to which he always returned a general answer, and diverted the conversation to some other topic.

'Amidst this willingness to be pleased, and labour to please, I had always reason to imagine that some painful sentiment pressed upon his mind. He often looked up earnestly towards the sun, and let his voice fall in the midst of his discourse. He would sometimes, when we were alone, gaze upon me in silence with the air of a man who longed to speak what he was yet resolved to suppress. He would sometimes send for me with vehement injunctions of haste, though, when I came to him, he had nothing extraordinary to say; and, sometimes, when I was leaving him, would call me back, pause a few moments, and then dismiss me.

CHAPTER XLI

The astronomer discovers the cause of his uneasiness

'At last the time came when the secret burst his reserve. We were sitting together last night in the turret of his house, watching the emersion of a satellite of Jupiter. A sudden tempest clouded the sky, and disappointed our observation. We sat awhile silent in the dark, and then he addressed himself to me in these words: "Imlac, I have long considered thy friendship as the greatest blessing of my life. Integrity without knowledge is weak and useless, and knowledge without integrity is dangerous and dreadful. I have found in thee all the qualities requisite for trust; benevolence, experience, and fortitude. I have long discharged an office which I must soon quit at the call of nature, and shall rejoice in the hour of imbecility and pain to devolve it upon thee."

'I thought myself honoured by this testimony, and protested

that whatever could conduce to his happiness would add like-wise to mine.

' "Hear, Imlac, what thou wilt not without difficulty credit. I have possessed for five years the regulation of weather and the distribution of the seasons: the sun has listened to my dic-tates, and passed from tropic to tropic by my direction; the clouds, at my call, have poured their waters, and the Nile has overflowed at my command; I have restrained the rage of the Dog-star, and mitigated the fervours of the Crab. The winds alone, of all the elemental powers, have hitherto refused my authority, and multitudes have perished by equinoctial tem-pests which I found myself unable to prohibit or restrain. I have administered this great office with exact justice, and made to the different nations of the earth an impartial dividend of rain and sunshine. What must have been the misery of half the globe, if I had limited the clouds to particular regions, or con-fined the sun to either side of the equator?"

CHAPTER XLII

The astronomer justifies his account of himself

'I suppose he discovered in me, through the obscurity of the room, some tokens of amazement and doubt, for, after a short pause, he proceeded thus:

' "Not to be easily credited will neither surprise nor offend me; for I am, probably, the first of human beings to whom this trust has been imparted. Nor do I know whether to deem this distinction a reward or punishment; since I have possessed it I have been far less happy than before, and nothing but the consciousness of good intention could have enabled me to support the weariness of unremitted vigilance."

' "How long, Sir," said I, "has this great office been in your hands?"

' "About ten years ago," said he, "my daily observations of the changes of the sky led me to consider, whether, if I had the power of the seasons, I could confer greater plenty upon the inhabitants of the earth. This contemplation fastened on my mind, and I sat days and nights in imaginary dominion, pouring upon this country and that the showers of fertility, and seconding every fall of rain with a due proportion of sunshine. I had yet only the will to do good, and did not imagine that I should ever have the power.

' "One day, as I was looking on the fields withering with heat, I felt in my mind a sudden wish that I could send rain on the southern mountains, and raise the Nile to an inundation. In the hurry of my imagination I commanded rain to fall, and, by comparing the time of my command with that of the inundation, I found that the clouds had listened to my lips."

' "Might not some other cause", said I, "produce this concurrence? The Nile does not always rise on the same day."

' "Do not believe", said he with impatience, "that such objections could escape me: I reasoned long against my own conviction, and laboured against truth with the utmost obstinacy. I sometimes suspected myself of madness, and should not have dared to impart this secret but to a man like you, capable of distinguishing the wonderful from the impossible, and the incredible from the false."

' "Why, Sir," said I, "do you call that incredible which you know, or think you know, to be true?"

' "Because", said he, "I cannot prove it by any external evidence; and I know too well the laws of demonstration to think that my conviction ought to influence another, who cannot, like me, be conscious of its force. I, therefore, shall not attempt to gain credit by disputation. It is sufficient that I feel this power—that I have long possessed and every day exerted it. But the life of man is short, the infirmities of age increase upon me, and the time will soon come when the regulator of the year must mingle with the dust. The care of appointing a successor has long disturbed me; the night and the day have been spent in comparisons of all the characters which have come to my knowledge, and I have yet found none so worthy as thyself.

I

CHAPTER XLIII

The astronomer leaves Imlac his directions

' "Hear, therefore, what I shall impart, with attention, such as the welfare of a world requires. If the task of a king be considered as difficult, who has the care only of a few millions to whom he cannot do much good or harm, what must be the anxiety of him on whom depend the action of the elements and the great gifts of light and heat?—Hear me therefore with attention.

' "I have diligently considered the position of the earth and sun, and formed innumerable schemes in which I changed their situation. I have sometimes turned aside the axis of the earth, and sometimes varied the ecliptic of the sun: but I have found it impossible to make a disposition by which the world may be advantaged; what one region gains, another loses, by any imaginable alteration, even without considering the distant parts of the solar system with which we are unacquainted. Do not, therefore, in thy administration of the year, indulge thy pride by innovation; do not please thyself with thinking that thou canst make thyself renowned to all future ages by disordering the seasons. The memory of mischief is no desirable fame. Much less will it become thee to let kindness or interest prevail. Never rob other countries of rain to pour it on thine own. For us the Nile is sufficient."

'I promised that when I possessed the power, I would use it with inflexible integrity, and he dismissed me, pressing my hand. "My heart", said he, "will be now at rest, and my benevolence will no more destroy my quiet: I have found a man of wisdom and virtue, to whom I can cheerfully bequeath the inheritance of the sun." '

The prince heard this narration with very serious regard, but the princess smiled, and Pekuah convulsed herself with laughter. 'Ladies,' said Imlac, 'to mock the heaviest of human afflictions is neither charitable nor wise. Few can attain this man's knowledge, and few practise his virtues; but all may suffer his calamity. Of the uncertainties of our present state, the most dreadful and alarming is the uncertain continuance of reason.'

The princess was recollected, and the favourite was abashed. Rasselas, more deeply affected, enquired of Imlac whether he thought such maladies of the mind frequent, and how they were contracted.

CHAPTER XLIV

The dangerous prevalence of imagination

'Disorders of intellect', answered Imlac, 'happen much more often than superficial observers will easily believe. Perhaps, if we speak with rigorous exactness, no human mind is in its right state. There is no man whose imagination does not sometimes predominate over his reason, who can regulate his attention wholly by his will, and whose ideas will come and go at his command. No man will be found in whose mind airy notions do not sometimes tyrannise, and force him to hope or fear beyond the limits of sober probability. All power of fancy over reason is a degree of insanity; but while this power is such as we can control and repress it is not visible to others, nor considered as any depravation of the mental faculties: it is not pronounced madness but when it comes ungovernable, and apparently influences speech or action.

'To indulge the power of fiction, and send imagination out upon the wing, is often the sport of those who delight too much in silent speculation. When we are alone we are not always busy; the labour of excogitation is too violent to last long; the ardour of enquiry will sometimes give way to idleness or satiety. He who has nothing external that can divert him must find pleasure in his own thoughts, and must conceive himself what he is not; for who is pleased with what he is? He then expatiates in boundless futurity, and culls from all imaginable conditions that which for the present moment he should most desire, amuses his desires with impossible enjoyments, and confers upon his pride unattainable dominion. The mind dances from scene to scene, unites all pleasures in all combinations, and riots in delights which nature and fortune, with all their bounty, cannot bestow.

'In time some particular train of ideas fixes the attention; all other intellectual gratifications are rejected; the mind, in weariness or leisure, recurs constantly to the favourite conception, and feasts on the luscious falsehood whenever she is offended with the bitterness of truth. By degrees the reign of fancy is confirmed; she grows first imperious, and in time despotic. Then fictions begin to operate as realities, false opinions fasten upon the mind, and life passes in dreams of rapture or of anguish.

'This, Sir, is one of the dangers of solitude, which the hermit has confessed not always to promote goodness and the astronomer's misery has proved to be not always propitious to wisdom.'

'I will no more', said the favourite, 'imagine myself the queen of Abyssinia. I have often spent the hours which the princess gave to my own disposal in adjusting ceremonies and regulating the court; I have repressed the pride of the powerful, and granted the petitions of the poor; I have built new palaces in more happy situations, planted groves upon the tops of mountains, and have exulted in the beneficence of royalty, till, when the princess entered, I had almost forgotten to bow down before her.'

'And I', said the princess, 'will not allow myself any more to play the shepherdess in my waking dreams. I have often soothed my thoughts with the quiet and innocence of pastoral employments, till I have in my chamber heard the winds whistle and the sheep bleat; sometimes freed the lamb entangled in the thicket, and sometimes with my crook encountered the wolf. I have a dress like that of the village maids, which I put on to help my imagination, and a pipe on which I play softly, and suppose myself followed by my flocks.'

'I will confess', said the prince, 'an indulgence of fantastic delight more dangerous than yours. I have frequently endeavoured to image the possibility of a perfect government, by which all wrong should be restrained, all vice reformed, and all the subjects preserved in tranquillity and innocence. This thought produced innumerable schemes of reformation, and dictated many useful regulations and salutary edicts. This has been the sport, and sometimes the labour, of my solitude; and I start, when I think with how little anguish I once supposed the death of my father and my brothers.'

'Such', says Imlac, 'are the effects of visionary schemes: when we first form them we know them to be absurd, but familiarise them by degrees, and in time lose sight of their folly.'

CHAPTER XLV

They discourse with an old man

The evening was now far passed, and they rose to return home. As they walked along the bank of the Nile, delighted with the beams of the moon quivering on the water, they saw at a small distance an old man whom the prince had often heard in the assembly of the sages. 'Yonder', said he, 'is one whose years have calmed his passions, but not clouded his reason: let us close the disquisitions of the night by enquiring what are his sentiments of his own state, that we may know whether youth alone is to struggle with vexation, and whether any better hope remains for the latter part of life.'

Here the sage approached and saluted them. They invited him to join their walk, and prattled awhile as acquaintance that had unexpectedly met one another. The old man was cheerful and talkative, and the way seemed short in his company. He was pleased to find himself not disregarded, accompanied them to their house, and, at the prince's request, entered with them. They placed him in the seat of honour, and set wine and conserves before him.

'Sir,' said the princess, 'an evening walk must give to a man of learning, like you, pleasures which ignorance and youth can hardly conceive. You know the qualities and the causes of all that you behold, the laws by which the river flows, the

periods in which the planets perform their revolutions. Everything must supply you with contemplation, and renew the consciousness of your own dignity.'

'Lady,' answered he, 'let the gay and the vigorous expect
pleasure in their excursions; it is enough that age can obtain
ease. To me the world has lost its novelty: I look round, and
see what I remember to have seen in happier days. I rest against
a tree, and consider that in the same shade I once disputed
upon the annual overflow of the Nile with a friend who is now
silent in the grave. I cast my eyes upwards, fix them on the
changing moon, and think with pain on the vicissitudes of life.
I have ceased to take much delight in physical truth; for what
have I to do with those things which I am soon to leave?'

'You may at least recreate yourself', said Imlac, 'with the
recollection of an honourable and useful life, and enjoy the
praise which all agree to give you.'

'Praise', said the sage, with a sigh, 'is to an old man an empty
sound. I have neither mother to be delighted with the reputation of her son, nor wife to partake the honours of her husband.
I have outlived my friends and my rivals. Nothing is now of
much importance, for I cannot extend my interest beyond
myself. Youth is delighted with applause, because it is considered as the earnest of some future good, and because the prospect of life is far extended: but to me, who am now declining
to decrepitude, there is little to be feared from the malevolence
of men, and yet less to be hoped from their affection or esteem.
Something they may yet take away, but they can give me nothing. Riches would now be useless, and high employment would
be pain. My retrospect of life recalls to my view many opportunities of good neglected, much time squandered upon trifles,
and more lost in idleness and vacancy. I leave many great designs unattempted, and many great attempts unfinished. My
mind is burthened with no heavy crime, and therefore I compose myself to tranquillity; endeavour to abstract my thoughts
from hopes and cares, which, though reason knows them to
be vain, still try to keep their old possession of the heart;
expect, with serene humility, that hour which nature cannot
long delay; and hope to possess in a better state that happiness

which here I could not find, and that virtue which here I have not attained.'

He rose and went away, leaving his audience not much elated with the hope of long life. The prince consoled himself with remarking that it was not reasonable to be disappointed by this account, for age had never been considered as the season of felicity, and, if it was possible to be easy in decline and weakness, it was likely that the days of vigour and alacrity might be happy; that the noon of life might be bright, if the evening could be calm.

The princess suspected that age was querulous and malignant, and delighted to repress the expectations of those who had newly entered the world. She had seen the possessors of estates look with envy on their heirs, and known many who enjoy pleasure no longer than they can confine it to themselves.

Pekuah conjectured that the man was older than he appeared, and was willing to impute his complaints to delirious dejection; or else supposed that he had been unfortunate and was therefore discontented: 'For nothing', said she, 'is more common than to call our own condition the condition of life.'

Imlac, who had no desire to see them depressed, smiled at the comforts which they could so readily procure to themselves, and remembered, that at the same age, he was equally confident of unmingled prosperity, and equally fertile of consolatory expedients. He forbore to force upon them unwelcome knowledge, which time itself would too soon impress. The princess and her lady retired; the madness of the astronomer hung upon their minds, and they desired Imlac to enter upon his office and delay next morning the rising of the sun.

CHAPTER XLVI

The princess and Pekuah visit the astronomer

The princess and Pekuah, having talked in private of Imlac's astronomer, thought his character at once so amiable and so strange that they could not be satisfied without a nearer knowledge, and Imlac was requested to find the means of bringing them together.

This was somewhat difficult; the philosopher had never received any visits from women, though he lived in a city that had in it many Europeans who followed the manners of their own countries, and many from other parts of the world that lived there with European liberty. The ladies would not be refused, and several schemes were proposed for the accomplishment of their design. It was proposed to introduce them as strangers in distress, to whom the sage was always accessible; but, after some deliberation, it appeared that by this artifice no acquaintance could be formed, for their conversation would be short, and they could not decently importune him often. 'This', said Rasselas, 'is true; but I have yet a stronger objection against the misrepresentation of your state. I have always considered it as treason against the great republic of human nature to make any man's virtues the means of deceiving him, whether on great or little occasions. All imposture weakens confidence and chills benevolence. When the sage finds that you are not what you seemed, he will feel the resentment natural to a man who, conscious of great abilities, discovers that he has been tricked by understandings meaner than his own, and, perhaps, the distrust, which he can never afterwards wholly lay aside, may stop the voice of counsel and close the hand of charity; and where will you find the power of restoring his benefactions to mankind, or his peace to himself?'

To this no reply was attempted, and Imlac began to hope that their curiosity would subside; but, next day, Pekuah told him she had now found an honest pretence for a visit to the astronomer, for she would solicit permission to continue under him the studies in which she had been initiated by the Arab, and the princess might go with her either as a fellow-student or because a woman could not decently come alone. 'I am afraid', said Imlac, 'that he will be soon weary of your company: men advanced far in knowledge do not love to repeat the elements of their art, and I am not certain that even of the elements as he will deliver them, connected with inferences and mingled with reflections, you are a very capable auditress.'

'That', said Pekuah, 'must be my care: I ask of you only to take me thither. My knowledge is, perhaps, more than you imagine it, and by concurring always with his opinions I shall make him think it greater than it is.'

The astronomer, in pursuance of this resolution, was told that a foreign lady, travelling in search of knowledge, had heard of his reputation and was desirous to become his scholar. The uncommonness of the proposal raised at once his surprise and curiosity, and when, after a short deliberation, he consented to admit her, he could not stay without impatience till the next day.

The ladies dressed themselves magnificently, and were attended by Imlac to the astronomer, who was pleased to see himself approached with respect by persons of so splendid an appearance. In the exchange of the first civilities he was timorous and bashful; but, when the talk became regular, he recollected his powers, and justified the character which Imlac had given. Enquiring of Pekuah what could have turned her inclination towards astronomy, he received from her a history of her adventure at the Pyramid and of the time passed in the Arab's island. She told her tale with ease and elegance, and her conversation took possession of his heart. The discourse was then turned to astronomy: Pekuah displayed what she knew: he looked upon her as a prodigy of genius, and entreated her not to desist from a study which she had so happily begun.

They came again and again, and were every time more welcome than before. The sage endeavoured to amuse them, that they might prolong their visits, for he found his thoughts grow brighter in their company; the clouds of solicitude vanished by degrees as he forced himself to entertain them, and he grieved when he was left at their departure to his old employment of regulating the seasons.

The princess and her favourite had now watched his lips for several months, and could not catch a single word from which they could judge whether he continued, or not, in the opinion of his preternatural commission. They often contrived to bring him to an open declaration, but he easily eluded all their attacks, and on which side soever they pressed him escaped from them to some other topic.

As their familiarity increased they invited him often to the house of Imlac, where they distinguished him by extraordinary respect. He began gradually to delight in sublunary pleasures. He came early and departed late; laboured to recommend himself by assiduity and compliance; excited their curiosity after new arts, that they might still want his assistance; and, when they made any excursion of pleasure or enquiry, entreated to attend them.

By long experience of his integrity and wisdom, the prince and his sister were convinced that he might be trusted without danger; and, lest he should draw any false hopes from the civilities which he received, discovered to him their condition, with the motives of their journey, and required his opinion on the *choice of life*.

'Of the various conditions which the world spreads before you, which you shall prefer', said the sage, 'I am not able to instruct you. I can only tell that I have chosen wrong. I have passed my time in study without experience; in the attainment of sciences which can, for the most part, be but remotely useful to mankind. I have purchased knowledge at the expense of all the common comforts of life: I have missed the endearing elegance of female friendship, and the happy commerce of domestic tenderness. If I have obtained any prerogatives above other students, they have been accompanied with fear, disquiet, and scrupulosity; but even of these prerogatives, whatever they were, I have, since my thoughts have been diversified by more intercourse with the world, begun to question the reality. When I have been for a few days lost in pleasing dissipation, I am always tempted to think that my enquiries have ended in error, and that I have suffered much and suffered it in vain.'

Imlac was delighted to find that the sage's understanding was breaking through its mists, and resolved to detain him from the planets till he should forget his task of ruling them, and reason should recover its original influence.

From this time the astronomer was received into familiar

friendship, and partook of all their projects and pleasures: his respect kept him attentive, and the activity of Rasselas did not leave much time unengaged. Something was always to be done; the day was spent in making observations which furnished talk for the evening, and the evening was closed with a scheme for the morrow.

The sage confessed to Imlac that, since he had mingled in the gay tumults of life and divided his hours by a succession of amusements, he found the conviction of his authority over the skies fade gradually from his mind, and began to trust less to an opinion which he never could prove to others and which he now found subject to variation from causes in which reason had no part. 'If I am accidentally left alone for a few hours,' said he, 'my inveterate persuasion rushes upon my soul, and my thoughts are chained down by some irresistible violence, but they are soon disentangled by the prince's conversation, and instantaneously released at the entrance of Pekuah. I am like a man habitually afraid of spectres, who is set at ease by a lamp and wonders at the dread which harassed him in the dark, yet, if his lamp be extinguished, feels again the terrors which he knows that when it is light he shall feel no more. But I am sometimes afraid lest I indulge my quiet by criminal negligence, and voluntarily forget the great charge with which I am entrusted. If I favour myself in a known error, or am determined by my own ease in a doubtful question of this importance, how dreadful is my crime!'

'No disease of the imagination', answered Imlac, 'is so difficult of cure as that which is complicated with the dread of guilt: fancy and conscience then act interchangeably upon us, and so often shift their places that the illusions of one are not distinguished from the dictates of the other. If fancy presents images not moral or religious, the mind drives them away when they give it pain, but, when melancholic notions take the form of duty, they lay hold on the faculties without opposition, because we are afraid to exclude or banish them. For this reason the superstitious are often melancholy, and the melancholy almost always superstitious.

'But do not let the suggestions of timidity overpower your

better reason: the danger of neglect can be but as the probability of the obligation, which, when you consider it with freedom, you find very little, and that little growing every day less. Open your heart to the influence of the light, which, from time to time, breaks in upon you: when scruples importune you, which you in your lucid moments know to be vain, do not stand to parley, but fly to business or to Pekuah, and keep this thought always prevalent, that you are only one atom of the mass of humanity, and have neither such virtue nor vice as that you should be singled out for supernatural favours or afflictions.'

CHAPTER XLVII

The prince enters and brings a new topic

'All this', said the astronomer, 'I have often thought, but my reason has been so long subjugated by an uncontrollable and overwhelming idea that it durst not confide in its own decisions. I now see how fatally I betrayed my quiet by suffering chimeras to prey upon me in secret; but melancholy shrinks from communication, and I never found a man before to whom I could impart my troubles, though I had been certain of relief. I rejoice to find my own sentiments confirmed by yours, who are not easily deceived, and can have no motive or purpose to deceive. I hope that time and variety will dissipate the gloom that has so long surrounded me, and the latter part of my days will be spent in peace.'

'Your learning and virtue', said Imlac, 'may justly give you hopes.'

Rasselas then entered with the princess and Pekuah and enquired whether they had contrived any new diversion for the next day. 'Such', said Nekayah, 'is the state of life that none are happy but by the anticipation of change: the change itself is nothing; when we have made it, the next wish is to change again. The world is not yet exhausted; let me see something tomorrow which I never saw before.'

'Variety', said Rasselas, 'is so necessary to content that even the Happy Valley disgusted me by the recurrence of its luxuries; yet I could not forbear to reproach myself with impatience, when I saw the monks of St. Anthony support, without complaint, a life, not of uniform delight, but uniform hardship.'

'Those men', answered Imlac, 'are less wretched in their silent convent than the Abyssinian princes in their prison of pleasure. Whatever is done by the monks is incited by an adequate and reasonable motive. Their labour supplies them with necessaries; it therefore cannot be omitted, and is certainly rewarded. Their devotion prepares them for another state, and reminds them of its approach while it fits them for it. Their time is regularly distributed; one duty succeeds another, so that they are not left open to the distraction of unguided choice, nor lost in the shades of listless inactivity. There is a certain task to be performed at an appropriated hour; and their toils are cheerful, because they consider them as acts of piety by which they are always advancing towards endless felicity.'

'Do you think', said Nekayah, 'that the monastic rule is a more holy and less imperfect state than any other? May not he equally hope for future happiness who converses openly with mankind, who succours the distressed by his charity, instructs the ignorant by his learning, and contributes by his industry to the general system of life; even though he should omit some of the mortifications which are practised in the cloister, and allow himself such harmless delights as his condition may place within his reach?'

'This', said Imlac, 'is a question which has long divided the wise and perplexed the good. I am afraid to decide on either part. He that lives well in the world is better than he that lives well in a monastery. But, perhaps, everyone is not able to stem the temptations of public life; and, if he cannot conquer, he may properly retreat. Some have little power to do good, and have likewise little strength to resist evil. Many are weary of their conflicts with adversity, and are willing to eject those passions which have long busied them in vain. And many are dismissed by age and diseases from the more laborious duties of society. In monasteries the weak and timorous may be happily sheltered, the weary may repose, and the penitent may meditate. Those retreats of prayer and contemplation have something so congenial to the mind of man that, perhaps, there is scarcely one that does not purpose to close his life in pious abstraction with a few associates serious as himself.'

'Such', said Pekuah, 'has often been my wish, and I have heard the princess declare that she should not willingly die in a crowd.'

'The liberty of using harmless pleasures', proceeded Imlac, 'will not be disputed; but it is still to be examined what pleasures are harmless. The evil of any pleasure that Nekayah can image is not in the act itself but in its consequences. Pleasure, in itself harmless, may become mischievous, by endearing to us a state which we know to be transient and probatory, and withdrawing our thoughts from that of which every hour brings us nearer to the beginning, and of which no length of time will bring us to the end. Mortification is not virtuous in itself, nor has any other use but that it disengages us from the allurements of sense. In the state of future perfection, to which we all aspire, there will be pleasure without danger, and security without restraint.'

The princess was silent, and Rasselas, turning to the astronomer, asked him whether he could not delay her retreat by showing her something which she had not seen before.

'Your curiosity', said the sage, 'has been so general, and your pursuit of knowledge so vigorous, that novelties are not now very easily to be found: but what you can no longer procure from the living may be given by the dead. Among the wonders of this country are the catacombs, or the ancient repositories in which the bodies of the earliest generations were lodged, and where, by the virtue of the gums which embalmed them, they yet remain without corruption.'

'I know not', said Rasselas, 'what pleasure the sight of the catacombs can afford; but, since nothing else is offered, I am resolved to view them, and shall place this with many other things which I have done because I would do something.'

They hired a guard of horsemen, and the next day visited

the catacombs. When they were about to descend into the sepulchral caves, 'Pekuah,' said the princess, 'we are now again invading the habitations of the dead; I know that you will stay behind; let me find you safe when I return.' 'No, I will not be left,' answered Pekuah. 'I will go down between you and the prince.'

They then all descended, and roved with wonder through the labyrinth of subterraneous passages, where the bodies were laid in rows on either side.

CHAPTER XLVIII

Imlac discourses on the nature of the soul

'What reason', said the prince, 'can be given, why the Egyptians should thus expensively preserve those carcasses which some nations consume with fire, others lay to mingle with the earth, and all agree to remove from their sight as soon as decent rites can be performed?'

'The original of ancient customs', said Imlac, 'is commonly unknown; for the practice often continues when the cause has ceased; and concerning superstitious ceremonies it is vain to conjecture, for what reason did not dictate, reason cannot explain. I have long believed that the practice of embalming arose only from tenderness to the remains of relations or friends, and to this opinion I am more inclined because it seems impossible that this care should have been general: had all the dead been embalmed, their repositories must in time have been more spacious than the dwellings of the living. I suppose only the rich or honourable were secured from corruption, and the rest left to the course of nature.

'But it is commonly supposed that the Egyptians believed the soul to live as long as the body continued undissolved, and therefore tried this method of eluding death.'

'Could the wise Egyptians', said Nekayah, 'think so grossly of the soul? If the soul could once survive its separation, what could it afterwards receive or suffer from the body?'

'The Egyptians would doubtless think erroneously', said the astronomer, 'in the darkness of heathenism and the first dawn of philosophy. The nature of the soul is still disputed amidst all our opportunities of clearer knowledge: some yet say that it may be material, who, nevertheless, believe it to be immortal.'

'Some', answered Imlac, 'have indeed said that the soul is material, but I can scarcely believe that any man has thought it, who knew how to think; for all the conclusions of reason enforce the immateriality of the mind, and all the notices of sense and investigations of science concur to prove the unconsciousness of matter.

'It was never supposed that cogitation is inherent in matter, or that every particle is a thinking being. Yet, if any part of matter be devoid of thought, what part can we suppose to think? Matter can differ from matter only in form, density, bulk, motion, and direction of motion: to which of these, however varied or combined, can consciousness be annexed? To be round or square, to be solid or fluid, to be great or little, to be moved slowly or swiftly one way or another, are modes of material existence, all equally alien from the nature of cogitation. If matter be once without thought, it can only be made to think by some new modification, but all the modifications which it can admit are equally unconnected with cogitative powers.'

'But the materialists', said the astronomer, 'urge that matter may have qualities with which we are unacquainted.'

'He who will determine', returned Imlac, 'against that which he knows because there may be something which he knows not, he that can set hypothetical possibility against acknowledged certainty, is not to be admitted among reasonable beings. All that we know of matter is that matter is inert, senseless and lifeless; and if this conviction cannot be opposed but by referring us to something that we know not, we have all the evidence that human intellect can admit. If that which is known may be over-ruled by that which is unknown, no being, not omniscient, can arrive at certainty.'

'Yet let us not', said the astronomer, 'too arrogantly limit the Creator's power.'

'It is no limitation of omnipotence', replied the poet, 'to suppose that one thing is not consistent with another, that the same proposition cannot be at once true and false, that the same number cannot be even and odd, that cogitation cannot be conferred on that which is created incapable of cogitation.'

'I know not', said Nekayah, 'any great use of this question. Does that immateriality, which, in my opinion, you have sufficiently proved, necessarily include eternal duration?'

'Of immateriality', said Imlac, 'our ideas are negative, and therefore obscure. Immateriality seems to imply a natural power of perpetual duration as a consequence of exemption from all causes of decay: whatever perishes is destroyed by the solution of its contexture, and separation of its parts; nor can we conceive how that which has no parts, and therefore admits no solution, can be naturally corrupted or impaired.'

'I know not', said Rasselas, 'how to conceive anything without extension: what is extended must have parts, and you allow that whatever has parts may be destroyed.'

'Consider your own conceptions,' replied Imlac, 'and the difficulty will be less. You will find substance without extension. An ideal form is no less real than material bulk: yet an ideal form has no extension. It is no less certain, when you think on a pyramid, that your mind possesses the idea of a pyramid than that the pyramid itself is standing. What space does the idea of a pyramid occupy more than the idea of a grain of corn? Or how can either idea suffer laceration? As is the effect such is the cause; as thought is, such is the power that thinks; a power impassive and indiscerptible.'

'But the Being', said Nekayah, 'whom I fear to name, the Being which made the soul, can destroy it.'

'He, surely, can destroy it,' answered Imlac, 'since, however unperishable in itself, it receives from a higher nature its power of duration. That it will not perish by any inherent cause or principle of corruption may be collected from philosophy; but philosophy can tell no more. That it will not be annihilated by him that made it, we must humbly learn from higher authority.'

The whole assembly stood a while silent and collected. 'Let

K

us return', said Rasselas, 'from this scene of mortality. How gloomy would be these mansions of the dead to him who did not know that he shall never die; that what now acts shall continue its agency, and what now thinks shall think on for ever. Those that lie here stretched before us, the wise and the powerful of ancient times, warn us to remember the shortness of our present state: they were, perhaps, snatched away while they were busy, like us, in the *choice of life.*'

'To me', said the princess, 'the *choice of life* is become less important; I hope hereafter to think only on the choice of eternity.'

They then hastened out of the caverns, and, under the protection of their guard, returned to Cairo.

CHAPTER XLIX

The conclusion, in which nothing is concluded

It was now the time of the inundation of the Nile: a few days after their visit to the catacombs, the river began to rise.

They were confined to their house. The whole region being under water gave them no invitation to any excursions, and, being well supplied with materials for talk, they diverted themselves with comparisons of the different forms of life which they had observed, and with various schemes of happiness which each of them had formed.

Pekuah was never so much charmed with any place as the convent of St. Anthony, where the Arab restored her to the princess, and wished only to fill it with pious maidens, and to be made prioress of the order: she was weary of expectation and disgust, and would gladly be fixed in some unvariable state.

The princess thought, that of all sublunary things, knowledge was the best. She desired first to learn all sciences, and then purposed to found a college of learned women, in which she would preside, that, by conversing with the old and educating the young, she might divide her time between the acquisition and communication of wisdom, and raise up for the next age models of prudence and patterns of piety.

The prince desired a little kingdom, in which he might administer justice in his own person and see all the parts of government with his own eyes; but he could never fix the limits of his dominion, and was always adding to the number of his subjects.

Imlac and the astronomer were contented to be driven along the stream of life without directing their course to any particular port.

Of these wishes that they had formed they well knew that none could be obtained. They deliberated a while what was to be done, and resolved, when the inundation should cease, to return to Abyssinia.

FINIS

ESSAYS

THE RAMBLER

No. 12. Saturday, April 28, 1750

. . . Miserum parva stipe focillat, ut pudibundos
Exercere sales inter convivia possit. . . .
. . . Tu mitis, et acri
Asperitate carens, positoque per omnia fastu,
Inter ut aequales unus numeraris amicos,
Obsequiumque doces, et amorem quaeris amando.
LUCANUS ad Pisonem.

To the RAMBLER

SIR,

As you seem to have devoted your labours to virtue, I cannot forbear to inform you of one species of cruelty with which the life of a man of letters perhaps does not often make him acquainted, and which, as it seems to produce no other advantage to those that practise it than a short gratification of thoughtless vanity, may become less common when it has been once exposed in its various forms, and its full magnitude.

I am the daughter of a country gentleman, whose family is numerous, and whose estate, not at first sufficient to supply us with affluence, has been lately so much impaired by an unsuccessful lawsuit, that all the younger children are obliged to try such means as their education affords them for procuring the necessaries of life. Distress and curiosity concurred to bring me to London, where I was received, with the coldness which misfortune generally finds, by a relation. A week, a long week, I lived with my cousin, before the most vigilant enquiry could procure us the least hopes of a place, in which time I was much better qualified to bear all the vexations of servitude. The first two days she was content to pity me, and only wished I had not been quite so well bred, but people must comply with their circumstances. This lenity, however, was soon at an end; and, for the remaining part of the week, I heard every hour of the pride of my family, the obstinacy of my father, and of people better born than myself that were common servants.

At last, on Saturday noon, she told me, with very visible satisfaction, that Mrs. Bombasine, the great silk-mercer's lady, wanted a maid, and a fine place it would be; for there would be nothing to do but to clean my mistress's room, get up her linen, dress the young ladies, wait at tea in the morning, take care of a little miss just come from nurse, and then sit down to my needle. But madam was a woman of great spirit, and would not be contradicted, and therefore I should take care, for good places were not easily to be got.

With these cautions I waited on Madam Bombasine, of whom the first sight gave me no ravishing ideas. She was two yards round the waist, her voice was at once loud and squeaking, and her face brought to my mind the picture of the full-moon. 'Are you the young woman', says she, 'that are come to offer yourself? It is strange when people of substance want a servant, how soon it is the town-talk. But they know they shall have a bellyful that live with me. Not like people at the other end of the town, we dine at one o'clock. But I never take anybody without a character; what friends do you come of?' I then told her that my father was a gentleman, and that we had been unfortunate. 'A great misfortune, indeed, to come to me and have three meals a day! So your father was a gentleman, and you are a gentlewoman I suppose—such gentlewomen!' 'Madam, I did not mean to claim any exemptions; I only answered your enquiry.' 'Such gentlewomen! People should set their children to good trades, and keep them off the parish. Pray go to the other end of the town; there are gentlewomen, if they would pay their debts; I am sure we have lost enough by gentlewomen.' Upon this, her broad face grew broader with triumph, and I was afraid she would have taken me for the pleasure of continuing her insult: but happily the next word was, 'Pray, Mrs. Gentlewoman, troop downstairs.' You may believe I obeyed her.

I returned and met with a better reception from my cousin than I expected; for, while I was out, she had heard that Mrs. Standish, whose husband had lately been raised from a clerk in an office to be commissioner of the excise, had taken a fine house, and wanted a maid.

To Mrs. Standish I went, and, after having waited six hours, was at last admitted to the top of the stairs, when she came out of her room, with two of her company. There was a smell of punch. 'So, young woman, you want a place; whence do you come?' 'From the country, Madam.' 'Yes, they all come out of the country. And what brought you to town, a bastard? Where do you lodge? At the Seven Dials? What, you never heard of the Foundling House?' Upon this, they all laughed so obstre-perously, that I took the opportunity of sneaking off in the tumult.

I then heard of a place at an elderly lady's. She was at cards; but in two hours, I was told, she would speak to me. She asked me if I could keep an account, and ordered me to write. I wrote two lines out of some book that lay by her. She wondered what people meant, to breed up girls to write at that rate. 'I suppose, Mrs. Flirt, if I was to see your work, it would be fine stuff!— You may walk. I will not have love-letters written from my house to every young fellow in the street.'

Two days after, I went on the same pursuit to Lady Lofty, dressed, as I was directed, in what little ornaments I had, because she had lately got a place at court. Upon the first sight of me, she turns to the woman that showed me in. 'Is this the lady that wants a place? Pray what place would you have, Miss? A maid of honour's place? Servants nowadays!' 'Madam, I heard you wanted——' 'Wanted what? Somebody finer than myself? A pretty servant indeed—I should be afraid to speak to her. I suppose, Mrs. Minx, these fine hands cannot bear wetting. A servant indeed! Pray move off—I am resolved to be the head person in this house. You are ready dressed; the taverns will be open at night.'

I went to enquire for the next place in a clean linen gown, and heard the servant tell his lady, there was a young woman but he saw she would not do. I was brought up however. 'Are

you the trollop that has the impudence to come for my place?
What! you have hired that nasty gown, and are come to steal
a better.' 'Madam, I have another, but being obliged to
walk——' 'Then these are your manners, with your blushes
and your courtesies, to come to me in your worst gown.'
'Madam, give me leave to wait upon you in my other.' 'Wait
on me, you saucy slut! Then you are sure of coming. I could
not let such a drab come near me. Here, you girl that came up
with her, have you touched her? If you have, wash your hands
before you dress me. Such trollops! Get you down. What,
whimpering? Pray walk!'

I went away with tears; for my cousin had lost all patience.
However, she told me that she had a respect for my relations,
was willing to keep me out of the street, and would let me have
another week.

The first day of this week I saw two places. At one I was
asked where I had lived. And, upon my answer, was told by the
lady that people should qualify themselves in ordinary places,
for she should never have done if she was to follow girls about.
At the other house, I was a smirking hussy, and that sweet face
I might make money of. For her part, it was a rule with her
never to take any creature that thought herself handsome.

The next three days were spent in Lady Bluff's entry, where
I waited six hours every day for the pleasure of seeing the
servants peep at me, and go away laughing. 'Madam will
stretch her small shanks in the entry; she will know the house
again.' At sunset the two first days I was told that my lady
would see me tomorrow; and, on the third, that her woman
stayed.

My week was now near its end, and I had no hopes of a
place. My relation, who always laid upon me the blame of
every miscarriage, told me that I must learn to humble myself,
and that all great ladies had particular ways; that if I went on
in that manner, she could not tell who would keep me; she had
known many, that had refused places, sell their clothes and
beg in the streets.

It was to no purpose that the refusal was declared by me to
be never on my side; I was reasoning against interest and

against stupidity; and therefore I comforted myself with the
hope of succeeding better in my next attempt, and went to
Mrs. Courtly, a very fine lady, who had routs at her house, and
saw the best company in town.

I had not waited two hours before I was called up, and found
Mr. Courtly and his lady at piquet, in the height of good
humour. This I looked on as a favourable sign, and stood at
the lower end of the room, in expectation of the common
questions. At last Mr. Courtly called out, after a whisper,
'Stand facing the light, that one may see you.' I changed my
place, and blushed. They frequently turned their eyes upon
me, and seemed to discover many subjects of merriment; for
at every look they whispered, and laughed with the most
violent agitations of delight. At last Mr. Courtly cried out, 'Is
that colour your own, child?' 'Yes,' says the lady, 'if she has
not robbed the kitchen hearth.' This was so happy a conceit,
that it renewed the storm of laughter, and they threw down
their cards in hopes of better sport. The lady then called me to
her, and began with an affected gravity to enquire what I could
do. 'But first turn about, and let us see your fine shape. Well,
what are you fit for, Mrs. Mum? You would find your tongue,
I suppose, in the kitchen.' 'No, no,' says Mr. Courtly, 'the
girl's a good girl yet, but I am afraid a brisk young fellow, with
fine tags on his shoulder—— Come, child, hold up your head.
What! You have stole nothing.' 'Not yet,' says the lady, 'but
she hopes to steal your heart quickly.' Here was a laugh of
happiness and triumph, prolonged by the confusion which I
could now no longer repress. At last the lady recollected herself: 'Stole? No! But if I had her, I should watch her. For that
downcast eye—— Why cannot you look people in the face?'
'Steal!' says her husband. 'She would steal nothing but perhaps a
few ribbons before they were left off by her lady.' 'Sir,' answered
I, 'why should you, by supposing me a thief, insult one from
whom you have received no injury?' 'Insult!' says the lady.
'Are you come here to be a servant, you saucy baggage, and
talk of insulting? What will this world come to, if a gentleman
may not jest with a servant? Well, such servants! Pray be gone,
and see when you will have the honour to be so insulted again.

Servants insulted! A fine time! Insulted! Get downstairs, you slut, or the footman shall insult you.'

The last day of the last week was now coming, and my kind cousin talked of sending me down in the wagon to preserve me from bad courses. But in the morning she came and told me that she had one trial more for me; Euphemia wanted a maid, and perhaps I might do for her; for, like me, she must fall her crest, being forced to lay down her chariot upon the loss of half her fortune by bad securities, and with her way of giving her money to everybody that pretended to want it, could have little beforehand; therefore I might serve her; for, with all her fine sense, she must not pretend to be nice.

I went immediately, and met at the door a young gentle-woman, who told me she had herself been hired that morning, but that she was ordered to bring any that offered upstairs. I was accordingly introduced to Euphemia, who, when I came in, laid down her book, and told me that she sent for me not to gratify an idle curiosity, but lest my disappointment might be made still more grating by incivility; that she was in pain to deny anything, much more what was no favour; that she saw nothing in my appearance which did not make her wish for my company; but that another, whose claims might perhaps be equal, had come before me. The thought of being so near to such a place, and missing it, brought tears into my eyes, and my sobs hindered me from returning my acknowledgements. She rose up confused, and supposing by my concern that I was distressed, placed me by her, and made me tell her my story; which when she had heard, she put two guineas in my hand, ordering me to lodge near her, and make use of her table till she could provide for me. I am now under her protection, and know not how to show my gratitude better than by giving this account to the Rambler.

ZOSIMA

No. 47. Tuesday, August 28, 1750

Quanquam his solatiis acquiescam, debilitor et frangor
eadem illa humanitate quae me, ut hoc ipsum permitterem,
induxit, non ideo tamen velim durior fieri: nec ignoro alios
huiusmodi casus nihil amplius vocare quam damnum:
eoque sibi magnos homines et sapientes videri. Qui an magni
sapientesque sint, nescio: homines non sunt. Hominis est
enim affici dolore, sentire: resistere tamen, et solatia
admittere, non solatiis non egere.

PLINY

Of the passions with which the mind of man is agitated, it may be observed that they naturally hasten towards their own extinction, by inciting and quickening the attainment of their objects. Thus fear urges our flight, and desire animates our progress; and if there are some which perhaps may be indulged till they outgrow the objects appropriated to their satisfaction, as is frequently observed of avarice and ambition, yet their immediate tendency is to some object really existing, and generally within the prospect. The miser always imagines that there is a certain sum that will fill his heart to the brim, and the ambitious man, like King Pyrrhus, has always a scheme that is to terminate his labours; after which he shall pass the rest of his life in ease or gaiety, in repose or devotion.

Sorrow is perhaps the only affection of the breast that can be excepted from this general remark, and it therefore deserves the particular attention of those who have assumed the arduous province of preserving the balance of our mental constitution and of administering physic to the soul. The other passions are diseases indeed, but they necessarily direct us to their proper cure. A man at once feels the pain and knows the medicine, to which he is carried with greater haste as the evil which requires it is more excruciating, and cures himself by instinct, as the wounded stags of Crete are related by Ælian to have recourse to vulnerary herbs. But for sorrow there is no remedy provided by nature; it is often occasioned by accidents irreparable, and dwells upon objects that have changed their existence; it requires what it cannot hope—that the laws of nature should be repealed, that the dead should return, or the past should be recalled.

Sorrow is not that regret for negligence or error which may animate us to future care or activity, or that repentance of crimes for which, however irrevocable, our Creator has promised to accept it as an atonement; the pain which arises from these causes has very salutary effects, and is every hour extenuating itself by the reparation of those miscarriages that produce it. Sorrow is properly that state of the mind in which our desires are fixed upon the past without looking forward to the future, an incessant wish that something were otherwise than it has been, a tormenting and harassing want of some enjoyment or possession which we have lost and which no endeavours can possibly regain. Into such anguish many have sunk upon sudden diminutions of their fortune, an unexpected blast of their reputation, or loss of children or of friends. They have cut off by one stroke all sensibility of pleasure, have given up for ever the hopes of substituting any other object in the room of that which they lament, and have resigned the remaining part of their lives to gloom and solitude, complaints and despondency, worn themselves out in unavailing misery, and sunk down at last under their burthen.

Yet so much is this passion the natural consequence of tenderness and endearment, that, however painful and however useless, it is justly reproachful not to feel it on some occasions; and so universally is it known to prevail, that the laws of some nations and the customs of others have limited a time for the external appearances of that grief caused by the dissolution of close alliances, and the breach of domestic union.

It seems determined by the general suffrage of mankind that sorrow is to a certain point laudable, as the offspring of love, or at least pardonable, as the effect of weakness; but that, however, it ought not to be suffered to increase by indulgence, but to give way, after a stated time, to social duties, and the common avocations of life. It is at first unavoidable, and therefore must be allowed, whether with or without our choice; it may afterwards be admitted as a decent and affectionate testimony of kindness and esteem; something will be extorted by nature, and something may be given to the world. But all beyond that is not only useless, but culpable; for we have no right to sacrifice, to the vain longings of affection, that time which Providence allows us for the task of our station.

But it too often happens that sorrow, thus lawfully entering, gains such a firm possession of the mind, that it is not afterwards to be ejected; the mournful ideas, first violently impressed and afterwards willingly received, have so much engrossed the attention as to be predominant in every meditation, to intrude uncalled to darken gaiety, or perplex ratiocination. An habitual sadness seizes upon the soul, and the faculties are chained to a single object, which can never be contemplated but with hopeless uneasiness.

This is a state of dejection from which it is often very difficult to rise to cheerfulness and alacrity, and therefore many who have laid down rules of speculative prudence think preservatives easier than remedies, and teach us not to trust ourselves with too much fondness, but to keep our minds always suspended in such a state of indifference that we may change any of the objects about us without inconvenience or emotion.

An exact compliance with this rule might, perhaps, contritribute to tranquillity, but surely it would never produce happiness. He that regards none so much as to be afraid of losing them must live for ever without the gentle pleasures of sympathy and confidence; he must feel no melting fondness, no warmth of benevolence, nor any of those nameless joys which arise from the power of pleasing. And as no man can justly claim more tenderness than he pays, he must forfeit his share in all that officious and watchful kindness which love only can dictate, and all those lenient endearments by which love only can soften life, and may justly be overlooked by such as have more warmth in their nature; for who would be the friend of him whom, with whatever assiduity he may be courted, and with whatever services obliged, his principles will not suffer to make equal returns, and who, when you have exhausted all the instances of good-will, can only be prevailed on not to be an enemy?

An attempt to preserve life in a state of neutrality and indifference is unreasonable and vain. If by excluding joy we could shut out grief, the scheme would deserve very serious attention; but since, however we may debar ourselves from happiness, misery will find its way at many inlets, and the assaults of pain will force our regard, though we may withhold it from the invitations of pleasure, we may surely endeavour to raise life above the middle point of apathy at one time, since it will necessarily sink below it at another.

But though it cannot be reasonable not to gain happiness for fear of losing it, yet it must be confessed that in proportion to the pleasure of possession will be for some time our sorrow for the loss; but it is to be tried whether that pain may not quickly give way to mitigation. Some have thought that the most certain way to clear the heart from its embarrassment is to drag it by force into scenes of merriment. Others imagine that such a transition is too violent, and recommend rather to soothe it into tranquillity by making it acquainted with miseries more dreadful and afflictive, and diverting to the calamities of others the regard which we are inclined to fix too closely upon our own misfortunes.

It may be doubted whether either of these remedies will be sufficiently powerful. The efficacy of mirth it is not easy always to try, and the indulgence of melancholy seems to be one of those medicines which, if it happens not to cure, will destroy.

The safe and general antidote against sorrow is employment. It is commonly observed that among soldiers and seamen, though there is much kindness, there is little grief; they see their friend fall without any of that lamentation which is indulged in security and idleness, because they have no leisure to spare from the care of themselves; and whoever shall keep his thoughts equally busy, will find himself equally unaffected with irretrievable losses.

Time is observed generally to wear out sorrow, and its

effects might doubtless be accelerated by quickening the succession and enlarging the variety of objects.

> . . . *Si tempore longo*
> *Leniri poterit luctus, tu sperne morari,*
> *Qui sapiet sibi tempus erit. . . .*

Sorrow is a kind of rust of the soul, which every new idea contributes in its passage to scour away. It is the putrefaction of stagnant life, and is remedied by exercise and motion.

No. 59. Tuesday, October 9, 1750.

> *Est aliquid fatale malum per verba levare,*
> *Hoc querulam Prognen Halcyonenque facit:*
> *Hoc erat in solo quare Pœantius antro*
> *Voce fatigaret Lemnia saxa sua.*
> *Strangulat inclusus dolor atque exæstuat intus,*
> *Cogitur et vires multiplicare suas.*

OVID

It is common to distinguish men by the names of animals which they are supposed to resemble. Thus a hero is frequently termed a lion, and a statesman a fox, an extortioner gains the appellation of vulture and a fop the title of monkey. There is also among the various anomalies of character, which a survey of the world exhibits, a species of beings in human form which may be properly marked out as the screech-owls of mankind.

These screech-owls seem to be settled in an opinion that the great business of life is to complain, and that they were born for no other purpose than to disturb the happiness of others, to lessen the little comforts, and shorten the short pleasures of our condition, by painful remembrances of the past, or melancholy prognostics of the future, and their only care is to crush the rising hope, to damp the kindling transport, and allay the golden hours of gaiety with the hateful dross of grief and suspicion.

To those whose weakness of spirits or timidity of temper subjects them to impressions from others, and who are apt to suffer by fascination, and catch the contagion of misery, it is extremely unhappy to live within the compass of a screech-owl's voice; for it will often fill their ears in the hour of dejection and terrify them with apprehensions, which their own thoughts would never have produced, and sadden, by intruded sorrows, the day which might have been passed in amusements or in business; it will fill the heart with unnecessary discontents, and weaken for a time that love of life which is necessary to the vigorous prosecution of any undertaking.

Though I have, like the rest of mankind, many failings and weaknesses, I have never yet, by either friends or enemies, been charged with superstition; I never count the company which I enter, and I look at the new moon indifferently over either shoulder. I have, like most other philosophers, often heard the cuckoo without money in my pocket, and have been sometimes reproached for foolhardy for not turning down my eyes when a raven flew over my head. I never go home abruptly because a snake crosses my way, nor have any particular dread of a climacterical year, but confess that, with all my scorn of old women and their tales, I always consider it as an unhappy day when I happen to be greeted, in the morning, by Suspirius, the screech-owl.

I have now known Suspirius fifty-eight years and four months, and have never yet passed an hour with him in which he has not made some attack upon my quiet. When we were first acquainted, his great topic was the misery of youth without a fortune; and whenever we walked out together he solaced me with a long enumeration of pleasures, which, as they were beyond the reach of my fortune, were without the verge of my desires, and which I should never have considered as the objects of a wish had not his unseasonable representations placed them in my sight.

Another of his topics is the neglect of merit, with which he never fails to amuse every man whom he sees not eminently fortunate. If he meets with a young officer, he always informs him of gentlemen whose personal courage is unquestioned, and whose military skill qualifies them to command armies, and who have, notwithstanding all their merit, grown old with subaltern commissions. For a genius in the church, he is always provided with a curacy for life. The lawyer he informs of many men of great parts and deep study, who have never had an opportunity to speak in the courts: and meeting Serenus the physician, 'Ah, Doctor,' says he, 'what a-foot still, when so many blockheads are rattling their chariots? I told you seven years ago you would never meet with encouragement, and I hope you will now take more notice when I tell you that your Greek, and your diligence, and your honesty, will never enable you to live like yonder apothecary, who prescribes to his own shop, and laughs at the physician.'

Suspirius has, in his time, intercepted fifteen authors in their way to the stage; persuaded nine and thirty merchants to retire from a prosperous trade for fear of bankruptcy; broke off an hundred and thirteen matches by prognostications of unhappiness, and enabled the small-pox to kill nineteen ladies, by perpetual alarms for fear of their beauty.

Whenever my evil stars bring us together, he never fails to represent to me the folly of my pursuits, and informs me that we are much older than when we began our acquaintance, that the infirmities of decrepitude are coming fast upon me, that whatever I now get I shall enjoy it but a little time, that fame is to a man tottering on the edge of the grave of very little importance, and that the time is now at hand when I ought to look for no other pleasures than a good dinner and an easy chair.

Thus he goes on in his unharmonious strain, displaying present miseries, and foreboding more, νυχτιχόραξ ἄδει θανα-τηφόρον; every syllable is loaded with misfortune, and death is always brought nearer to the view. Yet, what always raises my resentment and indignation, I do not perceive that his mournful meditations have much effect upon himself. He talks, and has long talked, of calamities, without discovering, otherwise than by the tone of his voice, that he feels any of the evils which he laments or threatens, but has the same habit of uttering lamentations as others of telling stories, and falls into expressions of condolence for past or apprehension of future

L

mischiefs as all men studious of their ease have recourse to those subjects upon which they can most fluently or copiously discourse.

It is reported of the Sybarites that they destroyed all their cocks, that they might dream out their morning dreams without disturbance. Though I would not so far promote effeminacy as to propose the Sybarites for an example, yet since there is no man so corrupt or foolish but something useful may be learned from him, I could wish that, in imitation of a people not often to be copied, some regulations might be made to exclude screech-owls from all company, as the enemies of mankind, and confine them to some proper receptacle, where they may mingle sighs at leisure, and thicken the gloom of one another.

Thou prophet of evil, says Homer's Agamemnon, *thou never foretellest me good, but the joy of thy heart is to predict misfortunes*. Whoever is of the same temper might there find the means of indulging his thoughts and improving his vein of denunciation, and the flock of screech-owls might hoot together without injury to the rest of the world.

Yet, though I have so little kindness for this dark generation, I am very far from intending to debar the soft and tender mind from the privilege of complaining, when the sigh rises from the desire not of giving pain but of gaining ease. To hear complaints with patience, even when complaints are vain, is one of the duties of friendship; and though it must be allowed that he suffers most like a hero that hides his grief in silence,

Spem vultu simulat, premit altum corde dolorem,

yet, it cannot be denied that he who complains acts like a man, like a social being who looks for help from his fellow-creatures. Pity is to many of the unhappy a source of comfort in hopeless distresses, as it contributes to recommend them to themselves by proving that they have not lost the regard of others; and heaven seems to indicate the duty even of barren compassion, by inclining us to weep for evils which we cannot remedy.

No. 155. Tuesday, September 10, 1751

——*Steriles transmisimus annos,*
Hæc ævi mihi prima dies, hæc limina vitæ.

STATIUS

None of the weaknesses of the human mind has more frequently incurred the animadversion of satirical writers than the negligence with which men overlook their own faults, however flagrant, and the easiness with which they pardon them, however frequently repeated.

It seems generally believed, that, as the eye cannot see itself, the mind has no faculties by which it can contemplate its own state, and that therefore we have not the means of becoming acquainted with our real characters; an opinion which, like innumerable other postulates, an enquirer finds himself inclined to admit with very little evidence, because it affords a ready solution of many moral difficulties. It will explain why the greatest abilities frequently fail to promote the happiness of those who possess them; why those who can distinguish with the utmost nicety the boundaries of vice and virtue suffer them to be confounded in their own conduct; why the active and vigilant resign their affairs implicitly to the management of others; and why the cautious and fearful make hourly approaches towards ruin without one sigh of solicitude or struggle of escape.

When a position teems thus with commodious consequences, who can without regret confess it to be false? Yet it is certain that the pleasure of wantoning in flowery periods, and the pride of swelling with airy declamation has produced a disposition to extend the dominion of the passions beyond the limits that nature has assigned. Self-love is very often rather arrogant than blind, and, though it does not hide our faults from ourselves, persuades us that they escape the notice of others, and disposes us to resent censures which we feel to be just, and to claim honours which, in our own opinion, we do not merit. We are conscious of innumerable defects and vices which we hope to conceal from the public eye, and please ourselves with the success of innumerable impostures by which, in reality, nobody is deceived.

In proof of the dimness of our internal sight, or the general inability of man to determine rightly concerning his own character, it is common to urge the success of the most absurd and incredible flattery, and the resentment which is always raised by advice, however soft, benevolent, and reasonable. But flattery, if its operation be more nearly examined, will be found to owe its acceptance not to our ignorance but our knowledge of our defects, and to delight us rather as it consoles our wants than celebrates our possessions. He that shall solicit the favour of his patron by praising him for qualities which he can find in himself, will always be defeated by the more daring panegyrist who enriches him with adscititious excellence, and plunders the sages and heroes of antiquity for the decoration of his name. Just praise is only a debt, but flattery is a present. The acknowledgement of those virtues on which conscience congratulates us, is a tribute that we can at any time exact with confidence, but the celebration of those which we only feign, or which we desire, without any vigorous endeavours to attain them, is received as a confession of sovereignty over regions that we never conquered, as a favourable decision of disputable claims, and is more welcome as it is more gratuitous.

Advice is generally offensive, not because it lays us open to regret, or convicts us of any fault which had escaped our notice, but because it shows us that we are known to others as well as to ourselves, that our artifices of hypocrisy have been detected, or that the fear of our resentment has lost its influence, and the officious monitor is persecuted with hatred, not because his accusation is considered as false, but because he assumes that superiority which we are not willing to grant him, has dared to detect what we endeavoured to conceal, and to utter what his awe or his tenderness ought to have suppressed.

For this reason advice is commonly ineffectual. If those who follow the call of their desires, without any enquiry whither they were going, had deviated ignorantly from the path of wisdom, and were rushing upon dangers which they had not foreseen, they would readily listen to any information that might recall them from their errors, and catch the first alarm by which destruction or infamy is denounced. But few wander in the wrong way because they mistake it for the right, but because it is more smooth and flowery; and therefore few are persuaded to quit it by admonition or reproof because they impress no new conviction, nor confer any new powers of action or resistance. He that is gravely informed how soon profusion will annihilate his fortune hears with very little advantage what he knew before, and catches at the next occasion of expense, because advice has no tendency to suppress his vanity. He that is told how certainly intemperance will hurry him to the grave runs with his usual speed to a new course of luxury, because his reason is not invigorated, nor his appetite weakened.

The mischief of flattery is that of suppressing the influence of honest ambition, by an opinion that honour may be gained without the toil of merit; and the benefit of advice arises commonly from the discovery which it affords of the public opinion. He that could withstand conscience is frighted at infamy, and shame prevails when reason is defeated.

As we all know our own faults, and know them generally with many aggravations which human perspicacity cannot discover, there is, perhaps, no man, however hardened by impudence or dissipated by levity, however sheltered by hypocrisy or blasted with disgrace, who does not intend some time to review his conduct, and to regulate the remaining part of his life by the laws of virtue. New temptations indeed attack him, new invitations are offered by pleasure and by interest, and the hour of reformation is always delayed; every delay gives vice another opportunity of fortifying itself by habit; and the change of manners, though sincerely intended and rationally planned, is referred to the time when some craving passion shall be fully gratified, or some powerful allurement cease its importunity.

Thus procrastination is accumulated on procrastination, and one impediment succeeds another, till age shatters our resolution, or death intercepts the project of amendment. Such is often the end of our salutary purposes, after they have long delighted the imagination, and appeased that disquiet which every mind feels from known misconduct, when the attention is not diverted by business or by pleasure.

Nothing surely can be more unworthy of a reasonable nature than to continue in a state so opposite to real happiness as that all the peace of solitude and all the felicity of meditation must arise from resolutions of forsaking it; yet the world will often afford opportunities of observing men who pass months and years in a continual war with their own convictions, and are every day dragged by habit or betrayed by passion into practices which they closed and opened their eyes with purposes to avoid, purposes which, though settled on conviction, the first impulse of momentary desire certainly overthrows.

The influence of custom is indeed such that to conquer it will require the utmost efforts of fortitude and virtue, nor can I think any man more worthy of veneration and renown, than those who have burst the shackles of habitual vice. This victory is more heroic as the objects of guilty gratification are more familiar, and the recurrence of solicitation more frequent. He that from conviction of the folly of ambition resigns his offices of power, sets himself free at once from any temptation to squander his life in courts, because he cannot easily regain his former station. He who is enslaved by an amorous passion may quit his tyrant in disgust, and absence will, without the help of reason, overcome by degrees the desire of returning. But those appetites to which every place affords their proper gratification, and which require no preparatory measures or gradual advances, are more tenaciously adhesive; the wish is so near the enjoyment that compliance often precedes consideration, and, before the powers of reason can be summoned, the time for employing them is past.

Indolence is therefore one of the vices from which those whom it once infects are seldom reformed. Every other species of luxury operates upon some appetite which is quickly satiated, and requires some concurrence of art or accident which every place will not supply; but the desire of ease acts equally at every hour, and the longer it is indulged is the more increased. To do nothing is in every man's power, and we can never want an opportunity of neglecting duties. The lapse to indolence is soft and imperceptible, because it is only a mere cessation of activity; but the return to diligence is difficult, because it implies a change from rest to motion, from privation to reality.

> ——*Facilis descensus Averni:*
> *Noctes atque dies patet atri janua Ditis:*
> *Sed revocare gradum, superasque evadere ad auras,*
> *Hoc opus, hic labor est.*——

It might perhaps be useful to the conquest of these en-snarers of the mind, if at certain stated periods life was to be reviewed. Many things necessary are neglected because we vainly imagine that they may be always performed, and what cannot be done without pain will certainly be delayed if the time of doing it be left unsettled. No corruption is great but by long negligence, which can scarcely prevail in a mind regu-larly and frequently awakened by the pain of remorse. He that thus breaks his life into parts will find in himself a desire to distinguish every stage of his existence by some improvement, and delight himself with the approach of the day of recollec-tion, as of the time which is to begin a new series of virtue and felicity.

THE ADVENTURER

No. 67. Tuesday, June 26, 1753

Inventas—vitam excoluere per artes.

VIRGIL

That familiarity produces neglect has been long observed. The effect of all external objects, however great or splendid, ceases with their novelty: the courtier stands without emotion in the royal presence; the rustic tramples under his foot the beauties of the spring, with little attention to their colours or their fragrance; and the inhabitant of the coast darts his eye upon the immense diffusion of waters, without awe, wonder, or terror.

Those who have passed much of their lives in this great city look upon its opulence and its multitudes, its extent and variety, with cold indifference; but an inhabitant of the remoter parts of the kingdom is immediately distinguished by a kind of dissipated curiosity, a busy endeavour to divide his attention amongst a thousand objects, and a wild confusion of astonishment and alarm.

The attention of a newcomer is generally first struck by the multiplicity of cries that stun him in the streets, and the variety of merchandise and manufactures which the shopkeepers expose on every hand; and he is apt, by unwary bursts of admiration, to excite the merriment and contempt of those who mistake the use of their eyes for effects of their understanding and confound accidental knowledge with just reasoning.

But, surely, these are subjects on which any man may without reproach employ his meditations: the innumerable occupations, among which the thousands that swarm in the streets of London are distributed, may furnish employment to minds of every cast, and capacities of every degree. He that contemplates the extent of this wonderful city finds it difficult to conceive by what method plenty is maintained in our markets, and how the inhabitants are regularly supplied with the necessaries of life; but when he examines the shops and warehouses, sees the immense stores of every kind of merchandise piled up for sale, and runs over all the manufactures of art and products of nature, which are everywhere attracting his eye and soliciting his purse, he will be inclined to conclude that such quantities cannot easily be exhausted, and that part of mankind must soon stand still for want of employment, till the wares already provided shall be worn out and destroyed.

As Socrates was passing through the fair at Athens, and casting his eyes over the shops and customers, 'How many things are here,' says he, 'that I do not want!' The same sentiment is every moment rising in the mind of him that walks the streets of London, however inferior in philosophy to Socrates: he beholds a thousand shops crowded with goods, of which he can scarcely tell the use, and which, therefore, he is apt to consider as of no value; and, indeed, many of the arts by which families are supported and wealth is heaped together are of that minute and superfluous kind, which nothing but experience could evince possible to be prosecuted with advantage, and which, as the world might easily want, it could scarcely be expected to encourage.

But so it is, that custom, curiosity, or wantonness supplies every art with patrons, and finds purchasers for every manufacture; the world is so adjusted that not only bread but riches may be obtained without great abilities or arduous performances: the most unskilful hand and unenlightened mind have sufficient incitements to industry; for he that is resolutely busy can scarcely be in want: there is, indeed, no employment, however despicable, from which a man may not promise himself more than competence, when he sees thousands and myriads raised to dignity by no other merit than that of contributing to supply their neighbours with the means of sucking smoke through a tube of clay; and others raising contributions upon those whose elegance disdains the grossness of smoky luxury, by grinding the same materials into a powder that may at once gratify and impair the smell.

Not only by these popular and modish trifles, but by a thousand unheeded and evanescent kinds of business are the multitudes of this city preserved from idleness, and consequently from want: in the endless variety of tastes and circumstances that diversify mankind, nothing is so superfluous but that someone desires it; or so common but that someone is compelled to buy it. As nothing is useless but because it is in improper hands, what is thrown away by one is gathered up by another; and the refuse of part of mankind furnishes a subordinate class with the materials necessary to their support.

When I look round upon those who are thus variously exerting their qualifications, I cannot but admire the secret concatenation of society, that links together the great and the mean, the illustrious and the obscure; and consider with benevolent satisfaction, that no man, unless his body or mind be totally disabled, has need to suffer the mortification of seeing himself useless or burdensome to the community: he that will diligently labour, in whatever occupation, will deserve the sustenance which he obtains and the protection which he enjoys, and may lie down every night with the pleasing consciousness of having contributed something to the happiness of life.

Contempt and admiration are equally incident to narrow minds: he whose comprehension can take in the whole subordination of mankind, and whose perspicacity can pierce to the real state of things through the thin veils of fortune or of fashion, will discover meanness in the highest stations, and dignity in the meanest; and find that no man can become venerable but by virtue, or contemptible but by wickedness.

In the midst of this universal hurry, no man ought to be so little influenced by example, or so void of honest emulation, as to stand a lazy spectator of incessant labour; or please himself with the mean happiness of a drone, while the active swarms are buzzing about him: no man is without some quality by the due application of which he might deserve well of the world; and whoever he be that has but little in his power should be in haste to do that little, lest he be confounded with him that can do nothing.

By this general concurrence of endeavours, arts of every kind have been so long cultivated that all the wants of man may be immediately supplied; idleness can scarcely form a wish which she may not gratify by the toil of others, or curiosity dream of a toy which the shops are not ready to afford her.

Happiness is enjoyed only in proportion as it is known; and such is the state or folly of man that it is known only by experience of its contrary: we who have long lived amidst the conveniencies of a town immensely populous have scarce an idea of a place where desire cannot be gratified by money. In order to have a just sense of this artificial plenty, it is necessary to have passed some time in a distant colony, or those parts of our island which are thinly inhabited: he that has once known how many trades every man in such situations is compelled to exercise, with how much labour the products of nature must be accommodated to human use, how long the loss or defect of any common utensil must be endured or by what awkward expedients it must be supplied, how far men may wander with money in their hands before any can sell them what they wish to buy, will know how to rate at its proper value the plenty and ease of a great city.

But that the happiness of man may still remain imperfect, as wants in this place are easily supplied, new wants likewise are easily created: every man, in surveying the shops of London, sees numberless instruments and conveniences, of which, while he did not know them, he never felt the need, and yet, when use has made them familiar, wonders how life could be supported without them. Thus it comes to pass that our desires always increase with our possessions; the knowledge that something remains yet unenjoyed impairs our enjoyment of the good before us.

They who have been accustomed to the refinements of science, and multiplications of contrivance soon lose their confidence in the unassisted powers of nature, forget the paucity of our real necessities, and overlook the easy methods by which they may be supplied. It were a speculation worthy of a philosophical mind, to examine how much is taken away from our native abilities, as well as added to them, by artificial expedients. We are so accustomed to give and receive assistance that each of us singly can do little for himself, and there is scarce anyone amongst us, however contracted may be his form of life, who does not enjoy the labour of a thousand artists.

But a survey of the various nations that inhabit the earth will inform us that life may be supported with less assistance, and that the dexterity, which practice enforced by necessity produces, is able to effect much by very scanty means. The nations of Mexico and Peru erected cities and temples without the use of iron; and at this day the rude Indian supplies himself with all the necessaries of life: sent like the rest of mankind naked into the world, as soon as his parents have nursed him up to strength, he is to provide by his own labour for his own support. His first care is to find a sharp flint among the rocks; with this he undertakes to fell the trees of the forest, he shapes his bow, heads his arrows, builds his cottage, and hollows his canoe, and from that time lives in a state of plenty and prosperity; he is sheltered from the storms, he is fortified against beasts of prey, he is enabled to pursue the fish of the sea and the deer of the mountains; and, as he does not know, does not envy the happiness of polished nations, where gold can supply the want of fortitude and skill, and he whose laborious ancestors have made him rich may lie stretched upon a couch, and see all the treasures of all the elements poured down before him.

This picture of a savage life, if it shows how much individuals may perform, shows likewise how much society is to be desired: though the perseverance and address of the Indian excite our admiration, they nevertheless cannot procure him the conveniences which are enjoyed by the vagrant beggar of a civilized country: he hunts like a wild beast to satisfy his hunger, and when he lies down to rest after a successful chase, cannot pronounce himself secure against the danger of perishing in a few days; he is, perhaps, content with his condition, because he knows not that a better is attainable by man, as he that is born blind does not long for the perception of light because he cannot conceive the advantages which light would afford him: but hunger, wounds, and weariness are real evils, though he believes them equally incident to all his fellow creatures; and when a tempest compels him to lie starving in his hut, he cannot justly be concluded equally happy with those whom art has exempted from the power of chance, and who make the foregoing year provide for the following.

To receive and to communicate assistance constitutes the happiness of human life: man may indeed preserve his existence in solitude, but can enjoy it only in society; the greatest understanding of an individual, doomed to procure food and clothing for himself, will barely supply him with expedients to keep off death from day to day; but, as one of a large community performing only his share of the common business, he gains leisure for intellectual pleasures, and enjoys the happiness of reason and reflection.

No. 84. Saturday, August 25, 1753

——*Tolle periclum,*
Jam vaga prosiliet frænis natura remotis.

HORACE

To the ADVENTURER

SIR,

It has been observed, I think, by Sir William Temple, and after him by almost every other writer, that England affords a greater variety of characters than the rest of the world. This is ascribed to the liberty prevailing amongst us, which gives every man the privilege of being wise or foolish his own way, and preserves him from the necessity of hypocrisy or the servility of imitation.

That the position itself is true, I am not completely satisfied. To be nearly acquainted with the people of different countries can happen to very few, and in life as in everything else beheld at a distance, there appears an even uniformity; the petty discriminations which diversify the natural character are not discoverable but by a close inspection; we therefore find them most at home, because there we have most opportunities of remarking them. Much less am I convinced that this peculiar diversification, if it be real, is the consequence of peculiar liberty: for where is the government to be found that super-intends individuals with so much vigilance as not to leave their private conduct without restraint? Can it enter into a reasonable mind to imagine that men of every other nation are not equally masters of their own time or houses with ourselves, and equally at liberty to be parsimonious or profuse, frolic or sullen, abstinent or luxurious? Liberty is certainly necessary to the full play of predominant humours, but such liberty is to be found alike under the government of the many or the few, in monarchies or in commonwealths.

How readily the predominant passion snatches an interval of liberty, and how fast it expands itself when the weight of restraint is taken away, I had lately opportunity to discover as I took a short journey into the country in a stage-coach, which, as every journey is a kind of adventure, may be very properly related to you, though I can display no such extraordinary assembly as Cervantes has collected at Don Quixote's inn.

In a stage-coach the passengers are for the most part wholly unknown to one another, and without expectation of ever meeting again when their journey is at an end; one should therefore imagine that it was of little importance to any of them what conjectures the rest should form concerning him. Yet so it is, that, as all think themselves secure from detection, all assume that character of which they are most desirous, and on no occasion is the general ambition of superiority more apparently indulged.

On the day of our departure, in the twilight of the morning, I ascended the vehicle, with three men and two women my fellow travellers. It was easy to observe the affected elevation of mien with which everyone entered, and the supercilious civility with which they paid their compliments to each other. When the first ceremony was despatched, we sat silent for a long time, all employed in collecting importance into our faces, and endeavouring to strike reverence and submission into our companions.

It is always observable that silence propagates itself, and that the longer talk has been suspended the more difficult it is to find anything to say. We began now to wish for conversation, but no one seemed inclined to descend from his dignity, or first to propose a topic of discourse. At last a corpulent gentleman, who had equipped himself for this expedition with a scarlet surtout and a large hat with a broad lace, drew out his watch, looked on it in silence, and then held it dangling at his finger. This was, I suppose, understood by all the company as an invitation to ask the time of the day, but nobody appeared to heed his overture, and his desire to be talking so far overcame his resentment that he let us know of his own accord it was past five, and that in two hours we should be at breakfast.

His condescension was thrown away; we continued all obdurate: the ladies held up their heads: I amused myself with watching their behaviour, and, of the other two, one seemed to employ himself in counting the trees as we drove by them, the other drew his hat over his eyes and counterfeited a slumber. The man of benevolence, to show that he was not depressed by our neglect, hummed a tune and beat time upon his snuff-box.

Thus universally displeased with one another, and not much delighted with ourselves, we came at last to the little inn appointed for our repast, and all began at once to recompense themselves for the constraint of silence by innumerable questions and orders to the people that attended us. At last, what everyone had called for was got, or declared impossible to be got at that time, and we were persuaded to sit round the same table, when the gentleman in the red surtout looked again upon his watch, told us that we had half an hour to spare, but he was sorry to see so little merriment among us; that all fellow travellers were for the time upon the level, and that it was always his way to make himself one of the company. 'I remember', says he, 'it was on just such a morning as this that I and my lord Mumble and the duke of Tenterden were out upon a ramble; we called at a little house as it might be this; and my landlady, I warrant you, not suspecting to whom she was talking, was so jocular and facetious, and made so many merry answers to our questions, that we were all ready to burst with laughter. At last the good woman happened to overhear me whispering to the duke and calling him by his title, was so surprised and confounded that we could scarcely get a word from her: and the duke never met me from that day to this but he talks of the little house, and quarrels with me for terrifying the woman.'

He had scarcely had time to congratulate himself on the veneration which this narrative must have procured him from the company, when one of the ladies, having reached out for a plate on a distant part of the table, began to remark the inconveniences of travelling, and the difficulty which they who never sat at home without a great number of attendants found in performing for themselves such offices as the road required: but that people of quality often travelled in disguise, and might be generally known from the vulgar by their condescension to poor inn-keepers, and the allowance which they made for any defect in their entertainment: that for her part, while people were civil and meant well, it was never her custom to find fault; for one was not to expect upon a journey all that one enjoyed at one's own house.

A general emulation seemed now to be excited. One of the men, who had hitherto said nothing, called for the last newspaper; and, having perused it awhile with deep pensiveness, 'It is impossible', says he, 'for any man to guess how to act with regard to the stocks; last week it was the general opinion that they would fall, and I sold out twenty thousand pound in order to a purchase: they have now risen unexpectedly, and I make no doubt but at my return to London I shall risk thirty thousand pound amongst them again.'

A young man, who had hitherto distinguished himself only by the vivacity of his look and a frequent diversion of his eyes from one object to another, upon this closed his snuff-box, and told us that he had a hundred times talked with the chancellor and the judges on the subject of the stocks; that for his part he did not pretend to be well acquainted with the principles on which they were established, but had always heard them reckoned pernicious to trade, uncertain in their produce,

M

and unsolid in their foundation; and that he had been advised by three judges, his most intimate friends, never to venture his money in the funds, but to put it out upon land security, till he could light upon an estate in his own country.

It might be expected that, upon these glimpses of latent dignity, we should all have began to look round us with veneration, and have behaved like the princes of romance when the enchantment that disguises them is dissolved and they discover the dignity of each other; yet it happened that none of these hints made much impression on the company; everyone was apparently suspected of endeavouring to impose false appearances upon the rest; all continued their haughtiness, in hopes to enforce their claims; and all grew every hour more sullen, because they found their representations of themselves without effect.

Thus we travelled on four days with malevolence perpetually increasing, and without any endeavour but to outvie each other in superciliousness and neglect; and, when any two of us could separate ourselves for a moment, we vented our indignation at the sauciness of the rest.

At length the journey was at an end, and time and chance, that strip off all disguises, have discovered that the intimate of lords and dukes is a nobleman's butler, who has furnished a shop with the money he has saved; the man who deals so largely in the funds is the clerk of a broker in Change-alley; the lady who so carefully concealed her quality keeps a cook-shop behind the Exchange; and the young man who is so happy in the friendship of the judges engrosses and transcribes for bread in a garret of the Temple. Of one of the women only I could make no disadvantageous detection, because she had assumed no character but accommodated herself to the scene before her, without any struggle for distinction or superiority.

I could not forbear to reflect on the folly of practising a fraud which, as the event showed, had been already practised too often to succeed, and by the success of which no advantage could have been obtained; of assuming a character which was to end with the day; and of claiming upon false pretences honours which must perish with the breath that paid them.

But, Mr. Adventurer, let not those who laugh at me and my companions think this folly confined to a stage-coach. Every man in the journey of life takes the same advantage of the ignorance of his fellow travellers, disguises himself in counterfeited merit, and hears those praises with complacency which his conscience reproaches him for accepting. Every man deceives himself while he thinks he is deceiving others, and forgets that the time is at hand when every illusion shall cease when fictitious excellence shall be torn away, and All must be shown to All in their real state.

> I am, Sir,
> Your humble servant,
> VIATOR

No. 126. Saturday, January 19, 1754

. . . Steriles nec legit arenas
Ut caneret paucis, mersitque hoc pulvere verum.

LUCAN

There has always prevailed among that part of mankind that addict their minds to speculation a propensity to talk much of the happiness of retirement, and some of the most pleasing compositions produced in every age contain descriptions of the peace and happiness of a country life.

I know not whether those who thus ambitiously repeat the praises of solitude have always considered how much they depreciate mankind by declaring that whatever is excellent or desirable is to be obtained by departing from them; that the assistance which we may derive from one another is not equivalent to the evils which we have to fear; that the kindness of a few is overbalanced by the malice of many; and that the protection of society is too dearly purchased by encountering its dangers and enduring its oppressions.

These specious representations of solitary happiness, however opprobrious to human nature, have so far spread their influence over the world, that almost every man delights his imagination with the hopes of obtaining some time an opportunity of retreat. Many, indeed, who enjoy retreat only in imagination, content themselves with believing that another year will transport them to rural tranquillity, and die while they talk of doing what if they had lived longer they would never have done. But many likewise there are, either of greater resolution or more credulity, who in earnest try the state which they have been taught to think thus secure from cares and dangers; and retire to privacy, either that they may improve their happiness, increase their knowledge, or exalt their virtue.

The greater part of the admirers of solitude, as of all other classes of mankind, have no higher or remoter view than the present gratification of their passions. Of these, some, haughty and impetuous, fly from society only because they cannot bear to repay to others the regard which themselves exact, and think no state of life eligible but that which places them out of the reach of censure or control, and affords them opportunities of living in a perpetual compliance with their own inclinations, without the necessity of regulating their actions by any other man's convenience or opinion.

There are others, of minds more delicate and tender, easily offended by every deviation from rectitude, soon disgusted by ignorance or impertinence, and always expecting from the conversation of mankind more elegance, purity, and truth than the mingled mass of life will easily afford. Such men are in haste to retire from grossness, falsehood, and brutality, and hope to find in private habitations at least a negative felicity, an exemption from the shocks and perturbations with which public scenes are continually distressing them.

To neither of these votaries will solitude afford that content which she has been taught so lavishly to promise. The man of arrogance will quickly discover that by escaping from his opponents he has lost his flatterers, that greatness is nothing where it is not seen, and power nothing where it cannot be felt: and he whose faculties are employed in too close an observation of failings and defects will find his condition very little mended by transferring his attention from others to himself;

he will probably soon come back in quest of new objects, and be glad to keep his captiousness employed on any character rather than his own.

Others are seduced into solitude merely by the authority of great names, and expect to find those charms in tranquillity which have allured statesmen and conquerors to the shades: these likewise are apt to wonder at their disappointment, from want of considering that those whom they aspire to imitate carried with them to their country seats minds full fraught with subjects of reflection, the consciousness of great merit, the memory of illustrious actions, the knowledge of important events, and the seeds of mighty designs to be ripened by future meditation. Solitude was to such men a release from fatigue, and an opportunity of usefulness. But what can retirement confer upon him, who having done nothing can receive no support from his own importance, who having known nothing can find no entertainment in reviewing the past, and who intending nothing can form no hopes from prospects of the future? He can, surely, take no wiser course than that of losing himself again in the crowd, and filling the vacuities of his mind with the news of the day.

Others consider solitude as the parent of philosophy, and retire in expectation of greater intimacies with science, as Numa repaired to the groves when he conferred with Egeria. These men have not always reason to repent. Some studies require a continued prosecution of the same train of thought, such as is too often interrupted by the petty avocations of common life: sometimes, likewise, it is necessary that a multiplicity of objects be at once present to the mind, and everything, therefore, must be kept at a distance which may perplex the memory, or dissipate the attention.

But though learning may be conferred by solitude, its application must be attained by general converse. He has learned to no purpose that is not able to teach; and he will always teach unsuccessfully, who cannot recommend his sentiments by his diction or address.

Even the acquisition of knowledge is often much facilitated by the advantages of society: he that never compares his notions with those of others readily acquiesces in his first thoughts, and very seldom discovers the objections which may be raised against his opinions; he, therefore, often thinks himself in possession when he is only fondling an error long since exploded. He that has neither companions nor rivals in his studies will always applaud his own progress and think highly of his performances, because he knows not that others have equalled or excelled him. And I am afraid it may be added that the student who withdraws himself from the world will soon feel that ardour extinguished which praise or emulation had enkindled, and take the advantage of secrecy to sleep rather than to labour.

There remains yet another set of recluses, whose intention entitles them to higher respect and whose motives deserve a more serious consideration. These retire from the world, not merely to bask in ease or gratify curiosity, but that, being disengaged from common cares, they may employ more time in the duties of religion; that they may regulate their actions with stricter vigilance, and purify their thoughts by more frequent meditation.

To men thus elevated above the mists of mortality, I am far from presuming myself qualified to give directions. On him that appears 'to pass through things temporary' with no other care than 'not to lose finally the things eternal', I look with such veneration as inclines me to approve his conduct in the whole, without a minute examination of its parts; yet I could never forbear to wish that, while vice is every day multiplying seducements, and stalking forth with more hardened effrontery, virtue would not withdraw the influence of her presence, or forbear to assert her natural dignity by open and undaunted perseverance in the right. Piety practised in solitude, like the flower that blooms in the desert, may give its fragrance to the winds of heaven, and delight those unbodied spirits that survey the works of God and the actions of men; but it bestows no assistance upon earthly beings, and, however free from taints of impurity, yet wants the sacred splendour of beneficence.

Our Maker, who, though he gave us such varieties of temper and such differences of powers, yet designed us all for happiness, undoubtedly intended that we should obtain that happiness by different means. Some are unable to resist the temptations of importunity or the impetuosity of their own passions incited by the force of present temptations: of these it is undoubtedly the duty to fly from enemies which they cannot conquer, and to cultivate, in the calm of solitude, that virtue which is too tender to endure the tempests of public life. But there are others, whose passions grow more strong and irregular in privacy, and who cannot maintain an uniform tenor of virtue but by exposing their manners to the public eye and assisting the admonitions of conscience with the fear of infamy: for such, it is dangerous to exclude all witnesses of their conduct till they have formed strong habits of virtue and weakened their passions by frequent victories. But there is a higher order of men so inspirited with ardour, and so fortified with resolution, that the world passes before them without influence or regard: these ought to consider themselves as appointed the guardians of mankind; they are placed in an evil world to exhibit public examples of good life, and may be said, when they withdraw to solitude, to desert the station which Providence assigned them.

THE IDLER

Among the innumerable mortifications that waylay human arrogance on every side may well be reckoned our ignorance of the most common objects and effects, a defect of which we become more sensible by every attempt to supply it. Vulgar and inactive minds confound familiarity with knowledge and conceive themselves informed of the whole nature of things when they are shown their form or told their use; but the speculatist who is not content with superficial views harasses himself with fruitless curiosity, and still as he enquires more perceives only that he knows less.

Sleep is a state in which a great part of every life is passed. No animal has been yet discovered whose existence is not varied with intervals of insensibility, and some late philosophers have extended the empire of sleep over the vegetable world.

Yet of this change so frequent, so great, so general, and so necessary, no searcher has yet found either the efficient or final cause; or can tell by what power the mind and body are thus chained down in irresistible stupefaction; or what benefits the animal receives from this alternate suspension of its active powers.

Whatever may be the multiplicity or contrariety of opinions upon this subject, nature has taken sufficient care that theory shall have little influence on practice. The most diligent enquirer is not able long to keep his eyes open; the most eager disputant will begin about midnight to desert his argument; and, once in four and twenty hours, the gay and the gloomy, the witty and the dull, the clamorous and the silent, the busy and the idle, are all overpowered by the gentle tyrant, and all lie down in the equality of sleep.

Philosophy has often attempted to repress insolence by

ESSAYS の部分

asserting that all conditions are levelled by death, a position which, however it may deject the happy, will seldom afford much comfort to the wretched. It is far more pleasing to consider that sleep is equally a leveller with death; that the time is never at a great distance, when the balm of rest shall be effused alike upon every head, when the diversities of life shall stop their operation, and the high and the low shall lie down together.

It is somewhere recorded of Alexander, that, in the pride of conquests and intoxication of flattery, he declared that he only perceived himself to be a man by the necessity of sleep. Whether he considered sleep as necessary to his mind or body, it was indeed a sufficient evidence of human infirmity; the body which required such frequency of renovation gave but faint promises of immortality; and the mind which, from time to time, sank gladly into insensibility, had made no very near approaches to the felicity of the supreme and self-sufficient Nature.

I know not what can tend more to repress all the passions that disturb the peace of the world than the consideration that there is no height of happiness or honour from which man does not eagerly descend to a state of unconscious repose; that the best condition of life is such that we contentedly quit its good to be disentangled from its evils; that in a few hours splendour fades before the eye, and praise itself deadens in the ear; the senses withdraw from their objects, and reason favours the retreat.

What then are the hopes and prospects of covetousness, ambition, and rapacity? Let him that desires most have all his desires gratified, he never shall attain a state, which he can, for a day and a night, contemplate with satisfaction, or from which, if he had the power of perpetual vigilance, he would not long for periodical separations.

All envy would be extinguished if it were universally known that there are none to be envied, and surely none can be much envied who are not pleased with themselves. There is reason to suspect that the distinctions of mankind have more show than value, when it is found that all agree to be weary alike of pleasures and of cares, that the powerful and the weak, the celebrated and obscure, join in one common wish, and implore from nature's hand the nectar of oblivion.

Such is our desire of abstraction from ourselves that very few are satisfied with the quantity of stupefaction which the needs of the body force upon the mind. Alexander himself added intemperance to sleep, and solaced with the fumes of wine the sovereignty of the world. And almost every man has some art by which he steals his thoughts away from his present state.

It is not much of life that is spent in close attention to any important duty. Many hours of every day are suffered to fly away without any traces left upon the intellects. We suffer phantoms to rise up before us, and amuse ourselves with the dance of airy images, which, after a time, we dismiss for ever, and know not how we have been busied.

Many have no happier moments than those that they pass in solitude, abandoned to their own imagination, which sometimes puts sceptres in their hands or mitres on their heads, shifts the scene of pleasure with endless variety, bids all the forms of beauty sparkle before them, and gluts them with every change of visionary luxury.

It is easy in these semi-slumbers to collect all the possibilities of happiness, to alter the course of the sun, to bring back the past and anticipate the future, to unite all the beauties of all seasons and all the blessings of all climates, to receive and bestow felicity, and forget that misery is the lot of man. All this is a voluntary dream, a temporary recession from the realities of life to airy fictions, an habitual subjection of reason to fancy.

Others are afraid to be alone, and amuse themselves by a perpetual succession of companions, but the difference is not great; in solitude we have our dreams to ourselves, and in company we agree to dream in concert. The end sought in both is forgetfulness of ourselves.

No. 49. Saturday, March 24, 1759

I supped three nights ago with my friend Will Marvel. His affairs obliged him lately to take a journey into Devonshire, from which he has just returned. He knows me to be a very patient hearer, and was glad of my company as it gave him an opportunity of disburthening himself by a minute relation of the casualties of his expedition.

Will is not one of those who go out and return with nothing to tell. He has a story of his travels which will strike a home-bred citizen with horror, and has in ten days suffered so often the extremes of terror and joy that he is in doubt whether he shall ever again expose either his body or mind to such danger and fatigue.

When he left London, the morning was bright and a fair day was promised. But Will is born to struggle with difficulties. That happened to him which has sometimes, perhaps, happened to others. Before he had gone more than ten miles it began to rain. What course was to be taken? His soul disdained to turn back. He did what the king of Prussia might have done; he flapped his hat, buttoned up his cape, and went forwards, fortifying his mind by the stoical consolation, that whatever evil is violent will be short.

His constancy was not long tried; at the distance of about half a mile he saw an inn, which he entered wet and weary, and found civil treatment and proper refreshment. After a respite of about two hours, he looked abroad, and, seeing the sky clear, called for his horse, and passed the first stage without any other memorable accident.

Will considered that labour must be relieved by pleasure, and that the strength which great undertakings require must be maintained by copious nutriment; he therefore ordered himself an elegant supper, drank two bottles of claret, and passed the beginning of the night in sound sleep; but, waking before light, was forewarned of the troubles of the next day by a shower beating against his windows with such violence as to threaten the dissolution of nature. When he arose, he found what he expected—that the country was under water. He joined himself, however, to a company that was travelling the same way, and came safely to the place of dinner, though every step of his horse dashed the mud into the air.

In the afternoon, having lost his company, he set forward alone, and passed many collections of water, of which it was impossible to guess the depth and which he now cannot review without some censure of his own rashness; but what a man undertakes he must perform, and Marvel hates a coward at his heart.

Few that lie warm in their beds think what others undergo who have, perhaps, been as tenderly educated and have as acute sensations as themselves. My friend was now to lodge the second night almost fifty miles from home, in a house which he had never seen before, among people to whom he was totally a stranger, not knowing whether the next man he should meet would prove good or bad; but, seeing an inn of a good appearance, he rode resolutely into the yard, and, knowing that respect is often paid in proportion as it is claimed, delivered his injunction to the hostler with spirit, and, entering the house, called vigorously about him.

On the third day up rose the sun and Mr. Marvel. His troubles and his dangers were now such as he wishes no other man ever to encounter. The ways were less frequented, and the country more thinly inhabited. He rode many a lonely hour through mire and water, and met not a single soul for two miles together with whom he could exchange a word. He cannot deny that, looking round upon the dreary region and seeing nothing but bleak fields and naked trees, hills obscured by fogs, and flats covered with inundations, he did for some time suffer melancholy to prevail upon him, and wished himself again safe at home. One comfort he had, which was to consider that none of his friends were in the same distress, for whom, if they had been with him, he should have suffered more than for himself; he could not forbear sometimes to consider how happily the Idler is settled in an easier condition, who, surrounded like him with terrors, could have done nothing but lie down and die.

Amidst these reflections he came to a town, and found a dinner which disposed him to more cheerful sentiments; but the joys of life are short, and its miseries are long. He mounted and travelled fifteen miles more through dirt and desolation.

At last the sun set, and all the horrors of darkness came upon him. He then repented the weak indulgence by which he had gratified himself at noon with too long an interval of rest. Yet he went forward along a path which he could no longer see, sometimes rushing suddenly into water and sometimes encumbered with stiff clay, ignorant whither he was going, and uncertain whether his next step might not be the last.

In this dismal gloom of nocturnal peregrination, his horse unexpectedly stood still. Marvel had heard many relations of the instinct of horses, and was in doubt what danger might be at hand. Sometimes he fancied that he was on the bank of a river, still and deep, and sometimes that a dead body lay across the track. He sat still awhile to recollect his thoughts, and, as he was about to alight and explore the darkness, out stepped a man with a lanthorn and opened the turnpike. He hired a guide to the town, arrived in safety, and slept in quiet.

The rest of his journey was nothing but danger. He climbed and descended precipices on which vulgar mortals tremble to look; he passed marshes like the *Serbonian bog, where armies whole have sunk*; he forded rivers where the current roared like the eagre of the Severn; or ventured himself on bridges that trembled under him, from which he looked down on foaming whirlpools or dreadful abysses: he wandered over houseless heaths, amidst all the rage of the elements, with the snow driving in his face, and the tempest howling in his ears.

Such are the colours in which Marvel paints his adventures. He has accustomed himself to sounding words and hyperbolical images till he has lost the power of true description. In a road through which the heaviest carriages pass without difficulty, and the post-boy every day and night goes and returns, he meets with hardships like those which are endured in Siberian deserts, and misses nothing of romantic danger but a giant and a dragon. When his dreadful story is told in proper terms, it is only that the way was dirty in winter, and that he experienced the common vicissitudes of rain and sunshine.

No. 50. Saturday, March 31, 1759

The character of Mr. Marvel has raised the merriment of some and the contempt of others, who do not sufficiently consider how often they hear and practise the same arts of exaggerated narration.

There is not, perhaps, among the multitudes of all conditions that swarm upon the earth, a single man who does not believe that he has something extraordinary to relate of himself, and who does not, at one time or other, summon the attention of his friends to the casualties of his adventures and the vicissitudes of his fortune; casualties and vicissitudes that happen alike in lives uniform and diversified—to the commander of armies and the writer at a desk, to the sailor who resigns himself to the wind and water, and the farmer whose longest journey is to the market.

In the present state of the world man may pass through Shakespeare's seven stages of life and meet nothing singular or wonderful. But such is every man's attention to himself, that what is common and unheeded when it is only seen becomes remarkable and peculiar when we happen to feel it.

It is well enough known to be according to the usual process of nature that men should sicken and recover; that some designs should succeed and others miscarry; that friends should be separated and meet again; that some should be made angry by endeavours to please them and some be pleased when no care has been used to gain their approbation; that men and women should at first come together by chance, like each other so well as to commence acquaintance, improve acquaintance into fondness, increase or extinguish fondness by marriage, and have children of different degrees of intellects and virtue, some of whom die before their parents and others survive them.

Yet let any man tell his own story and nothing of all this has ever befallen him according to the common order of things; something has always discriminated his case; some unusual concurrence of events has always appeared which made him more happy or more miserable than other mortals; for in pleasures or calamities, however common, everyone has comforts and afflictions of his own.

It is certain that without some artificial augmentations many of the pleasures of life and almost all its embellishments would fall to the ground. If no man was to express more delight than he felt, those who felt most would raise little envy. If travellers were to describe the most laboured performances of art with the same coldness as they survey them, all expectation of happiness from change of place would cease. The pictures of Raphael would hang without spectators, and the gardens of Versailles might be inhabited by hermits. All the pleasure that is received ends in an opportunity of splendid falsehood, in the power of gaining notice by the display of beauties which the eye was weary of beholding and a history of happy moments of which, in reality, the most happy was the last.

The ambition of superior sensibility and superior eloquence disposes the lovers of art to receive rapture at one time and communicate it at another, and each labours first to impose upon himself, and then to propagate the imposture.

Pain is less subject than pleasure to caprices of expression. The torments of disease and the grief for irremediable misfortunes sometimes are such as no words can declare, and can only be signified by groans, or sobs, or inarticulate ejaculations. Man has from nature a mode of utterance peculiar to pain, but he has none peculiar to pleasure, because he never has pleasure but in such degrees as the ordinary use of language may equal or surpass.

It is nevertheless certain that many pains, as well as pleasures, are heightened by rhetorical affectation, and that the picture is, for the most part, bigger than the life.

When we describe our sensations of another's sorrows, either in friendly or ceremonious condolence, the customs of the world scarcely admit of rigid veracity. Perhaps the fondest friendship would enrage oftener than comfort were the tongue on such occasions faithfully to represent the sentiments of the heart; and I think the strictest moralists allow forms of address to be used without much regard to their literal acceptation, when either respect or tenderness requires them, because they are universally known to denote not the degree but the species of our sentiments.

But the same indulgence cannot be allowed to him who aggravates dangers incurred or sorrow endured by himself, because he darkens the prospect of futurity, and multiplies the pains of our condition by useless terror. Those who magnify their delights are less criminal deceivers, but they raise hopes which are sure to be disappointed. It would be undoubtedly best if we could see and hear everything as it is, that nothing might be too anxiously dreaded, or too ardently pursued.

No. 70. Saturday, August 18, 1759

Few faults of style, whether real or imaginary, excite the malignity of a more numerous class of readers than the use of hard words.

If an author be supposed to involve his thoughts in voluntary obscurity, and to obstruct, by unnecessary difficulties, a mind eager in pursuit of truth; if he writes not to make others learned, but to boast the learning which he possesses himself, and wishes to be admired rather than understood, he counteracts the first end of writing and justly suffers the utmost severity of censure, or the more afflictive severity of neglect.

But words are only hard to those who do not understand them; and the critic ought always to enquire whether he is incommoded by the fault of the writer or by his own.

Every author does not write to every reader; many questions are such as the illiterate part of mankind can have neither interest nor pleasure in discussing, and which therefore it would be an useless endeavour to level with common minds by tiresome circumlocutions or laborious explanations; and

N

many subjects of general use may be treated in a different manner, as the book is intended for the learned or the ignorant. Diffusion and explication are necessary to the instruction of those who, being neither able nor accustomed to think for themselves, can learn only what is expressly taught; but they who can form parallels, discover consequences, and multiply conclusions, are best pleased with involution of argument and compression of thought; they desire only to receive the seeds of knowledge which they may branch out by their own power, to have the way to truth pointed out which they can then follow without a guide.

The *Guardian* directs one of his pupils 'to think with the wise, but speak with the vulgar'. This is a precept specious enough, but not always practicable. Difference of thoughts will produce difference of language. He that thinks with more extent than another will want words of larger meaning; he that thinks with more subtlety will seek for terms of more nice discrimination; and where is the wonder, since words are but the images of things, that he who never knew the originals should not know the copies?

Yet vanity inclines us to find faults anywhere rather than in ourselves. He that reads and grows no wiser seldom suspects his own deficiency, but complains of hard words and obscure sentences, and asks why books are written which cannot be understood.

Among the hard words which are no longer to be used, it has been long the custom to number terms of art. 'Every man', says Swift, 'is more able to explain the subject of an art than its professors; a farmer will tell you in two words that he has broken his leg; but a surgeon, after a long discourse, shall leave you as ignorant as you were before.' This could only have been said, by such an exact observer of life, in gratification of malignity, or in ostentation of acuteness. Every hour produces instances of the necessity of terms of art. Mankind could never conspire in uniform affectation; it is not but by necessity that every science and every trade has its peculiar language. They that content themselves with general ideas may rest in general terms; but those whose studies or employments force them upon closer inspection must have names for particular parts, and words by which they may express various modes of combination, such as none but themselves have occasion to consider.

Artists are, indeed, sometimes ready to suppose that none can be strangers to words to which themselves are familiar, talk to an incidental enquirer as they talk to one another, and make their knowledge ridiculous by injudicious obtrusion. An art cannot be taught but by its proper terms, but it is not always necessary to teach the art.

That the vulgar express their thoughts clearly is far from true, and what perspicuity can be found among them proceeds not from the easiness of their language but the shallowness of their thoughts. He that sees a building as a common spectator contents himself with relating that it is great or little, mean or splendid, lofty or low; all these words are easily understood, because they convey no distinct or limited ideas; but if he attempts, without the terms of architecture, to delineate the parts or enumerate the ornaments, his narration at once becomes unintelligible. The terms, indeed, generally displease, because they are understood by few; but they are so little understood only because few that look upon an edifice examine its parts or analyse its columns into their members.

The state of every other art is the same; as it is cursorily surveyed or accurately examined, different forms of expression become proper. In morality it is one thing to discuss the niceties of the casuist, and another to direct the practice of common life. In agriculture, he that instructs the farmer to plough and sow may convey his notions without the words which he would find necessary in explaining to philosophers the process of vegetation; and if he who has nothing to do but to be honest by the shortest way will perplex his mind with subtle speculations, or if he whose task is to reap and thrash will not be contented without examining the evolution of the seed and circulation of the sap, the writers whom either shall consult are very little to be blamed, though it should sometimes happen that they are read in vain.

No. 71. Saturday, August 25, 1759

Dick Shifter was born in Cheapside, and, having passed
reputably through all the classes of St. Paul's school, has been
for some years a student in the Temple. He is of opinion that
intense application dulls the faculties, and thinks it necessary
to temper the severity of the law by books that engage the
mind but do not fatigue it. He has therefore made a copious
collection of plays, poems, and romances, to which he has
recourse when he fancies himself tired with statutes and reports;
and he seldom enquires very nicely whether he is weary or
idle.

Dick has received from his favourite authors very strong
impressions of a country life, and, though his furthest excursions have been to Greenwich on one side and to Chelsea on
the other, he has talked for several years with great pomp of
language and elevation of sentiments, about a state too high
for contempt and too low for envy, about homely quiet and
blameless simplicity, pastoral delights and rural innocence.

His friends who had estates in the country had often invited
him to pass the summer among them, but something or other
had always hindered him; and he considered that to reside in
the house of another man was to incur a kind of dependence
inconsistent with that laxity of life which he had imaged as the
chief good.

This summer he resolved to be happy, and procured a lodging to be taken for him at a solitary house, situated about
thirty miles from London on the banks of a small river, with
cornfields before it, and a hill on each side covered with wood.
He concealed the place of his retirement that none might
violate his obscurity, and promised himself many a happy day
when he should hide himself among the trees, and contemplate the tumults and vexations of the town.

He stepped into the post-chaise with his heart beating and
his eyes sparkling, was conveyed through many varieties of
delightful prospects, saw hills and meadows, cornfields and
pastures, succeed each other, and for four hours charged none

of his poets with fiction or exaggeration. He was now within six miles of happiness, when, having never felt so much agitation before, he began to wish his journey at an end, and the last hour was passed in changing his posture and quarrelling with his driver.

An hour may be tedious but cannot be long; he at length alighted at his new dwelling and was received as he expected; he looked round upon the hills and rivulets, but his joints were stiff and his muscles sore, and his first request was to see his bed-chamber.

He rested well, and ascribed the soundness of his sleep to the stillness of the country. He expected from that time nothing but nights of quiet and days of rapture, and, as soon as he had risen, wrote an account of his new state to one of his friends in the Temple.

> Dear Frank,
>
> I never pitied thee before. I am now, as I could wish every man of wisdom and virtue to be, in the regions of calm content and placid meditation, with all the beauties of nature soliciting my notice, and all the diversities of pleasure courting my acceptance; the birds are chirping in the woods, and the flowers blooming in the mead; the breeze is whistling in the woods, and the sun dancing on the water. I can now say with truth that a man, capable of enjoying the purity of happiness, is never more busy than in his hours of leisure, nor ever less solitary than in a place of solitude.
>
> I am, dear Frank, &c.

When he had sent away his letter, he walked into the wood, with some inconvenience from the furze that pricked his legs and the briars that scratched his face; he at last sat down under a tree, and heard with great delight a shower, by which he was not wet, rattling among the branches: 'This', said he, 'is the true image of obscurity; we hear of troubles and commotions but never feel them.'

His amusement did not overpower the calls of nature, and he therefore went back to order his dinner. He knew that the country produces whatever is eaten or drank, and, imagining that he was now at the source of luxury, resolved to indulge himself with dainties which he supposed might now be procured at a price next to nothing, if any price at all was expected, and intended to amaze the rustics with his generosity by paying more than they would ask. Of twenty dishes which he named, he was amazed to find that scarce one was to be had, and heard, with astonishment and indignation, that all the fruits of the earth were sold at a higher price than in the streets of London.

His meal was short and sullen, and he retired again to his tree to enquire how dearness could be consistent with abundance, or how fraud should be practised by simplicity. He was not satisfied with his own speculations, and, returning home early in the evening, went awhile from window to window, and found that he wanted something to do.

He enquired for a newspaper, and was told that farmers never minded news, but that they could send for it from the ale-house. A messenger was despatched, who ran away at full speed, but loitered an hour behind the hedges, and at last comin back with his feet purposely bemired, instead of expressing the gratitude which Mr. Shifter expected for the bounty of a shilling, said that the night was wet and the way dirty, and he hoped that his worship would not think it much to give him half-a-crown.

Dick now went to bed with some abatement of his expectations, but sleep, I know not how, revives our hopes and rekindles our desires. He rose early in the morning, surveyed the landscape, and was pleased. He walked out, and passed from field to field, without observing any beaten path, and wondered that he had not seen the shepherdesses dancing nor heard the swains piping to their flocks.

At last he saw some reapers and harvest-women at dinner. 'Here', said he, 'are the true Arcadians', and advanced courteously towards them, as afraid of confusing them by the dignity of his presence. They acknowledged his superiority by no other token than that of asking him for something to drink. He imagined that he had now purchased the privilege of discourse, and began to descend to familiar questions, endeavouring to accommodate his discourse to the grossness of rustic understandings. The clowns soon found that he did not know wheat from rye, and began to despise him; one of the boys, by pretending to show him a bird's nest, decoyed him into a ditch; and one of the wenches sold him a bargain.

This walk had given him no great pleasure, but he hoped to find other rustics less coarse of manners and less mischievous of disposition. Next morning he was accosted by an attorney, who told him that, unless he made Farmer Dobson satisfaction for trampling his grass, he had orders to indict him. Shifter was offended but not terrified, and, telling the attorney that he was himself a lawyer, talked so volubly of pettifoggers and barrators that he drove him away.

Finding his walks thus interrupted, he was inclined to ride, and, being pleased with the appearance of a horse that was grazing in a neighbouring meadow, enquired the owner, who warranted him sound, and would not sell him but that he was too fine for a plain man. Dick paid down the price, and, riding out to enjoy the evening, fell with his new horse into a ditch; they got out with difficulty, and, as he was going to mount again, a countryman looked at the horse and perceived him to be blind. Dick went to the seller and demanded back his money, but was told that a man who rented his ground must do the best for himself, that his landlord had his rent though the year was barren, and that, whether horses had eyes or no, he should sell them to the highest bidder.

Shifter now began to be tired with rustic simplicity, and on the fifth day took possession again of his chambers, and bade farewell to the regions of calm content and placid meditation.

From a review of Soame Jenyns's
A Free Enquiry into
the Nature and Origin of Evil

We are next entertained with Pope's alleviations of those evils which we are doomed to suffer.

'Poverty, or the want of riches, is generally compensated by having more hopes and fewer fears, by a greater share of health, and a more exquisite relish of the smallest enjoyments, than those who possess them are usually blessed with. The want of taste and genius, with all the pleasures that arise from them, are commonly recompensed by a more useful kind of common-sense, together with a wonderful delight, as well as success, in the busy pursuits of a scrambling world. The sufferings of the sick are greatly relieved by many trifling gratifications imper-ceptible to others, and sometimes almost repaid by the incon-ceivable transports occasioned by the return of health and vigour. Folly cannot be very grievous, because imperceptible; and I doubt not but there is some truth in that rant of a mad poet, that there is a pleasure in being mad, which none but madmen know. Ignorance, or the want of knowledge and litera-ture, the appointed lot of all born to poverty and the drudgeries of life, is the only opiate capable of infusing that insensibility which can enable them to endure the miseries of the one and the fatigues of the other. It is a cordial administered by the gracious hand of providence, of which they ought never to be deprived by an ill-judged and improper education. It is the basis of all subordination, the support of society, and the privilege of individuals: and I have ever thought it a most remarkable instance of the divine wisdom that, whereas in all animals, whose individuals rise little above the rest of their species, knowledge is instinctive, in man, whose individuals are so widely different, it is acquired by education; by which means the prince and the labourer, the philosopher and the peasant, are in some measure fitted for their respective situations.'

Much of these positions is perhaps true, and the whole paragraph might well pass without censure were not objections necessary to the establishment of knowledge. *Poverty* is very gently paraphrased by *want of riches*. In that sense almost every man may in his own opinion be poor. But there is another poverty which is *want of competence*, of all that can soften the miseries of life, of all that can diversify attention or delight imagination. There is yet another poverty which is *want of necessaries*, a species of poverty which no care of the public, no charity of particulars, can preserve many from feeling openly, and many secretly.

That hope and fear are inseparably or very frequently connected with poverty and riches, my surveys of life have not informed me. The milder degrees of poverty are sometimes supported by hope, but the more severe often sink down in motionless despondence. Life must be seen before it can be known. This author and Pope perhaps never saw the miseries which they imagine thus easy to be borne. The poor indeed are insensible of many little vexations which sometimes embitter the possessions and pollute the enjoyments of the rich. They are not pained by casual incivility, or mortified by the mutilation of a compliment; but this happiness is like that of a malefactor who ceases to feel the cords that bind him when the pincers are tearing his flesh.

That want of taste for one enjoyment is supplied by the pleasures of some other may be fairly allowed. But the compensations of sickness I have never found near to equivalence, and the transports of recovery only prove the intenseness of the pain.

With folly no man is willing to confess himself very intimately acquainted, and therefore its pains and pleasures are kept secret. But what the author says of its happiness seems applicable only to fatuity or gross dullness, for that inferiority of understanding which makes one man without any other reason the slave, or tool, or property of another, which makes him sometimes useless and sometimes ridiculous, is often felt with very quick sensibility. On the happiness of madmen, as the case is not very frequent, it is not necessary to raise a disquisition, but I cannot forbear to observe that I never yet knew disorders of mind increase felicity: every madman is either arrogant and irascible, or gloomy and suspicious, or possessed by some passion or notion destructive to his quiet. He has always discontent in his look, and malignity in his bosom. And, if we had the power of choice, he would soon repent who should resign his reason to secure his peace.

Concerning the portion of ignorance necessary to make the condition of the lower classes of mankind safe to the public and tolerable to themselves, both morals and policy exact a nicer enquiry than will be very soon or very easily made. There is undoubtedly a degree of knowledge which will direct a man to refer all to providence, and to acquiesce in the condition which omniscient goodness has determined to allot him; to consider this world as a phantom that must soon glide from before his eyes, and the distresses and vexations that encompass him, as dust scattered in his path, as a blast that chills him for a moment and passes off for ever.

Such wisdom, arising from the comparison of a part with the whole of our existence, those that want it most cannot possibly obtain from philosophy, nor, unless the method of education and the general tenor of life are changed, will very easily receive it from religion. The bulk of mankind is not likely to be very wise or very good: and I know not whether there are not many states of life in which all knowledge less than the highest wisdom will produce discontent and danger. I believe it may be sometimes found that a *little learning* is to a poor man a *dangerous thing*. But such is the condition of humanity, that we easily see or quickly feel the wrong, but cannot always distinguish the right. Whatever knowledge is superfluous in irremediable poverty is hurtful, but the difficulty is to determine when poverty is irremediable, and at what point superfluity begins. Gross ignorance every man has found equally dangerous with perverted knowledge. Men left wholly to their appetites and their instincts, with little sense of moral or religious obligation and with very faint distinctions of right and wrong, can never be safely employed or confidently trusted: they can be honest only by obstinacy, and diligent only by compulsion or caprice. Some instruction, therefore, is necessary, and much perhaps may be dangerous.

Though it should be granted that those who are *born to poverty and drudgery* should not be *deprived* by an *improper education* of the *opiate* of *ignorance*, even this concession will not be of much use to direct our practice, unless it be determined who are those that are *born to poverty*. To entail irreversible poverty upon generation after generation only because the ancestor happened to be poor is in itself cruel, if not unjust, and is wholly contrary to the maxims of a commercial nation, which always suppose and promote a rotation of property, and offer every individual a chance of mending his condition by his diligence. Those who communicate literature to the son of a poor man consider him as one not born to poverty but to the necessity of deriving a better fortune from himself. In this attempt, as in others, many fail and many succeed. Those that fail will feel their misery more acutely; but since poverty is now confessed to be such a calamity as cannot be born without the opiate of insensibility, I hope the happiness of those whom education enables to escape from it may turn the balance against that exacerbation which the others suffer.

I am always afraid of determining on the side of envy or cruelty. The privileges of education may sometimes be improperly bestowed, but I shall always fear to withhold them, lest I should be yielding to the suggestions of pride, while I persuade myself that I am following the maxims of policy; and, under the appearance of salutary restraints, should be indulging the lust of dominion and that malevolence which delights in seeing others depressed.

*   *   *

Having thus despatched the consideration of particular evils, he comes at last to a general reason for which *evil* may be said to be *our good*. He is of opinion that there is some inconceivable benefit in pain abstractedly considered; that pain, however inflicted or wherever felt, communicates some good to the general system of being, and that every animal is some way or other the better for the pain of every other animal. This opinion he carries so far as to suppose that there passes some principle of union through all animal life, as attraction is communicated to all corporeal nature, and that the evils suffered on this globe may, by some inconceivable means, contribute to the felicity of the inhabitants of the remotest planet.

How the origin of evil is brought nearer to human conception by any *inconceivable* means, I am not able to discover. We believed that the present system of creation was right, though we could not explain the adaptation of one part to the other, or for the whole succession of causes and consequences. Where has this enquirer added to the little knowledge that we had before? He has told us of the benefits of evil, which no man feels, and relations between distant parts of [the] universe, which he cannot himself conceive. There was enough in this question inconceivable before, and we have little advantage from a new inconceivable solution.

I do not mean to reproach this author for not knowing what is equally hidden from learning and from ignorance. The shame is to impose words for ideas upon ourselves or others; to imagine that we are going forward when we are only turning round; to think that there is any difference between him that gives no reason, and him that gives a reason which by his own confession cannot be conceived.

But that he may not be thought to conceive nothing but things inconceivable, he has at last thought on a way by which human sufferings may produce good effects. He imagines that as we have not only animals for food, but choose some for our diversion, the same privilege may be allowed to some beings above us, *who may deceive, torment, or destroy us for the ends only of their own pleasure or utility*. This he again finds impossible to be conceived, *but that impossibility lessens not the probability of the conjecture, which by analogy is so strongly confirmed.*

I cannot resist the temptation of contemplating this analogy, which I think he might have carried further very much to the advantage of his argument. He might have shown that these *hunters whose game is man* have many sports analogous to our own. As we drown whelps and kittens, they amuse themselves now and then with sinking a ship, and stand round the fields of Blenheim or the walls of Prague as we encircle a cock-pit. As we shoot a bird flying, they take a man in the midst of his business or pleasure, and knock him down with an apoplexy. Some of them, perhaps, are virtuosi, and delight in the operations of an asthma, as a human philosopher in the effects of the air pump. To swell a man with a tympany is as good sport as to blow a frog. Many a merry bout have these frolic beings at the vicissitudes of an ague, and good sport it is to see a man tumble with an epilepsy, and revive and tumble again, and all this he knows not why. As they are wiser and more powerful than we, they have more exquisite diversions, for we have no way of procuring any sport so brisk and so lasting as the paroxysms of the gout and stone which undoubtedly must make high mirth, especially if the play be a little diversified with the blunders and puzzles of the blind and deaf. We know not how far their sphere of observation may extend. Perhaps now and then a merry being may place himself in such a situation as to enjoy at once all the varieties of an epidemical disease, or amuse his leisure with the tossings and contortions of every possible pain exhibited together.

One sport the merry malice of these beings has found means of enjoying to which we have nothing equal or similar. They now and then catch a mortal proud of his parts, and flattered either by the submission of those who court his kindness, or the notice of those who suffer him to court theirs. A head thus prepared for the reception of false opinions and the projection of vain designs, they easily fill with idle notions, till in time they make their plaything an author: their first diversion commonly begins with an ode or an epistle, then rises perhaps to a political irony, and is at last brought to its height by a treatise of philosophy. Then begins the poor animal to entangle himself in sophisms, and flounder in absurdity, to talk confidently of the scale of being, and to give solutions which himself confesses impossible to be understood. Sometimes, however, it happens that their pleasure is without much mischief. The author feels no pain, but while they are wondering at the extravagance of his opinion and pointing him out to one another as a new example of human folly, he is enjoying his own applause, and that of his companions, and perhaps is elevated with the hope of standing at the head of a new sect.

Many of the books which now crowd the world may be justly suspected to be written for the sake of some invisible order of beings, for surely they are of no use to any of the corporeal inhabitants of the world. Of the productions of the last bounteous year, how many can be said to serve any purpose of use or pleasure. The only end of writing is to enable the readers better to enjoy life, or better to endure it: and how will either of those be put more in our power by him who tells us that we are puppets, of which some creature not much wiser than ourselves manages the wires: that a set of beings, unseen and unheard, are hovering about us, trying experiments upon our sensibility, putting us in agonies to see our limbs quiver, torturing us to madness that they may laugh at our vagaries; sometimes obstructing the bile, that they may see how a man looks when he is yellow, sometimes breaking a traveller's bones to try how he will get home, sometimes wasting a man to a skeleton, and sometimes killing him fat for the greater elegance of his hide?

This is an account of natural evil which though, like the rest, not quite new is very entertaining, though I know not how much it may contribute to patience. The only reason why we should contemplate evil is that we may bear it better, and I am afraid nothing is much more placidly endured for the sake of making others sport.

NOTES ON THE TEXT

All texts are from the first editions, though spelling, punctuation, and typography have been modernised, and a few obvious printers' errors silently corrected. When the *Idler* essays were printed as a collection, *No. 22*, a bitter animal fable satirising war, was omitted, and the numbers of subsequent essays changed. The numbers of the *Idler* essays in this volume are those familiarised by the collected editions, not those of the original edition.

Johnson revised both *Rasselas* and the periodical essays (though only *The Rambler* was extensively rewritten), and nearly all modern editions are based, reasonably enough, on the revised texts. Yet Johnson's speed in composition, so frequently referred to by editors and critics, cannot fairly be illustrated by writings corrected and revised at leisure, and there is some interest in seeing exactly what he was offering to the public week by week. Little is lost by using the first editions, and the original text of a work as important as *Rasselas* should at least be available.

Johnson's works have, as a rule, been rather sparingly annotated. The notes in this edition have been written for a reader not already familiar with eighteenth-century usage or background, and less likely to be irritated by a superfluous note than by the absence of required information or explanation. The varied indebtedness of the notes to earlier editors, critics, and commentators is obvious and inevitable, but I have made specific acknowledgement only in a few places where some particular information has been recently supplied. An edition of *Rasselas* by A. J. F. Collins (University Tutorial Press, 1910), apparently designed for correspondence-course students, has the merit of being the most thorough attempt at annotation, and, although some of its information is now out of date, the editor shows a sharp awareness of the difficulties which a non-specialist reader may encounter, and I have found him a useful guide in this respect.

WORD USAGE

The difficulty an inexperienced reader meets with in Johnson's writings is less a matter of 'hard words' and recondite allusions

O

than of more or less familiar words of which the significance or connotations have changed in the course of two centuries. Often the eighteenth-century writer, and Johnson in particular, used words with a sharper sense of their etymologies than we do now; usages which were then slangy or impolite have now established themselves, and have often ousted the polite forms of Johnson's time; certain senses of a word which were then uncommon have now become dominant. For instance, *want* more frequently meant *lack* than *wish for*, and while this is of little consequence when we are being told that Mrs. Bombasine *wanted a maid* it can lead to misunderstanding of the statement in *The Adventurer No. 67* that *the world might easily want* certain apparently unnecessary trades.

To explain these words on each occurrence would produce a proliferation of notes or cross-references; to put them in an appended glossary would hardly meet the case, for the heart of the problem is that the reader is likely to think that he knows what the words mean. For this reason it seemed best to prefix to the particular explanatory notes some general comments on the words most frequently encountered and misunderstood. The list is not complete, although I think it includes the most common traps, and the notes are not full definitions but brief warnings. Where possible I have used materials from Johnson's *Dictionary*, and these, both in the general and the particular notes, are enclosed in single quotes. Thus, although Johnson's explanations are rarely given in full, the notes may give some notion of his manner and quality as a lexicographer.

accident: 'that which happens unforeseen', i.e., any chance occurrence, not necessarily an unpleasant one. In a philosophical context *accident* is opposed to *essence* or *substance*, and means 'the property or quality of anything which may be separated from it at least in thought'. Thus the colour of an object is not essential but accidental. Usually *accidental* means *chance*.

accommodation: anything provided for comfort, refreshment, or even entertainment.

address: 'skill; dexterity'.

admire: usually 'to regard with wonder'. Similarly, *admiration* normally means *wonder*.

affection: may mean 'passion of any kind' or 'state of mind in general'.

airy: in a favourable sense, 'gay; sprightly; full of mirth; vivacious; lively; spirited; light of heart', or, unfavourably, 'without reality; without any steady foundation in truth or nature; vain; trifling'.

amuse: frequently means merely *occupy the mind.*

art: The basic meaning is 'the power of doing something not taught by nature or instinct'. Hence it can mean any skill, trade, craft, or acquired expertise. An *artist* may therefore be any man of trained or acquired ability: 'a skilful man; not a novice'. *Terms of art* means simply *technical terms.*

avocation: any business or occupation. Johnson is conscious of the Latin etymology: 'the act of calling aside or the business that calls, or the call that summons away'. He sometimes uses the word for those ordinary daily occupations which take us out of ourselves.

candour: 'sweetness of temper; purity of mind; openness; kindness'. The word never refers to mere outspokenness, but rather to a disposition to think and speak well of others. It was opposed not only to *deceit* but also to *malice.* Similarly *candid.*

careless: occasionally has the modern meaning 'negligent; thoughtless', but very often is close in meaning to *carefree* ('cheerful; undisturbed'), and can mean 'unmoved by; unconcerned at'.

casualty: usually *chance,* or 'a thing happening by chance, not design'.

ceremony: any kind of formal behaviour.

chariot: 'a carriage of pleasure or state' or 'a lighter kind of coach with only back seats'.

competence: 'such a quantity of anything as is sufficient, without superfluity', or 'such a fortune as . . . is equal to the necessities of life'.

concatenation: 'a series of links; an uninterrupted unvariable succession'. (From Latin *catena,* a chain.)

condition: frequently means *social position, rank,* or *circumstances.*

confidence: trust. Similarly *confide.*

confound: usually 'to mingle things so that their several forms or natures cannot be discerned'. Sometimes 'to perplex'.

contemn: despise, consider of little value.

conveniency (or *convenience*): very similar in meaning to *accommodation* (see above): anything which makes for ease or comfort.

conversation: may mean, as now, 'easy talk', but does not necessarily refer to speech. It frequently means 'behaviour; manner of acting in common life'; or *the ordinary daily intercourse of people in society.* Similarly *converse.*

curiosity: besides *inquisitiveness*, may mean *any kind of interest*, or 'fastidious delicacy', or 'accuracy; exactness'.

demonstration: 'the highest degree of deducible or argumental evidence; the strongest degree of proof; such proof as not only evinces the position proved to be true, but shows the contrary position to be absurd or impossible'. (See 'the laws of demonstration': *Rasselas*, p. 87.) Similarly *demonstrative.*

discover: usually used in a sense related to *uncover*: 'to show; to disclose; to bring to light'; occasionally means *perceive.*

disgust: not such a violent reaction as in modern usage; often it means little more than *distaste* or *dislike.*

dissipate: Three meanings are common: 'to scatter every way; to scatter the attention; to spend a fortune'.

easy: often 'without constraint; without formality', as in the expression *free and easy.*

elegance: The word did not connote, as it usually does today, an almost foppish refinement. Johnson defined it as 'beauty of art, rather soothing than striking; beauty without grandeur'. *Art* is the key-word in the definition; *elegance* would refer to works of high finish which delighted the viewer or reader without transporting him.

event: Besides the modern meaning ('an incident; anything that happens'), this frequently means 'the consequence of an action; the conclusion; the upshot'. This second meaning still survives in a few expressions, but normally we would use *outcome.*

faction: 'a party in a state', or 'tumult; discord; dissension'. The two meanings were usually combined to refer to any party, especially political or religious, to which the speaker himself did not belong.

happy: 'lucky; successful; fortunate'. Similarly *unhappy* means *unfortunate.*

idea: Johnson defines the word as 'mental imagination', and quotes Locke in illustration: 'Whatsoever the mind perceives in itself, or is the immediate object of perception, thought or understanding, that I call an idea.'

illiterate: 'unlettered; untaught; unlearned'. It does not necessarily mean *unable to read or write.* (See *Idler No. 70,* p. 151.)

imbecility: 'weakness; feebleness of mind or body'.

insensibility: 'dullness of mental perception, or dullness of corporal sense'.

intercept: frequently means 'to obstruct; to cut off; to stop from being communicated'.

intestine: 'internal; inward'.

irregular: 'deviating from rule, custom, or nature'.

issue: often 'to come out; to pass out from any place'.

just: The meaning of this common word is often 'exact; proper; accurate', or 'true'.

liberality: 'bounty; generosity'. Similarly *liberal.*

luxury: usually 'voluptuousness; addictedness to pleasure', but can refer specifically to the pleasures of the table—'delicious fare'. (See *Rasselas,* p. 4, and *Idler No. 71,* p. 156.)

manners: 'general way of life; morals; habits', or 'ceremonious behaviour; studied civility'.

mean: then, as now, a word of many meanings. Common meanings in Johnson are: 'of low rank or birth'; 'low-minded; base; contemptible'. But sometimes it means 'middle; moderate'. Similarly *meanness.*

nature: an important word, capable of a wide variety of meanings. (For a full analysis see ' "Nature" as Aesthetic Norm' in *Essays in the History of Ideas,* by Arthur O. Lovejoy, O.U.P 1948.) When opposed to *art,* it means the artist's innate gifts as opposed to his acquired skills. In the most general sense it can mean the whole cosmic order. More familiarly it refers to external nature, the natural world as opposed to what man has made. But frequently and importantly it means all that is fundamental and unchanging in human nature and experience—what is true of and has been known to all men, at all times, and in all places.

nice: generally 'scrupulously exact', or 'fastidious', even fussily so.

obsequious: 'obedient; compliant; not resisting'.

officious: sometimes used in the modern sense ('importunely forward'), but often means 'kind; doing good offices', as in *Rambler No. 47,* p. 115 ('all that officious and watchful kindness').

ostentation: besides the modern sense ('ambitious display; vain show'), may mean simply 'outward show; appearance'.

passions: In the *Dictionary*, Johnson quotes Watts: 'The word "passion" signifies the receiving any action in a large philosophical sense; in a more limited philosophical sense it signifies any of the affections of human nature, as love, fear, joy, sorrow, but the common people confine it only to anger.' The first sense is rare in Johnson except in religious contexts, and although he uses the singular form much as we do now for any 'violent commotion of the mind', the plural form usually refers to the whole emotional and motivating side of human nature, as opposed to the rational.

peculiar: 'appropriate; belonging to anyone with exclusion of others'.

policy: usually means 'prudence; management of affairs'.

pompous: 'splendid; magnificent; grand'. *Pomp*, besides meaning 'splendour', can mean 'a procession of splendour and ostentation'.

pretend: 'claim'. Similarly *pretensions* means *claims*.

privation: may mean 'removal or destruction of any thing or quality', rather like the modern *deprivation*. But sometimes it refers not to an action but a state. The *Dictionary* quotes Watts: 'A "privation" is the absence of what does naturally belong to the thing, or which ought to be present with it.'

profuse: 'lavish; extravagant'.

proper: usually should be understood as *appropriate*, but sometimes means *own*. Similarly *propriety*.

recollect: may mean, as now, *recall to memory*, but frequently means *regain one's self-possession* or *pull oneself together* ('to recover reason or resolution'). Similarly *recollection*.

regular: according to rule or established practice.

remark: notice; point out; observe. Similarly the noun *remark*.

reparation: often means simply *repair*.

riot: The verb usually means *to revel*, and the noun, 'wild, loose festivity'.

rude: The basic meaning is *crude; unimproved*. Applied to people it usually means *untaught; lacking in social refinement*.

science: knowledge as a whole, or any particular body of knowledge. It was not, as now, contrasted with *art*; indeed, the

Dictionary definitions include 'any art or species of knowledge', and 'one of the seven liberal arts'.

scrupulous: Besides meaning *exact or careful in matters of conduct*, it could also mean *fastidious, doubtful*, or 'given to
objections; captious'. Similarly *scrupulosity*.

secure: sometimes means, as now, 'free from danger; safe', but
can also mean 'free from fear', and, more unexpectedly,
'careless; wanting caution; wanting vigilance'. (Cf. Latin
securus.) Similarly *security*.

sensible: Of the meaning with which we are most familiar, the
Dictionary says, 'In low conversation it has sometimes the
sense of reasonable; judicious; wise', and Johnson never
employs it in this sense. There are two basic meanings:
'having the power of perceiving by the senses', and 'per-
ceptible to the senses'. These are extended to include perception or sensitivity in moral, aesthetic, or emotional
matters. Similarly *sensibility* can mean 'quickness of sensa-
tion', or 'quickness of perception', and is usually roughly
equivalent to the modern *sensitivity*.

sensitive: refers specifically to reception through the senses:
'having sense or perception, but not reason'. Similarly
sensitivity.

sentiments: feelings or opinions.

solicitude: often simply 'anxiety'. See *Rasselas*, p. 79.

specious: 'showy; pleasing to the view', or 'plausible; superfi-
cially, not solidly, right'.

subordination: can mean *a position of inferiority*, but usually in
Johnson means 'a series regularly descending', and in
particular, *the social hierarchy descending from kings to
beggars*, or *the whole principle of social order*. The order
of the universe was similarly based on *subordination*.

suffrage: strictly *vote*, but used for any considered opinion.

temper: usually *temperament* or *disposition*.

vulgar: usually 'plebeian; suiting to the common people; practised among the common people'. *The vulgar* means *the
common people*.

want: The verb usually means *lack, have need of* rather than
wish for.

wanton: sometimes means *lascivious*, but as often means merely
'unrestrained; sportive; frolicsome'. Similarly *wantonness*.
The verb *to wanton* may mean 'to move nimbly and irregu-
larly'.

RASSELAS

References to *Life* are to the edition of *Boswell's Life of Johnson* in the 'Oxford Standard Authors' series (O.U.P., new edition, 1953).

Chapter I

Page 1. Rasselas: Johnson gained much of his knowledge of Abyssinia from *A Voyage to Abyssinia by Father Jerome Lobo, A Portuguese Jesuit*, which he translated from the French of Le Grand in 1735, together with Le Grand's appended 'Dissertations'. In this translation reference is made to Rassela Christos, Lieutenant General to Sultan Segued (p. 102), and later to 'the title of *Ras*, or *Chief*' (p. 262). Johnson certainly used other sources, and there have been many recent critical attempts to identify them: see, for instance, J. R. Moore's '*Rasselas* and the Early Travellers to Abyssinia' (*Modern Language Quarterly*, XV, 36–41), Gwin J. Kolb's 'The "Paradise" in Abyssinia and the "Happy Valley" in *Rasselas*' (*Modern Philology*, LVI, 10–16), and Donald M. Lockhart's ' "The Fourth Son of the Mighty Emperor": The Ethiopian Background of Johnson's *Rasselas*' (*Publications of the Modern Language Association of America*, LXXVIII, 516–28). The difficulty is that early travel-writers borrowed very freely from their predecessors, so that it cannot be proved which Johnson was using. However, we can be sure that, besides *Lobo*, he knew Ludolph's *New History of Ethiopia* (1681), because he refers to it in his preface to *Lobo*, had a copy in his library, and seems to have taken the name 'Imlac' from it (see p. 15 note), and also *Purchas His Pilgrimage* (1612), a compilation which popularised a good deal of legendary as well as factual material. But the question of Johnson's sources chiefly relates to his procedures as a writer: in *Rasselas* the Abyssinian and Egyptian backgrounds have no importance in themselves, but provide convenient occasions for Johnson's moral discussions.

the Father of waters: From Lobo, Johnson learned that the Nile rose in the kingdom of Goiama in Abyssinia and that the natives called it '*Abavi*, that is the Father of Waters' (p. 97). The exact source in Abyssinia of the Blue Nile was

not known until later in the century. The source of the
White Nile was unknown until the mid-nineteenth century.

the streams of plenty: The Nile carried 'wealth and plenty into
Egypt, which owes to the annual inundations of this river
its envied fertility' (*Lobo*, p. 103).

torrid: 'particularly applied to the regions or zone between
the tropics'.

antiquity: 'the people of old times; the ancients'.

the residence of the Abyssinian princes: The story of the iso-
lation of the heirs to the Abyssinian throne was a famous
one and had been ornamented with legend. In one of the
'Dissertations' appended to Lobo's *Voyage* mention is made
of the 'famous rock' in Amhara 'on which the sons and
brothers of the emperor were confined till their accession
to the throne' (p. 200). But this rock was far from being a
Happy Valley: 'It was on the barren summit of Ambaguexa
that the princes of the blood-royal passed their melancholy life, being guarded by officers who treated them often
with great rigour and severity' (p. 204). Moreover, the
custom is said to have been abolished 'for two ages'. The
account given in *Purchas his Pilgrimage* (1612), where a
whole chapter is devoted to the subject ('Of the Hill Amara
and the rarities therein' (Bk. VII, Ch. 5)), is typical:

> Here in Amara is a steep hill, dilating itself in a round
> form, fifteen days' journey in compass, environing with
> the steep sides and impassable tops thereof many fruitful
> and pleasant valleys, wherein the kindred of the Prete
> [the emperor of Abyssinia] are kept, for the avoiding of
> all tumults and seditions. . . . Heaven and Earth, nature
> and industry, have all been corrivals to it, all presenting
> their best presents to make it of this so lovely presence,
> some taking this for the place of our forefathers'
> Paradise. And yet, though thus admired of others as a
> paradise, it is made a prison to some. . . . [The princes
> live] in great estate and majesty in royal palaces with
> spacious halls richly hanged . . . (pp. 561–8).

This same passage was referred to by Milton in *Paradise
Lost*, IV, 280–4, and seems to have been at the back of
Coleridge's mind when he was writing 'Kubla Khan'. To
create his Happy Valley, Johnson merely added further em-
broideries to an already much-embroidered story.

massy: 'heavy; weighty; ponderous; bulky'.

engines: An engine was 'any mechanical complication, in which various movements and parts concur to one effect'.

page 2. superfluities: overflowings (Latin *superfluere*, to overflow). In the next paragraph but one, the word has the more familiar meaning of 'more than enough'.

spices from the rocks: i.e. from the trees and plants growing there.

vacancies of attention: i.e. times when there was nothing to occupy the mind.

artificers of pleasure: Here we would say *performers* or *artistes*. But three paragraphs earlier the word means *craftsmen*.

these only: R. W. Chapman, in his edition of *Rasselas* (Clarendon Press: 1927), suggests '*these* should perhaps be *those*; the words are hardly distinguishable in Johnson's hand'. But a few lines later *those* has been correctly read, and this word was not corrected in the later revision.

page 3. paces: A pace is defined as 'a measure of five feet. The quantity supposed to be measured by the foot from the place where it is taken up to that where it is set down.'

solstitial rains and equinoctial hurricanes: Lobo describes the fierce downpour in Abyssinia at the summer solstice. The belief that gales were to be expected at the equinoxes was long-established.

an open and secret passage: i.e. two passages, one open and one concealed. Here, and in what follows, Johnson seems to be preparing the ground for some romantic adventure which he did not pursue.

Chapter II

public life: not in the modern sense of the expression: here, *life as lived by and among the general community.*

page 4. but passed: Johnson does not mean that *few passed* . . . but that *most passed* . . . cf. *The Rambler No. 155*, p. 123, '*few wander*'.

anon: sometimes; now and then.

humour: mood or disposition.

page 5. some latent sense: Some eighteenth-century philosophers, in particular Shaftesbury and Hutcheson, had maintained that man had an additional sense, a 'moral sense' by which he distinguished instinctively between right and wrong; but Rasselas seems to be thinking of a sense similar in kind to the normal five senses, since he opposes to it 'some desires distinct from sense', i.e. intellectual or spiritual.

Chapter III

page 6. conference: 'oral discussion'.

intellects: intellectual powers.

page 7. give me something to desire: This exchange is central to Johnson's whole view of the human condition. To bc happy, man needs something to desire, but as long as he has an unsatisfied desire he cannot be happy (see p. 5). Johnson's notion is that God gives man the desire for happiness in this world, and the satisfaction of that happiness in the next. Thus, *Rasselas* is, in a sense, an answer to those who ask why Providence denies man happiness. Here is a man with all earthly satisfactions, but still unhappy because his nature demands 'something to desire'. Similarly, Rasselas's conversion of the old man's argument relates to the more general concept. If, for Rasselas, an acquaintance with the miseries of this world is 'necessary to happiness', the same might be said of man in general—that in order to know the happiness of heaven he needs to know the miseries of earth.

Chapter IV

only: one.

whose views were extended to a wider space: i.e. who had more years of life ahead of him than had the old man.

page 8. run forward: The past tense *run* was being superseded by *ran.*

page 9. The consciousness of his own folly: Johnson is attributing to Rasselas his own obsession. Throughout his adult life he accused himself, in his diary and his prayers, of sloth, indolence, and waste of time, and resolved again and again to reform.

reasonable: based on reason.

Chapter V

page 10. bars: barriers.

grate: cage.

prominence: steepness and height.

page 11. spared to search: ceased searching.

Chapter VI

mechanic powers: mechanical forces. *run:* See p. 8 note.

page 12. migration of wings: In 'Johnson's *Dissertation on Flying*
and John Wilkins's *Mathematical Magick*' (*Modern Philology*,
XLVII, 24–39), Gwin J. Kolb has shown how Johnson used
materials from Wilkins's book (1648) for this chapter.

grosser . . . subtler: denser . . . less dense.

resistance: i.e. to gravity.

page 13. philosopher: The word was much less specialised than
now. Johnson is probably thinking of a *natural philosopher*,
whom we would call a *scientist* or *physicist*.

parallel: i.e. of latitude.

marts: markets.

speculation: Perhaps a double meaning is intended here. The
word can mean 'contemplation' and also *a purely hypothetical scheme* ('mental scheme not reduced to practice').

tenuity: thinness.

Nothing . . . first overcome: This has the ring of a true
Johnsonian aphorism. The comedy lies in its misapplica-
tion. The objection Rasselas has raised about the impossibility of breathing at the height where gravity ceases to
operate is not some quibble to be brushed aside. But Johnson is presenting the *artist* as an enthusiast of very limited
imagination, unwilling to consider anything which conflicts
with his fantasies.

volant: flying.

tower: soar. (A technical term from falconry.)

page 14. the southern sea: the South Pacific and Indian Oceans.

levity: lightness of weight. Elsewhere in *Rasselas* it has the
familiar meaning, 'trifling gaiety'.

Chapter VII

page 15. support himself: keep up his spirits. ('Support: to endure
anything painful without being overcome'.)

Imlac: Johnson seems to have taken the name from
Ludolph's *New History of Ethiopia*, where there is a reference to a prince named 'Icon Imlac'. (See page 1 note.)

Chapter VIII

page 16. the kingdom of Goiama: Gojjam is now a province on
the western border of Abyssinia, south of Amhara. Johnson

took the name from Lobo, who listed Goiama as one of the three richest kingdoms in the Abyssinian empire.

spoiled: plundered.

for fear of losing them: them was accidentally omitted in the first edition.

page 17. the supreme magistrate: a common expression in the seventeenth and eighteenth centuries for the sovereign, as chief executive of the government.

some desire is necessary: See page 7 and note.

invention: here, *original thinking* as contrasted with *intelligence* (i.e. *understanding* or *knowledge*).

grossness of conception: coarse, materialistic way of thinking.

course of gratifications: series of pleasures.

page 18. negotiate: do business.

to waste or to improve: to diminish or to increase.

We laid . . . cheap goods: The money was loaded on to camels, not expended on them. The clumsy construction absurdly suggests that it was the camels who were concealed.

obliged: bound.

regulate: 'direct'.

Surat: an Indian town north of Bombay.

Chapter IX

page 19. enlarged: may mean *made larger, amplified* or *set free.* As, at the end of the previous chapter, Rasselas felt like 'a prisoner escaped', the second meaning is probably intended.

for show: i.e. in order to seem to be engaged in trade.

page 20. delicate: fastidious, of refined tastes.

Agra . . . the great Mogul: From the middle of the sixteenth to the middle of the seventeenth century, Agra was the capital of the Mogul Empire in India. The word 'great' should probably have a capital letter, since the Indian emperor was usually referred to by Europeans as the Great Mogul.

to gain the dignity of instructing: Compare *The Adventurer No. 126*, p. 139: 'He has learned to no purpose that is not able to teach.'

recommended myself so much: i.e. made such a good impression (on).

he dismissed me astonished at his wisdom: Johnson (or Imlac) is laughing at the human tendency to exaggerate the virtues of the 'great' who condescend to us.

confidence of solicitation: i.e. boldness in asking favours (of one whom they had treated so badly).

Chapter X

page 21. the first writers: That in this passage Johnson was thinking primarily of Homer is evident from the terms in which that poet is praised in the *Preface to Shakespeare.* The stock comparison with Virgil is also clearly in his mind; Homer was supposed to have the advantage in 'nature' (i.e. both in natural gifts and in first-hand observation and understanding of human nature) and Virgil in 'art' (i.e. conscious artistry). The same comparison is made in *The Rambler No. 121*, and Boswell records a similar observation:

> We must consider (said he) whether Homer was not the greatest poet, though Virgil may have produced the finest poem. Virgil was indebted to Homer for the whole invention of the structure of an epic poem, and for many of his beauties. (*Life*, p. 870.)

page 22. strength and invention . . . elegance and refinement: This is an extension of the contrast between nature and art. 'Strength' probably refers to an energetic, forceful style, and 'invention' to imaginative power in the creation of character, incident, story, structure. Conversely, 'elegance' is the product of artistry in the handling of materials, and 'refinement' can refer equally to artistic subtlety and to the avoidance of anything in content or expression which damages the total effect.

suspended in the mosque of Mecca: Johnson is almost certainly thinking of the Mu'allaqat, the seven 'golden' or 'suspended' poems, still considered masterpieces of Arabic poetry. According to tradition these poems, belonging to the century before the coming of Mohammed, were chosen in an annual competition and were then written in golden letters and hung up in the Ka'aba, the famous shrine in the great mosque at Mecca. They have been translated into English verse by Lady Anne and Wilfred Scawen Blunt: (*The Seven Golden Odes of Pagan Arabia:* 1903).

page 23. he does not number the streaks of the tulip: This famous passage has often been quoted to suggest that Johnson required only vague generalities in the description of nature. But this would be inconsistent with the praise of Thomson's *Seasons:* 'He looks round on nature and on life with the eye which nature bestows only on the poet, the eye that distinguishes in everything presented to its view whatever there is on which imagination can delight to be detained, and with a mind that at once comprehends the vast and attends to the minute.' He goes on to praise 'Thomson's wide expansion of general views, and his enumeration of circumstantial varieties'. It may be supposed that Johnson's opinion changed between the writing of *Rasselas* and the *Lives of the Poets*, but the two statements are not essentially opposed. A poet does not normally number the streaks of a tulip; in this his description differs from that of the horticulturist or botanist. Scientific description is analytic, poetic description synthetic, using only such details as can be composed into the total picture. Attention to the minute must be reconciled with comprehension of the vast.

neglect the minuter discriminations: Again, this seems in conflict with the assertion that 'the reader of *The Seasons* wonders that he never saw before what Thomson shows him'. But Johnson was thinking of the combination in Thomson's vision of the general and the particular, and not of minute details which some may have noticed and others not. Of course, the real point which Imlac wishes to make here is that the poet should always seek the general truth in the complex particulars of experience. Where Johnson differs from later critics is not so much in this view as in his tendency to wish for such general truths to be made explicit.

character: i.e. his role as a poet.

transcendental: 'general; pervading many particulars'.

the legislator of mankind: It has been observed that this anticipates Shelley's concluding sentence in his *Defence of Poetry:* 'Poets are the unacknowledged legislators of the world.'

Chapter XI

page 24. the enthusiastic fit: In the eighteenth century the word *enthusiasm* generally had a bad connotation since it was associated with the religious enthusiasts who had 'a vain belief of private revelation'. Imlac's enthusiasm is mere 'heat of imagination', but there is still the implication that he has lost control and is overstating his case. Rasselas's comment makes the point bluntly but humorously.

natural: native.

page 25. representations: descriptive accounts.

  our religion: The Abyssinians have been Christians since the fourth century.

  some places . . . uncommon manner: This thought was developed in a famous passage in *A Journey to the Western Islands*:

> To abstract the mind from all local emotion would be impossible if it were endeavoured, and would be foolish if it were possible. Whatever withdraws us from the power of our senses, whatever makes the past, the distant, or the future predominate over the present, advances us in the dignity of thinking beings. Far from me and from my friends be such frigid philosophy as may conduct us indifferent and unmoved over any ground which has been dignified by wisdom, bravery, or virtue. That man is little to be envied whose patriotism would not gain force upon the plain of Marathon, or whose piety would not grow warmer among the ruins of Iona!

page 26. privacies of life: private life.

Chapter XII

page 28. addressed: courted.

  replete with images: The common psychology of the time, largely derived from Locke, held that all mental activity consisted of the combination and interaction of materials derived through the senses. Having a mind full of recorded sense-experiences, gained in his travels, Imlac was well equipped for thinking as well as for remembering.

page 29. impotence precludes malice: i.e. ill-will is prevented because it has no opportunity to express itself in action.

page 30. experiment: 'trial of anything'.

Chapter XIII

page 31. conies: rabbits.

  prominence: the steep projecting part of the summit.

  mine: tunnel.

  experiment: attempt.

page 32. walk with vigour: Imlac's notion of a vigorous pace is little more than 3 m.p.h.

Chapter XV

page 34. vacuity: unoccupied space.
  stations: positions in society, ranks.
  dignity: 'high place'.
page 35. unpractised: inexperienced.

Chapter XVI

Commerce is here honourable: For such information as he
  required about Egypt Johnson may have depended on
  George Sandys's *A Relation of a Journey* (1615), a book
  which he included in a recommended reading-list (*Life*, p.
  1306). Sandys writes of Cairo at length, emphasising its
  populousness and business: 'Most of the inhabitants of
  Cairo consist of merchants and artificers' (p. 126).
offended: troubled, bothered.
undistinguished: 'not treated with any particular respect'.
her favourite: In the second edition the name, Pekuah, was
  introduced at this point.
page 36. traffic: trade, or trading.
  politeness: 'elegance of manners'.
  acquaintance: Johnson normally uses this singular form where
  we would say 'acquaintances'. (See *Rasselas*, p. 91.)
  dependants: i.e. would-be retainers.
  places of resort: places where people met.

Chapter XVII

page 38. Their mirth was without images: Johnson probably means
  that it did not derive from anything in their experience
  (compare Imlac's mind 'replete with images', p. 30): i.e.
  their mirth was pointless frivolity as their laughter was
  unmotivated.
  'Happiness . . . uncertainty': This account of happiness is
  extremely important, for, if Johnson is allowed his definition, few readers would want to deny that happiness is not
  to be found on earth.
frankness: open-heartedness rather than plain speaking.

Chapter XVIII

page 39. school of declamation: It has been suggested that Johnson
  was thinking of the Roman Schools of Rhetoric, but it is
  more likely that he had in mind Gresham College in the City
  P

London. By the will of Sir Thomas Gresham seven professors were appointed to give free public lectures. These were given in the original building in Bishopsgate Street up to 1768.

Chapter XVIII

auditory: audience.

the lower faculties predominate over the higher: What distinguished man from beasts was his possession of reason. This, then, was the higher faculty, and passions and fancy (or imagination), which were shared with beasts, the lower faculties. Johnson himself believed that to allow the imagination to rule the reason was the way to madness (see p. 89); his chief criticism of this rationalist stoic philosopher is directed against the easy assumption that man can (or should) eliminate his fancy and his passions.

page 40. modes or accidents: two philosophical terms for the inessential qualities of a substance. Here, of course, the philosopher is saying that pain and pleasure, good and evil, are not parts of the essence of what happens in life; they are merely qualities which irrational human beings attribute to such events.

joy and wonder: The Stoic's detachment from human passions immediately collapses when he is offered money, but, although Rasselas 'had now learned the power of money', he as yet fails to perceive the discrepancy between precept and practice.

conviction closes his periods: i.e. each sentence, as he utters it, convinces his listeners.

page 41. enforced: urged.

Chapter XIX

the lowest cataract of the Nile: i.e. at Asswan.

page 42. the life which has been often celebrated: Johnson had a particular dislike of unreal rhapsodies about country life and, in particular, of pastoral poetry. This was one of the reasons for his attack on Milton's *Lycidas:* 'Its form is that of a pastoral; easy, vulgar, and therefore disgusting.' See also *The Adventurer No. 126* (pp. 137 ff.) and *The Idler No. 71* (pp. 154 ff.).

Chapter XX

page 43. skilful enough in appearances: i.e. he was a good enough judge of people's rank by their outward appearance and behaviour.

offered: made as if to.

Bassa of Egypt: Egypt was part of the Turkish Empire. The Turkish governor was entitled the Pasha or Bassa.

page 44. deprecating his exile: expressing their hope (or praying) that his exile would not take place.

Chapter XXI

rude essay: uncultivated attempt.

page 45. regularity: orderliness.

enthusiasm: See p. 24 note.

professed arms: entered the military profession.

preferment: promotion.

vanities of imagination: empty imaginings.

Chapter XXII

page 46. controvertist: disputant.

had been justly punished: i.e. would have been, etc.

page 47. 'This', said a philosopher: This philosopher has been identified as Leibniz, Shaftesbury, Pope, and Rousseau, but Johnson is not attacking a particular writer; he is exposing a set of ideas, largely derived from Leibniz, which appeared variously in the writings of many eighteenth-century optimists. The basic notion was that the universe, whether viewed scientifically or theologically, was a complete system of interdependent parts, of which the ruling principle was harmony. Man, therefore, performed his proper duty and found his proper happiness in recognising and accepting his place in this great universal order. Johnson had already attacked Soame Jenyns's glib applications and extensions of this notion, and, later, in the 'Life of Pope', he ridiculed the poet's exposition in the *Essay on Man* of 'much that every man knows, and much that he does not know himself'. Indeed, as the most widely read version of these ideas, the *Essay on Man* was probably in the forefront of Johnson's mind when he wrote this chapter. The motives for his hostility were numerous: he distrusted metaphysical philosophy, which purported to explain things beyond man's understanding and had no relevance to how a man should live; he saw in these philosophisings an attempt to replace the Christian revelation with some kind of 'natural religion'; and, as this chapter makes evident, he believed that such speculations were ultimately no more than fine-sounding nonsense. The Stoic philosopher of Chapter XVIII was rejected because he recommended a course of conduct which no man could possibly follow; the philosopher of this chapter is rejected because his speculations have no intelligible bearing on human behaviour.

Chapter XXIII

page 48. as he was yet young: As in Chapter II it is stated that Rasselas was in his twenty-sixth year and various indications of the passage of time have been given, it has been calculated that at this point Rasselas must be at least thirty-two. But Johnson is interested in time only as something which can be wasted or well spent, and not in the kind of time-scheme with which a novelist might be concerned.

Chapter XXIV

page 49. distinguished: noticed among others.

page 50. Janissaries: the private army of the Turkish Sultan. Originally formed from converted Christians, this army became the most powerful military force in Turkey. It was a constant threat to the ruling powers and was finally abolished in 1826 after a great revolt.

Chapter XXV

competitions: rivalries.

page 51. countenance: 'patronage; support'.

  thy native king: i.e. king of the place where you are born or originate.

  partition of our provinces: division of our duties or areas of investigation.

  some fiend: Johnson is thinking not of a person but of a feeling or spirit. In the second edition he replaced *fiend* by *fury*.

Chapter XXVI

page 52. allayed: alloyed. See *The Rambler No. 59*, p. 117 note.

  artifices: schemings.

page 53. magnanimity: boldness.

page 54. Marriage . . . pleasures: This sentence is recalled by Jane Austen in *Mansfield Park* when Fanny Price realises that 'though Mansfield Park might have some pains, Portsmouth could have no pleasures'.

Chapter XXVII

the prospects of futurity: what lies before us in the future.

page 55. inferior desert: i.e. those of less merit.

preference: promotion. (See p. 45 note.)

page 56. incident: 'apt to happen'.

patience must suppose pain: The *Dictionary* defines *patience* as 'the power of suffering'. *Pain*, here, means any kind of distress. The existence of the first implies the presence of the second.

Chapter XXVIII

horrid: 'hideous; dreadful; shocking'. (Johnson also records the meaning, 'unpleasing, in women's cant', which has survived.)

a siege like that of Jerusalem: Jerusalem was many times besieged, but the most famous and prolonged siege was that by the Romans under Titus, which ended in the destruction of the city in A.D. 70.

every blast . . . south: Plagues were supposed to be brought on the south wind.

page 57. intestine competitions: internal rivalries.

casuists: The *Dictionary* defines *casuist* as 'one that studies and settles cases of conscience'.

even now: just now.

page 58. discriminations: differences.

in its full compass . . . complication: i.e. in its total extent and with all its numerous complexities.

Chapter XXIX

page 59. necessary: inevitable. The point Rasselas is making is that the disadvantages of the single state are essential to its very nature, while those of the married state, however common, are 'accidental' (i.e. inessential) and may therefore be avoided.

collect: a technical term from logic. The *Dictionary* defines *to collect* as 'to infer as a consequence; to gather from premises'.

page 61. attrition: 'the act of wearing things by rubbing one against another'.

Chapter XXX

page 62. civil society: civilised society.

page 63. the future of hope and fear: i.e. the future is the object of hope and fear. The sentence is a chiasmus.

respect: concern (i.e. are in respect to).

page 64. antiquity: See p. 1 note.

Chapter XXXI

the Great Pyramid: the Great Pyramid of Cheops, the only one of the 'Seven Wonders of the World' which remains. It is at Gizeh.

page 65. 'That the dead are seen no more': Imlac's views are like Johnson's own. Talking of the appearance of ghosts, he said: 'All argument is against it; but all belief is for it.' (*Life*, p. 900.)

page 66. leave at last undone: i.e. finish by not doing.

Chapter XXXII

surveyed the vaults of marble: It has been pointed out that the vaults are lined not with marble but with granite. But this tends to confirm Johnson's reliance, for information about the Pyramid, on George Sandys (see p. 35 note), because Sandys describes the marble chambers in some detail. Moreover, the reference to 'the chest in which the body of the founder is supposed to have been reposited' may be indebted to Sandys's account of the empty sarcophagus: 'In this no doubt lay the body of the builder' (p. 130).

their ignorance made it efficacious: i.e. they did not know the machinery of war by which the wall could have been breached or undermined.

Chapter XXXIII

page 67. train: 'a retinue; a number of followers or attendants'.

Chapter XXXIV

page 68. form: 'empty show'.

page 69. memorial: a written statement of the facts.

presently: may have the old meaning, 'immediately', but already in Johnson's time the meaning 'soon after' was current.

intelligence: information.

sunk down: an alternative past tense to *sank* Cf. *run,* p. 8 note.

page 70. how would you have borne: not a question. We would say 'how you would have borne'.

   the present reward: i.e. the reward which is paid in this life.

Chapter XXXV

page 71. condition: rank.

   remit her curiosity: abandon her interest.

   convenience: opportunity.

   excursions: digressions to other subjects.

   adventitious: usually means *chance,* but here *additional.*

page 72. but as it is communicated: In the second edition Johnson made this point clearer by adding, 'They must therefore be imparted to others; and to whom could I now delight to impart them?'

   the fabulous inhabitants: Probably Johnson was thinking of Lucretius (*De Rerum Natura,* v, 973–6), although the story is also referred to by Manilius (*Astronomicon,* I, 66 70) and Statius (*Thebaid,* iv, 282–4). Lucretius, however, is dismissing the story, as though it was, even in his time, an old legend. In a letter to *The Times Literary Supplement* (3 April 1959), E. E. Duncan Jones mentioned the three classical antecedents and also drew attention to the use of the same story in Marvell's poem, *The First Anniversary of the government under Oliver Cromwell* (1655), lines 325–42.

Chapter XXXVI

page 74. art of intelligence: means of acquiring information.

Chapter XXXVII

   the borders of Nubia: Nubia lies between Egypt and Abyssinia.

page 75. the lower country: The control of the central government was exercised only in the plains on either side of the lower Nile.

   the monastery of St. Anthony: St. Anthony of Egypt (*c.* 250–355) was the first Christian monk. The monastery (Der Mar Antonios) stands in the desert not far from the Red Sea.

Chapter XXXVIII

page 77. vest: an outer garment.

The sons of Ishmael: Ishmael was the son of Abraham and the Egyptian Hagar. Of him the angel of the Lord said: 'And he will be a wild man; his hand will be against every man, and every man's hand against him' (*Genesis*, XVI, 12). The Arabs claim descent from him and claim that he and his mother lie buried at Mecca.

late invaders: i.e. the Turks.

page 78. had been exempt: i.e. would have been, etc.

civil life: i.e. civilised life. (See p. 62 note.)

passport: a safe-conduct.

stipulation: bargain.

punctuality: 'scrupulous exactness'.

page 79. erratic: wandering.

passenger: 'a traveller; one who is upon the road; a wayfarer'.

porphyry: 'marble of a particular kind'.

Chapter XXXIX

since I found: i.e. since I had found. *Since*, here, is a temporal, not a causal, conjunction.

page 80. under the tropic: on the tropic of Capricorn.

crocodiles and river-horses: Johnson could have learned from Father Lobo that the Nile was 'full of hippopotames, or river-horses, and crocodiles'.

mermaids and tritons: In the preface to his translation of Lobo's *Voyage to Abyssinia*, Johnson compared the truthfulness of the Jesuit with the lies and exaggerations of other travellers. Here he may be thinking of *Purchas his Pilgrimage* (see p. 1 note), for Purchas says that the Nile 'comes from two lakes . . . in which (report goeth) that mermaids, tritons or men-fishes are seen'. But other authors give similar misinformation.

page 81. As I bore a superior character: i.e. as I was considered to be of a higher social position.

Chapter XL

page 84. has drawn out his soul: may mean that the astronomer has drawn out his mind like a wire, ready to snap, or that he has racked his spirit.

page 85. sublime: lofty.

Chapter XLI

the emersion of a satellite of Jupiter: the emergence, from behind the planet, of one of Jupiter's moons.

page 86. the rage of the Dog-star: The heat of July and August was attributed to the rising of Sirius, the dog-star, with the sun.

the fervours of the Crab: The period of the zodiacal sign of Cancer (the Crab) is from 21 June to 20 July.

equinoctial tempests: See p. 3 note.

dividend: 'share'.

Chapter XLII

page 87. seconding: means *supporting* as well as *following*.

Chapter XLIII

page 88. the ecliptic of the sun: the apparent path through the heavens followed annually by the sun.

page 89. the uncertain continuance of reason: Johnson himself was greatly troubled by this thought:

> To Johnson, whose supreme enjoyment was the exercise of his reason, the disturbance or obscuration of that faculty was the evil most to be dreaded. Insanity, therefore, was the object of his most dismal apprehension; and he fancied himself seized by it, or approaching to it, at the very time when he was giving proofs of a more than ordinary soundness and vigour of judgement. (*Life*, p. 49.)

Chapter XLIV

fancy: Johnson does not distinguish between *fancy* and *imagination*. He defines the former as 'imagination; the power by which the mind forms to itself images and representations of things, persons, or scenes of being'. He once said that madness was 'occasioned by too much indulgence of imagination' (*Life*, p. 1225).

depravation: 'degeneracy'.

comes: i.e. becomes.

apparently: 'evidently; openly'.

fiction: 'the art of feigning or inventing'.

expatiates: ranges freely.

page 90. adjusting: Here the verb means 'to regulate; to put in order; to settle in the right form'.

fantastic: fanciful.

Chapter XLV

page 91. acquaintance: See page 36 note.

    not disregarded: i.e. treated with attention and respect.

    conserves: preserves.

page 92. excursions: walks out of doors.

    physical truth: the truth about the physical world.

    I have neither mother . . . her husband: Johnson is probably thinking of himself. His wife had died in 1752 and his mother in 1759, just before the completion of *Rasselas*. The preface to his *Dictionary* (1755) had concluded:

> I have protracted my work till most of those whom I wished to please have sunk into the grave, and success and miscarriage are empty sounds: I therefore dismiss it with frigid tranquillity, having little to fear or hope from censure or from praise.

    pain: 'uneasiness of mind'.

    expect: wait for.

page 93. malignant: 'envious'.

Chapter XLVI

page 95. My knowledge . . . greater than it is: Whatever the limits of Pekuah's knowledge of astronomy, there is little wrong with her understanding of human nature.

    stay: wait.

    which she had so happily begun: in which she had made such a promising start.

    contrived: schemed.

page 97. respect kept him attentive: i.e. kept his mind occupied with the business in hand (and thus prevented the flights of fancy which had resulted in his delusion).

    inveterate: 'long established; obstinate by long continuance'.

page 98. scruples: doubts.

    business: employment, occupation.

Chapter XLVII

    chimeras: The *Dictionary* explains *chimera* as 'a vain and wild fancy, as remote from reality as the existence of the poetical chimera, a monster feigned to have the head of a lion, the belly of a goat, and the tail of a dragon'.

though I had been certain: i.e. even if I had been certain.

page 99. stem: 'to oppose a current'.

page 100. probatory: serving to try or test us.

    delay her retreat: Nekayah has not talked seriously of retiring from the world since Pekuah returned from captivity. This is presumably a teasing reference to Pekuah's remark about her mistress's unwillingness to 'die in a crowd', together with a reference to Nekayah's statement at the beginning of the chapter.

    the catacombs: Johnson may have in mind Sandys's account of the underground sepulchres he visited 'where the corpses lie ranked one by another' (*A Relation of a Journey*, p. 133). Sandys also follows this account with a description of the methods of embalming and the reasons for it.

    the virtue of the gums: Sandys describes how the bodies were eviscerated and wrapped in linen 'besmeared with gum' (p. 134).

Chapter XLVIII

page 101. only the rich or honourable: Sandys says that the rich were embalmed with 'a composition of cassia, myrrh and other odours' and 'the poorer sort of people with bitumen'.

    it is commonly supposed . . . eluding death: 'The idea was either that the Ba [the soul] would ultimately return and cause the dead to live again, or that the existence of the soul in the Nether World depended upon the existence of the body upon earth.' (*Egyptian Myth and Legend*, D. A. Mackenzie: Gresham: 1913.)

page 102. 'Some', answered Imlac . . . is material: Although much of the following discussion has been related to Locke, Johnson is not answering any particular philosopher but the arguments and assertions of a number of more or less 'materialist' philosophers. The materiality of the soul had been asserted by Lucretius (*De Rerum Natura*, III, 161–2) among others.

notices of sense: what our senses observe.

    It was never supposed . . . : Imlac's argument begins with an attempt to show that the soul or mind is immaterial. The power of thinking is not a part of the essential nature of matter. No one believes that every particle of matter can think. But if it is agreed that some material particles cannot think, how can it be held that any particle does, since matter can differ from matter only in respect of 'form, density, bulk, motion, and direction of motion'? None of these and no possible modification of them is in any way related to thinking. This part of the argument is conducted along the lines followed by Locke to show that the eternal mind is not material: 'Not material: First, because every particle of matter is not cogitative . . . Secondly, one particle alone of matter cannot be cogitative. . . . Thirdly, a system of incogitative matter cannot be cogitative.' (*Essay Concerning Human Understanding*, IV, ch. 10, 14–16.) The astronomer makes two objections: first, that matter may have qualities of which we are ignorant; and, second, that although we may consider that it is impossible for matter to think, all things are possible to God. Imlac answers, first, that it is unreasonable to reject all that we know of matter simply because of some assumed possibility of which we are ignorant, and, second, that it is no limitation of God's power to say that a statement cannot be both true and false, i.e. if God created matter incapable of thought it cannot be given the power of thought and remain matter. All of this argument relates directly to Locke's *Essay Concerning Human Understanding*, Book IV, Ch. 3, section 6, and Johnson was probably thinking of Locke and this section when he referred earlier to some who 'say it may be material, who nevertheless believe it to be immortal'. The section at once involved Locke in a controversial exchange with the Bishop of Worcester, and their arguments, many of which are reflected in this discussion, are printed in editions of the *Essay*. The case presented by Imlac is a strangely circular one, for once matter has been defined as 'incapable of cogitation' and differing only in respects 'unconnected with cogitative powers', there is no case to argue. Johnson is infinitely more at home as a moral philosopher than as a metaphysician.

page 103. I know not . . . this question: Nekayah reaches a conclusion very like that reached by Locke in the section referred to above:

> All the great ends of morality and religion are well enough secured without philosophical proofs of the soul's immateriality; since it is evident that he who made us at first begin to subsist here sensible intelligent beings, and for several years continued us in such a state, can and

will restore us to the like state of sensibility in another world, and make us capable there to receive the retribution he has designed to men according to their doings in this life. And therefore it is not of such mighty necessity to determine one way or the other. . . .

'Of immateriality', said Imlac . . .: The second stage of Imlac's argument attempts to proceed from the immateriality of the soul (a point now considered, by Nekayah at least, sufficiently proved) to its immortality. The first point is one that had been made in Plato's *Phaedo* and by many other philosophers and theologians, including Aquinas. Decay is the dissolution of something into its constituent parts ('the solution of its contexture'), and, therefore, that which is immaterial and has no constituent parts cannot decay. Again, this is only a verbal quibble: the definition of decay is derived from the decay of material substance and cannot logically be applied to those things which are held to be immaterial. The objection of Rasselas turns on the philosophical term 'extension', a term which Locke rejected as 'insignificant' (*Essay*, II, Ch. 13, 15). As used here it seems to mean 'spatial magnitude'. Imlac deals with the objection by saying that the idea of a thing is as real as the material thing, yet occupies no space. As it occupies no space, it cannot be said to have parts, and therefore it is incapable of decay. What is said of the *effect* (i.e. the thought) is equally true of the *cause* (i.e. the mind).

impassive: incapable of being injured physically.

indiscerptible: 'not to be separated; incapable of being broken or destroyed by dissolution of parts'.

'He, surely, can destroy it,': Having proved that the soul has 'a natural power of perpetual duration', Imlac has to allow that God could destroy it by withdrawing that power. Only divine revelation can tell us that God will not do so. But one might ask why, if it is necessary to depend on revelation for the crowning point of the argument, the whole argument is not rendered unnecessary, for revelation would have declared what Imlac's tortuous arguments have tried to prove.

collected from: See page 59 note.

collected: contained within their own thoughts.

page 104. the choice of eternity: This is the point to which the whole book has been leading. Man can find happiness not by any choice of life on earth but only by so living as to ensure that eternal happiness will be given him after death.

Chapter XLIX

page 105. to return to Abyssinia: Most commentators have assumed that this means a return to the Happy Valley, but a few have argued that such a return is impossible and that the travellers are only going back to live in their native land. As they are the first to have escaped from the valley, there are presumably no rules to deal with them. Imlac's speech on pp. 29–30 seems to imply that there can be no return, though his fears 'lest they should be discovered' (p. 35) may suggest that in that event they would have been returned to the valley. It is unlikely that Johnson thought the matter out, though the circular *motif* implicit in *The conclusion, in which nothing is concluded* seems to demand a return of the travellers to their starting-point. This is not a novel but a philosophic fiction: the sequence of events is not determined by an action and does not culminate in a catastrophe: there is no need to think in terms of a happy or an unhappy ending—indeed both terms are suspect in the context of *Rasselas*. The argument is concluded with Nekayah's resolve 'to think only the choice of eternity', but, immediately afterwards, she, like the others, develops a new dream. Imlac tired of the world and entered the valley, but soon tired of the valley and re-entered the world, and, if one needs to imagine a future for Rasselas and his companions, it would be consistent with the whole cast of the book and with Johnson's view of human nature to suppose that any return to the valley would soon be followed by a renewed desire to see the world. (Compare the comment about the hermit made by the man who was 'more affected with the narrative' in Chapter XXII.)

ESSAYS

The Rambler No. 12.

page 107. Motto: In the first collected editions of *The Rambler* and *The Adventurer*, sheets were included giving translations of the mottos, and in later editions these translations were inserted in their respective papers. They are given

here in the notes, but where, as often, they are mere para-
phrases or approximations, a closer modern translation
follows.

Unlike the ribald, whose licentious jest
Pollutes his banquet and insults his guest,
From wealth and grandeur easy to descend
Thou joy'st to lose the master in the friend:
We round thy board the cheerful menials see,
Gay with the smile of bland equality;
No social care the gracious lord disdains;
Love prompts to love, and rev'rence rev'rence gains.

'He bestows upon the poor wretch a little cash so that he
can make shameful jokes (against him) among the guests.
. . . You, kindly, without any harsh severity, and with all
pride laid aside, so that you are counted one among
equal friends, teach complaisance, and seek love by
loving.'
The passage is from *Ad Calpurnium Pisonem Panegyricum*
(ll. 114–15 and 117–20), attributed to Lucan. In the text I
consulted the reading was *munerat*, not *focillat*, in the first
line.

page 108. Bombasine: 'a slight silken stuff'.

  get up her linen: Strictly *getting up* is the technical term for
    dressing linen, but here the reference is more general. The
    maid's duties will include preparing all her mistress's under-
    clothes for wearing.

  we dine at one o'clock: Mrs. Bombasine is a city-merchant's
    wife pretending to a contempt for the aristocracy and
    fashionable families who lived in the West End. During the
    eighteenth century the fashionable dinner-hour grew later
    and later. At the beginning of the century Steele had re-
    marked in *The Tatler No. 263*, 'In my own memory the
    dinner has crept by degrees from twelve o'clock to three,
    and where it will fix nobody knows.' By mid-century it was
    already supplanting supper as the evening meal.

  off the parish: Each parish was responsible for the distribution
    of relief to its own poor.

  if they would pay their debts: As the wife of a silk-merchant
    Mrs. Bombasine is particularly resentful of those who fail to
    pay debts.

  porto downstairs: In most eighteenth-century houses (of the well-to-do) the family's accommodation was above ground-floor level.

page 109. Standish: a desk-set containing pens, ink, and other writing materials.

commissioner of the excise: Johnson had a special detestation for the men who held this office. In the *Dictionary* he defined *excise* as 'a hateful tax levied upon commodities, and ad-judged, not by the common judges of property, but wretches hired by those to whom excise is paid'. In *The Idler No. 65* he refers to 'the two lowest of all human beings, a scribbler for a party, and a commissioner of excise'.

the Seven Dials: an area between Charing Cross Road and New Oxford Street, which during the eighteenth and nineteenth centuries was a slum, notorious as the home of criminals and prostitutes.

Foundling House: In 1745 Captain Coram established the famous Foundling Hospital, on the site now occupied by Coram's Fields. No questions were asked of women who came to leave babies there.

work: i.e. needlework.

the taverns will be open: The implication is that as the girl is smartly dressed she must be a prostitute.

page 110. nasty: 'dirty; filthy'.

courtesies: A *courtesy* may be 'an act of civility or respect' or 'the reverence made by women', i.e. a curtsy. Probably the latter is intended.

interest: i.e. it was to the interest or profit of the relation to get the girl off her hands.

page 111. routs: fashionable gatherings or parties.

piquet: 'a game at cards'.

robbed the kitchen hearth: The husband's joke is to ask whether the girl is blushing or wearing rouge. The wife's joke is that the colour in the girl's face may come from the heat of the kitchen fire.

Mrs. Mum: The girl is silent or 'mum'.

tags: the shoulder-knots on a footman's livery.

page 112. A fine time!: another way of saying 'What is the world coming to!'

sending me down in the wagon: Wagons were used for trans-porting goods about the country. Only the poor would travel in them.

Euphemia: means *of good reputation, well spoken of.*

fall her crest: humble her pride.

beforehand: 'in a state of accumulation, or so as that more has been received than expended', i.e. with money in hand.

Zosima: a reference to a Greek epitaph praised by Johnson in his *Essay on Epitaphs* (1740). Zosima was apparently a slave, and Johnson translates her epitaph, 'Zosima, who in her life could only have her body enslaved, now finds her body likewise at liberty.' He comments:

> It is impossible to read this epitaph without being animated to bear the evils of life with constancy, and to support the dignity of human nature under the most pressing afflictions, both by the example of the heroine whose grave we behold, and the prospect of that state in which, to use the language of the inspired writers, 'The poor cease from their labours, and the weary be at rest.'

The Rambler No. 47.

page 113. Motto:

> These proceedings have afforded me some comfort in my distress; notwithstanding which I am still dispirited and unhinged by the same motives of humanity that induced me to grant such indulgences. However, I by no means wish to become less susceptible of tenderness. I know these kind of misfortunes would be estimated by other persons only as common losses, and from such sensations they would conceive themselves great and wise men. I shall not determine either their greatness or their wisdom; but I am certain they have no humanity. It is the part of a man to be affected with grief, to feel sorrow, at the same time that he is to resist it, and to admit of comfort.—*Earl of Orrery.*

The quotation is from the *Letters* of Pliny the Younger. In the letter in question (Bk. VIII, xvi) Pliny speaks of the death of some of his servants, and consoles himself by remembering that he had very readily allowed his slaves their freedom and had granted certain other privileges.

within the prospect: i.e. in sight as a future possibility.

King Pyrrhus: Johnson is presumably thinking of the conversation described in Plutarch's *Life of Pyrrhus* between the great Greek general and his friend, Cineas. Pyrrhus was planning to attack Rome, and Cineas asked, 'What next?'

Q

Pyrrhus said he would conquer Italy, and, as Cineas continued to repeat his question, went on to talk of conquering Sicily, the countries of North Africa, and finally Macedon and the whole of Greece:

> Cineas said 'And when all these are in our power what shall we do then?' Said Pyrrhus, smiling, 'We will live at our ease, my dear friend, and drink all day, and divert ourselves with pleasant conversation.' When Cineas had led Pyrrhus with his argument to this point: 'And what hinders us now, sir, if we have a mind to be merry, and entertain one another, since we have at hand without trouble all those necessary things, to which through much blood and great labour, and infinite hazards and mischief done to ourselves and to others, we design at last to arrive?' (*Plutarch's Lives:* The Dryden Plutarch revised by Arthur Hugh Clough. Dent (Everyman's Library): 1910. Vol. II, p. 53.)

those who have assumed . . .: i.e. moralists.

wounded stags of Crete: Johnson's memory seems to have combined two stories from Aelian's *Varia Historia*. Book I, Ch. 10, tells of Cretan goats 'which being hurt, immediately eat of the herb Dittany, which as soon as they have tasted, the arrow drops out'; and Book XIII, Ch. 35 describes how 'harts' purge themselves by eating the herb 'seselis'. (Translation from *Claudius Aelianus: His Various History* (1665) by Thomas Stanley.)

vulnerary: 'useful in the cure of wounds.'

page 115. many who have . . . speculative prudence: i.e. Stoic philosophers. (See *Rasselas* Ch. XVIII.) *Speculative* here means *hypothetical, unrelated to practice,* Johnson's usual objection to stoicism.

page 116. instances: persuasions.

page 117. Si tempore longo . . .: From *Consolatoria Oratio ad Patrem super morte Francisci Fratris,* in Grotius's *Poemata,* 1739. According to this edition the lines should begin 'Si tempore reddi/Pax animo tranquilla potest, tu sperne morari'. The general sense remains unchanged: 'If by a long period of time sorrow can be alleviated, cast aside all delay: a man of good sense makes time pass for himself.' The collected *Rambler* prints the following translation:

> 'Tis long e'er time can mitigate your grief;
> To wisdom fly, she quickly brings relief.—*F. Lewis*

The Rambler No. 59.

page 117. Motto:

> Complaining oft, gives respite to our grief;
> From hence the wretched Progne sought relief;
> Hence the Poeantian chief his fate deplores,
> And vents his sorrow to the Lemnian shores:
> In vain by secrecy we would assuage
> Our cares; concealed they gather tenfold rage.
>
> *F. Lewis.*

The passage is from Ovid's *Tristia*, V, i, 59–64. The translation by A. L. Wheeler, in *Ovid: Tristia. Ex Ponto*, (Heinemann Loeb Classical Library), 1924, reads:

> 'Tis something to lighten with words a fated evil; to this are due the complaints of Procne and Halcyone. This was why the son of Poeas in his chill cave wearied with his outcries the Lemnian rocks. A suppressed sorrow chokes and seethes within, multiplying perforce its own strength.

(The Loeb text has *gelido*, 'chill', where Johnson has *solo*, 'lonely'.) Procne (or Progne) was the wife of Tereus. When Tereus raped her sister, Philomela, the two sisters killed Tereus's son, cooked the body, and served it to Tereus at a feast. According to many authors, Procne became a swallow and Philomela a nightingale, but Ovid followed a tradition in which Procne became a nightingale. Halcyone (or Alcyone), when her husband was drowned in a shipwreck, leapt into the sea; both were transformed into kingfishers, and each winter the female bird was supposed to lament for her mate. Philoctetes, son of Poeas, was afflicted, when on his way to the siege of Troy, with an agonising and evil-smelling wound. He was put ashore on the island of Lemnos and left there for ten years.

allay: alloy. Johnson's image is of alloying gold with cheap waste metal. See *Rasselas*, p. 52 note.

page 118. superstition: Some of the superstitions to which Johnson refers are still current—avoiding thirteen in company, or looking at the new moon over the left shoulder, for instance. Less familiar, perhaps, is the old saying 'Turn your money when you hear the cuckoo, and you'll have money in your purse till he come again'. Ravens and snakes have always been regarded as creatures of ill-omen. The climacteric years (i.e. the seventh, ninth, twenty-first, twenty-seventh, thirty-fifth, forty-fifth, forty-ninth, and sixty-third) were regarded by astrologers as critical and dangerous periods in life, especially the sixty-third, or Grand Climacteric.

Suspirius: from Latin *suspirium*, a sigh.

without the verge: beyond the range.

page 119. subaltern: inferior, or subordinate.

For a genius: i.e. As for a man of genius etc.

Serenus: Latin *serenus*, figuratively *of a cheerful, tranquil disposition.*

foreboding more: The Greek quotation is from an epigram attributed to Nicarchus: 'The night-raven's song bodes death'. The translation by W. R. Paton is in *The Greek Anthology* (5 Vols.): Heinemann (Loeb Classical Library), 1916–18: Vol. IV, p. 161.

page 120. Sybarites: the inhabitants of the city of Sybaris in Southern Italy who became notorious for their love of idle luxury and pleasure. I have not found the source of this particular story.

receptacle: 'a vessel or place into which anything is received'.

Homer's Agamemnon: Iliad, I, 106–7.

Spem vultu . . . dolorem: In later editions Johnson inserted a line of Dryden's translation of the *Aeneid:* 'His outward smiles concealed his inward smart.' The reference is to *Aeneid,* 1, 209. A more literal translation would be, 'He pretends to hope in his face, and suppresses the deep grief in his heart.'

The Rambler No. 155.

page 121. Motto:

. . . Our barren years are past:
Be this of life the first, of sloth the last.
Elphinston.

The quotation is from Statius (*Silvae,* IV, ii, ll. 12–13) and may be translated: 'We have spent barren years; this is the first day of a new age for me, the threshold of life.'

page 122. adscititious: 'that which is taken in to complete something else, though originally extrinsic; supplemental; additional'.

page 124. Indolence: See *Rasselas,* p. 9 note.

page 125. Facilis descensus . . . labor est: In later editions Johnson added Dryden's translation of these lines (*Aeneid*, VI, 126–9):

> The gates of Hell are open night and day;
> Smooth the descent, and easy is the way:
> But, to return, and view the cheerful skies;
> In this, the task and mighty labour lies.

More literally, 'The descent to Avernus (the Underworld of the dead) is easy; every night and day the door of gloomy Dis (King of the Underworld) stands open. But to retrace one's steps and ascend into the upper atmosphere—this is the difficult task, this the toil.'

if at certain stated days life was reviewed: This was Johnson's own practice at the New Year, at Easter, and on his birthday.

The Adventurer No. 67.

page 127. Motto: Aeneid, VI, 663 (with connectives, irrelevant to Johnson's purpose, omitted). Johnson supplied the translation, 'They polish life by useful arts', but a more literal translation would be 'They adorned life with the skills and knowledge they discovered'.

the multiplicity of cries: The noise of tradesmen and street-vendors was a feature of the London streets. Addison began *The Spectator No. 251:* 'There is nothing which more astonishes a foreigner, and frights a country squire, than the cries of London.'

use of their eyes: i.e. the fact that their eyes are used to the sight.

page 128. Socrates: The story is taken from the life of Socrates by Diogenes Laertius (*Lives of Eminent Philosophers*, II, 25). The word *want* here should be understood as *need* or *lack*.

might easily want: could easily do without.

raised to dignity: raised to a respected position in society.

raising contributions upon: getting money from.

a powder: snuff.

page 131. Mexico and Peru: That the Aztecs, and the Peruvians under the Incas had built great and elaborate cities without the use of iron was a continual source of wonder. They had, of course, other metals, and used tools of a copper and tin alloy.

the rude Indian: Johnson is thinking of the American Indian.

page 132. can enjoy it only in society: Though not born there, Johnson was a Londoner by adoption. He told Boswell, 'No, sir, when a man is tired of London, he is tired of life; for there is in London all that life can afford' (*Life*, p. 859).

The Adventurer No. 84.

Motto:

> But take the danger and the shame away,
> And vagrant nature bounds upon her prey.
>   Francis.

The quotation is from Horace's *Satires*, II, vii, 73–4. More literally it can be translated: 'Take away the risk, and at once, with the curbs removed, runaway human nature springs forth.'

Sir William Temple: in his essay *Of Poetry*. The remark became part of the stock of writers on manners.

page 133. a short journey: In the second edition *short* was properly omitted. Towards the end of the essay we are told that the journey lasted four days.

Cervantes . . . Don Quixote's inn: Don Quixote, Part I, Chs. 32–47. This is a famous section where Cervantes inserts, into his narrative, tales and verses exchanged by the 'extraordinary assembly' he gathers together in the inn.

page 134. surtout: overcoat.

a broad lace: The hats of the well-to-do were trimmed with braid.

page 135. in order to a purchase: i.e. to make a purchase of land or some other commodity more substantial than stocks.

chancellor: The young man is pretending to an acquaintance with the Lord Chancellor, the head of the judiciary.

page 136. funds: i.e. stocks.

his own country: i.e. his own part of the country. The expression would ordinarily be used by the landed gentry.

began: another example of the variant past tenses and part participles of verbs like *begin* (p. 136 note) and *drink* (p. 156 note).

Change-alley: a lane near the Royal Exchange largely occupied by stock-brokers.

the Exchange: the Royal Exchange.

engrosses: To engross ('to copy in a large hand') was a principal occupation of lawyers' clerks.

the Temple: where lawyers had, and continued to have, their chambers.

page 137. Viator: wayfarer, traveller.

The Adventurer No. 126.

Motto:

Canst thou believe the vast eternal mind
Was e'er to Syrts and Lybyan sands confin'd?
That he would choose this waste, this barren ground,
To teach the thin inhabitants around,
And leave his truth in wilds and deserts drown'd?
(Johnson used the translation of the *Pharsalia* by Nicholas
Rowe.) In Lucan's *The Civil War* (or *Pharsalia*) IX, 576–7,
Cato passes the shrine of Jupiter Ammon in the North
African desert but refuses to consult the oracle: 'Did he
chose these barren sands, that a few might hear his voice?
did he bury truth in this desert?' (*Lucan: The Civil War*,
trans. J. D. Duff: Heinemann (Loeb Classical Library),
1928.) In the Loeb edition the passage begins: *Sterilesne
elegit*, etc.

page 138. eligible: 'fit to be chosen.'

page 139. Numa . . . Egeria: Numa Pompilius, a legendary king
of Rome, claimed to be loved and instructed by the nymph
Egeria, whom he visited in a grove near Rome. The story
is told in Livy's *History of Rome* (I, 21) and in Plutarch's
Lives ('Numa Pompilius').

page 140. 'to pass through . . . the things eternal': Johnson is
quoting from *The Book of Common Prayer*, the Collect for
the Fourth Sunday after Trinity: 'Increase and multiply
upon us thy mercy; that, thou being our ruler and our guide,
we may so pass through things temporal, that we finally
lose not the things eternal.'

The Idler No. 32.

page 143. speculatist: theorist, one who speculates about the
nature of things.

some late philosophers: Johnson is presumably referring to the
great botanists (Grew and Ray in the late seventeenth, and
Hales in the eighteenth century) who had revolutionised
man's understanding of plant physiology.

> *the efficient or final cause:* Johnson uses the philosophical terms: *the efficient cause* is the agency which produces the effect; *the final cause* is the purpose or end for which the effect is caused.

page 144. effused: poured out.

> *Alexander . . . the necessity of sleep:* The reference is to a remark recorded in Plutarch's *Life of Alexander:* 'He was wont to say that sleep and the act of generation chiefly made him sensible that he was mortal.' *Plutarch's Lives:* The Dryden Plutarch revised by Arthur Hugh Clough. Dent (Everyman's Library): 1910. Vol. II, p. 482.

> *the supreme and self-sufficient Nature:* i.e. God.

page 145. Alexander himself added intemperance . . . .: Accounts of Alexander's drinking-bouts occur in all the 'Lives'— those of Quintus Curtius, Plutarch, and Arrian—though the last two say that accounts of his drinking were exaggerated. But many stories were told of his excesses by later writers (for instance, Aelian in the *Varia Historia* III, xxiii), and Johnson referred to them again in *The Idler No. 51.*

The Idler No. 49.

page 146. the King of Prussia: At this time Frederick the Great of Prussia was engaged in the Seven Years' War. Again and again his persistence in the face of disaster had resulted in victory. In an essay on the king (printed in *The Literary Magazine* in 1756) Johnson had remarked on 'the rapidity which constituted his military character'.

> *flapped his hat:* Travellers often wore hats with flaps which could be let down in bad weather.

> *the dissolution of nature: Dissolution* means *destruction,* but in the watery context another meaning is partly involved: 'the act of liquefying by heat or moisture'.

page 147. lost his company: In the second edition Johnson made his sense clearer by amending this to 'parted from his company'. No suggestion is intended that Marvel met with any real misfortunes.

> *review:* look back on.

> *up rose the sun and Mr. Marvel:* It has been observed that Johnson seems to be parodying Chaucer: 'Up roos the sonne, and up roos Emilye' (*Canterbury Tales,* I, 2273). The line was familiar to the eighteenth century chiefly through

Dryden's version of *The Knight's Tale* which retained it unchanged (*Palamon and Arcite*, III, 190).

page 148. Serbonian bog . . . have sunk: from *Paradise Lost*, II, lines 592 and 594. The bog was on the Egyptian coast, separated from the sea by a narrow sand-bar.

    eagre: a bore; a large wave caused by the tide rushing in up a narrowing estuary.

    post-boy: a carrier on horseback of letters and newspapers to outlying towns and villages.

    romantic: 'resembling the tales of romances; wild' or 'improbable; false'. The two meanings are related and both are intended here.

The Idler No. 50.

page 149. Shakespeare's seven stages of life: As You Like It, II, vii, 142 ff.

page 150. the pictures of Raphael: Boswell says that Johnson 'had no taste for painting', but, when Johnson saw three Raphaels in Paris in 1775, he noted, 'I thought the pictures of Raphael fine' (*Life*, pp. 1312 and 649). Johnson's short-sightedness may have contributed to his coolness about the visual arts, but here he is criticising, not the art of painting, but what he took to be travellers' affectations.

    the gardens of Versailles: Laid out towards the end of the seventeenth century, these were considered one of the wonders of Europe. Johnson visited them in 1775 and made some notes without displaying any great enthusiasm.

The Idler No. 70.

page 152. Diffusion: the use of many words to convey the sense.
    involution: 'complication'.

    The Guardian: a reference to *The Guardian No. 24*, by Steele. The saying is proverbial, but based on the advice of Aristotle.

    '*Every man*', *says Swift:* Johnson is paraphrasing a passage in Swift's *Letter to a Young Gentleman, Lately Entered into Holy Orders:*

> . . . Professors in most arts and sciences are generally the worst qualified to explain their meanings to those who are not of their tribe: a common farmer shall make you understand in three words that his foot is out of joint, or his collar-bone broken; wherein a surgeon, after a

hundred terms of art, if you are not a scholar, shall leave
you to seek.

Swift's point, however, is not that specialists should not
use technical terms among themselves but that they should
not use them when talking to ordinary people. Johnson
makes this point himself in the next paragraph.

page 153. limited: specific.

 members: the technical term for the constituent parts of a
 column (base, shaft, capital, etc.).

 casuist: See *Rasselas* p. 57 note.

The Idler No. 71.

page 154. Dick Shifter . . . The Temple: In this opening sentence
 Johnson is making the point that Dick Shifter, despite his
 name, is a Londoner by birth, education, and profession.

 Greenwich . . . Chelsea: A boat-trip to Greenwich Park and
 a walk through the fields to Chelsea village were popular
 recreations in eighteenth-century London.

 too high . . . envy: a reference to Cowley:

> This only grant me, that my means may lie
> Too low for envy, for contempt too high.
>   *Of Myself.*

 laxity of life: relaxed way of life.

 the chief good: a term from moral philosophy, which was largely
 concerned with the *Summum Bonum* or the highest good
 available to man, or attainable by him.

 post-chaise: a carriage drawn by post-horses. A post-chaise
 with a postilion could be hired by those who did not wish
 (or were unable) to travel by stage-coach.

page 155. agitation: The preceding sentence leads one to read this
 word as referring to Dick's excitement of spirit, but what
 follows shows that Dick was being physically tossed about.

 chirping in the woods: Johnson's haste in composition is
 suggested by the clumsy repetition of 'in the woods'. In
 the second edition he corrected it by replacing *woods* with
 hedges here.

page 156. drank: Cf. *began*, p. 136 note.

 observing any beaten path: keeping to any footpath, or track.

 Arcadians: Arcadia was a region in Greece supposed to be the
 original home of the ideal rural life. The name of its people

was used of any folk imagined to be living in blissful rustic innocence.

page 157. sold him a bargain: 'Selling bargains' was a crude kind of joking. Johnson defines *bargain* as 'an unexpected reply, tending to obscenity'.

pettifoggers and barrators: lawyers guilty of shifty practices and of encouraging unnecessary and trivial lawsuits.

enquired the owner: asked who the owner was.

A review of Soame Jenyns's *A Free Enquiry into the Nature and Origin of Evil*

In his article 'Samuel Johnson' written for the *Encyclopaedia Britannica*, Lord Macaulay described this review as 'the very best thing that [Johnson] wrote, a masterpiece both of reasoning and satirical pleasantry', and certainly it is the most varied and energetic of Johnson's shorter pieces. Many of Jenyns's ideas were plainly borrowed from Pope's *Essay on Man*, and Johnson, who was contemptuous of Pope's thought although he admired his poetry ('Never were penury of knowledge and vulgarity of sentiment so happily disguised'), accused Jenyns of plagiarising, demolished his logic, showed the incompatibility of his theories with human experience, exposed the moral implications of some of his arguments, ridiculed his analogies, and found time to praise a few paragraphs.

Basic to the arguments of Pope and Jenyns was the famous and widely held notion of the 'Great Chain of Being'—that the universe was a full and complete system consisting of infinite gradations of existence from inanimate matter, through the levels of vegetable life to microscopic animals, thence by similar steps in the animal kingdom up to man, and from man through unknown spiritual existences to God. This Great Chain was divinely created and therefore the best of all possible universes, and for man to complain of his lot was both blasphemous and unreasonable.

The two extracts given here are the passages where Johnson's moral susceptibilities were most outraged and his own moral position made most clear. The first deals with Jenyns's attempt to explain away the evils of human life by arguing that every link in the Great Chain has its own special blessings to counterbalance its special pains or incapacities; the second pursues to an absurd, but bitter and logical, conclusion Jenyns's supposition that human pain may be of benefit to creatures higher in the Chain of Being than man, as the sufferings of lower animals benefit and entertain man.

The fullest account of the development of the notion is given by Arthur O. Lovejoy in *The Great Chain of Being* (Harvard University Press, 1936: republished Harper Torchbooks, 1960).

page 159. Pope's alleviations: mainly in Epistle IV of the *Essay on Man*.

    Folly: 'want of understanding; weakness of intellect'.

    that rant of a mad poet: in Dryden's play *The Spanish Friar*, II, i.

    literature: 'skill in letters', i.e. ability to read and write.

page 160. particulars: individuals.

    the mutilation of a compliment: Johnson's definition of *compliment* is 'an act, or expression of civility, usually understood to include some hypocrisy, and to mean less than it declares'. By *mutilation* Johnson means an error in polite behaviour, such as the use of the wrong form of address.

page 161. a little learning is . . . a dangerous thing: Pope's *Essay on Criticism.* l. 215.

page 164. Blenheim . . . Prague: The battles of Blenheim (1704) and Prague (1757) were two of the decisive and most bloody battles of the century.

    virtuosi: men interested in scientific experiment.

    philosopher: natural philosopher, or scientist.

    a tympany: swelling of the abdomen due to obstructed gas or air.

    to blow a frog: Johnson is referring to the cruel trick of distending a frog by blowing air into it through a quill.

    ague: 'an intermitting fever, with cold fits succeeded by hot.'

    the gout and stone: two extremely painful diseases, the first characterised by deposits in the joints and the second by the formation of 'stones' in various parts of the body.

    a mortal proud of his parts: What follows is intended as a sketch of the literary career of Jenyns.

    sophisms: over-subtle and fallacious arguments.

page 165. natural evil: i.e. evil in the natural order of things as opposed to evil produced by man.

FURTHER READING

JOHNSON'S WRITINGS

Johnson: Prose and Poetry, ed. by Mona Wilson, (1950) Hart-Davis.

Samuel Johnson: Rasselas, Poems, and Selected Prose, ed. by Bertrand H. Bronson (1958), Holt, Rinehart and Winston.

Selections from Samuel Johnson, 1709–1784, ed. by R. W. Chapman (1962), ('The World's Classics') Oxford University Press. (All three of these books contain excellent selections, though only Bronson supplies notes, and he has very few. But each illustrates admirably the range of Johnson's achievement.)

Volume I. Diaries, Prayers and Annals, ed. by E. L. McAdam, Jr., with Donald and Mary Hyde (1958), Yale University Press.

Volume II 'The Idler' and 'The Adventurer', ed. by W. J. Bate, John M. Bullett, and L. F. Powell (1963), Yale University Press. (These are the first two volumes of 'The Yale Edition of the Works of Samuel Johnson', which, when completed, will certainly be the standard text of Johnson's writings. Volume I is primarily of biographical interest though it illuminates Johnson's moral and religious concerns. Volume II presents the later periodical essays in a form both readable and scholarly.)

The Rambler, ed. by S. C. Roberts (1953), '(Everyman's Library') Dent. (A good selection of the essays.)

The Poems of Samuel Johnson, ed. by D. Nichol Smith and E. L. McAdam (1941), Oxford University Press.

The Letters of Samuel Johnson, ed. by R. W. Chapman (1952), 3 vols., Oxford University Press.

Johnson's 'Journey to the Western Islands of Scotland' and Boswell's 'Journal of a Tour to the Hebrides with Samuel Johnson, LL.D.', ed. by R. W. Chapman (1930): ('Oxford Standard Authors'), Oxford University Press. (There is no better introduction to the differing temperaments and geniuses of Johnson and Boswell, and to their curious relationship, than these two contrasting accounts of their tour.)

BIOGRAPHY

BOSWELL, JAMES, *Boswell's Life of Johnson* (1953 ed.), Oxford University Press.

HILL, G. B. (ed.), *Johnsonian Miscellanies* (1897), 2 vols., Oxford University Press. (A collection of Johnsonian materials including, in particular, Mrs. Thrale's *Anecdotes*.)

KRUTCH, J. W., *Samuel Johnson* (1948), Cassell. (The best modern biography of Johnson, drawing on all the sources and also commenting briefly but critically on the works.)

CLIFFORD, JAMES, *Young Samuel Johnson* (1955), Heinemann. (A very thorough and interesting account of the first forty years of Johnson's life.)

CRITICISM

BATE, W. J., *The Achievement of Samuel Johnson* (1955), Oxford University Press. (The best general critical introduction.)

WIMSATT, W. K., *The Prose Style of Samuel Johnson* (1942), Oxford University Press.

WIMSATT, W. K., *Philosophic Words; a study of style and meaning in 'The Rambler' and the 'Dictionary'* (1948), Oxford University Press.

HAGSTRUM, J. H., *Samuel Johnson's Literary Criticism* (1953), Oxford University Press.

CLIFFORD, JAMES (ed.), *Johnsonian Studies 1887–1950: A Survey and Bibliography* (1951), Oxford University Press. (This is an essential book for anyone wishing to explore the mass of writings about Johnson the man, his circle, his time or his writings. The survey indicates the important works of criticism and scholarship, and, in the bibliography, the more valuable books and articles are starred.)